HOME SCHOOLING:

The Fire Night Ball

Anne Carlisle

Thanks for being a reader...

Anne

Anne Carlisle 8/22/12

Copyright © 2012 Anne Carlisle

ISBN 978-1-62141-743-9

All rights reserved. No part of this publication may be reproduced, stored in a retrieval system, or transmitted in any form or by any means, electronic, mechanical, recording or otherwise, without the prior written permission of the author.

Printed in the United States of America.

The characters and events in this book are fictitious. Any similarity to real persons, living or dead, is coincidental and not intended by the author.

BookLocker.com, Inc.
2012

First Edition

Dedicated with all my love and gratitude
to my daughter, Zoe Carlisle, and my husband, Mark Leik.

"So we beat on, boats against the current,

borne back ceaselessly into the past."

F. Scott Fitzergerald, <u>The Great Gatsby</u>

"*To figure out what women are inclined to seek in a man,*

and vice versa, we'll need to think more carefully

about our ancestral social environment(s)."

Robert Wright, <u>The Moral Animal</u>

Prologue
Alta, Wyoming
October 28, 1900

The young woman who was the focus of all eyes sat down in the first row of the unadorned church. She bowed her head, clasped her gloved hands, and prayed for the one thing she wanted most.

She longed for desire's epiphany, passion as bright and all-consuming as the bonfires the natives had lit last evening on the first Fire Night of the new century.

Instinctively, though she was only an orphan now living atop a desolate mountain, she knew a blaze is better than a weak lantern lasting for many years. She missed the gay life she had known in Saratoga with her aunt, the theater, and the military men. But she wasn't without God-given powers to achieve her desires.

She had special gifts: perfect recall of all she'd witnessed or read and a siren's trick of focusing her will to stop a horse or fascinate a man. What she wanted was simple, one great love, and because of that wish she was exerting the force of her will every night on Curly Drake.

If tepid love was all fate had in store for her, then she would prefer the safe, solitary life she had with her grandfather, a retired sea captain out of Gloucester who'd retired to a stone home in the most blustery part of Wyoming.

Cassandra's prayer ran something like this: "O Lord, deliver me from the sadness and the loneliness I feel in the vast spaces of this awful place. Grant me a great love, or I shall die."

When the services were over, she was surprised to find her way was blocked when she stepped out into the aisle.

Standing there with folded arms was Goody Brown, who looked as if she might spit in her eye. The beauty with the flaming red-gold hair and the heavy-set matron stared at each other.

Goody felt she had every reason to object to the scarlet woman's being in church. Her carnal presence was a mark of sheer blasphemy that would bring the wrath of the Lord down on all, including the new baby in Goody's family who was about to be baptized. Goody couldn't afford any chances of the Lord's wrath being piqued.

The story she had heard, the gossip that was running like wildfire through the village, was reverberating in her pipes like a gong, and she felt compelled to speak.

Last evening, when the innkeeper and Miss Brighton were supposed to have been celebrating their nuptials, Curly Drake and Cassandra were meeting on Hatter's Field, Drake having been lured there by Cassandra's signal fire. The story confirmed Goody's darkest suspicions.

A Salem witch was in Cassandra's family tree; the sea captain had admitted as much.

And now the red-headed hussy was in church, acting out hypocritical piety. She'd been able to entice a bridegroom away from the pious widow's daughter, using witchcraft to carry on clandestinely on the very night he was to bed his bride. Surely this was Satan's work, and yet here she was, brazenly parading before them all in the Lord's own house!

If Cassandra Vye could cast a spell so strong as that, there was no telling what else she might do. The waters of the baptismal fount would surely be fouled as she walked past, endangering the soul of Goody's grand-daughter.

Anticipating the danger to her family, Goody had put a hex on the witch with a soap doll, as she'd been taught by a Lakota Sioux witch-doctor. There was nothing she could do that was powerful enough to kill the witch herself. But there might be a way to scare her off by afflicting the witch with a curse. The men who fell into the siren's clutches--also the sweethearts of her descendants--these unfortunate sinners would suffer untimely deaths, so the hexing went.

And now, while the eye of the Lord was upon her, Goody would show Him the stalwart loyalty of His servant by publicly exposing Cassandra as Satan's legion.

"Hu-sssss-y," Goody hissed, spraying spittle from her thick lips. "I know how to defend the natives against your wickedness. Thou art accursed, Satan's whore. Be gone, witch! Or else I predict two deaths on your head once the bonfires are extinguished."

Cassandra wiped her face with her gloved hand. Captain Vye now pushed forward and grabbed his grand-daughter out of harm's way. Her face was dead white, and her exotic cat's eyes blazed like burning coals as she marched down the aisle.

While the churchgoers gathered outside gawked and whispered among themselves, Cassandra stopped at the church door, flung off her bonnet, and let her shimmering mane of fiery-gold curls blow with the wind. Without a word, she got into the buggy.

No crazy hag is going to determine my fate. Damn the natives' opinions, and damn Goody Brown's curse.

Chapter One
Alta, Wyoming
December 20, 1977

The January issue of <u>Playboy</u> was in her hands. Marlena Bellum shuddered with anticipation as she opened it and began to thumb through the slick pages. There it was, a blurb under "Traveler's Report."

Her eyes raced through the first sentence:

"The place where the rich, the famous, and the wannabe depraved go to get fucked up these days is (drum roll) B. L. Zebub's Poolhall Saloon in Alta, Wyoming, where chic bordello meets devils' hideaway on the coldest, remotest mountain top of the Old West."

A smile of pure joy crossed her Cupid's bow lips, and her long-lashed, wide-set eyes sparkled. They were an alluring, blue-green hue, like the waters of the Mediterranean Sea.

"One enters through a secret door in the grand, castle-like, five-diamond Alta Hotel, the Xanadu of real estate mogul Harry Drake and brainchild of Pioneer Architectural Designs (PAD). Once inside, you'll hobnob with Hollywood, East Coast saloon society, and oil refinery executives dandling young playgirls."

Permeating the stale doctor's office air was the scent of jasmine. Marlena flipped back her shimmering mane of fiery-gold curls, crinkly as corn silk and rippling to the curve of her backside. She read on:

"If excess is your bag, a diamond-studded card can hold your place, or you may sit your butt on a vintage saddle stool for the price of a Maserati. No streakers reported; it's too freaking cold! Check your power ties at the door, gentlemen. Ladies (the term is loosely applied), bras and girdles are optional."

Now there's advertising you can't buy, she thought happily.

The 1978 promotional campaign was her most ambitious yet. And, if the numbers held up through the holidays, 1977 would be another record-breaking year for Drake Enterprises.

B. L. Zebub's was their baby, hers and Harry's. Since December, 1972, when the secret door first opened to a select few, any traveler of note passing through northeastern Wyoming was sure to turn up at what GQ dubbed "the sexiest private gentleman's club in America."

Its centerpiece, an oak bar she had nicknamed "B. L. Zebub" because of its intensely dark history, was an English colossus bought for only 40,000 pounds from the ancient proprietor of a dusty antique shop in the Cotswolds. Even the cherry bar in Cody's Irma Hotel, a gift Queen Victoria had sent Buffalo Bill, couldn't hold a candle to B. L. Zebub. Its woodcarver, so the story went, was a gifted young woman of 17th century England who was stoned to death in the public square of her Puritan village for crimes of adultery and witchcraft.

Marlena put aside the blurb that had taken her a year to secure and wondered how long she'd have to wait before she was called in to see the doctor.

Picking up an older issue of Cosmo from a side table, she glanced through the cover article, which offered advice to young women on how to marry a millionaire by becoming an expert on the great man's interests, ala Pamela Harriman. *How do I stack up?*

Chapter Two

At first, she'd taken Harry Drake for a limp-wristed fop. He was dressed in an Italian silk suit tailored at Savile Row; his cuff links were Cartier. His high forehead was feathered with luxuriant black curls, Napoleon style; his small nose was almost girlishly attractive; and his smile was sheepishly self-effacing. He was on the short side, though a long-waisted torso and upright posture made him appear taller than he was.

However, as Harry entered the reception room at the back of Bottomly's Cafe, where Drake Enterprises was hosting a soiree for the Alta community in advance of ground-breaking for the hotel project, Marlena's initial impression changed. His signature stroll exuded male power and authority, as did the cold, light-brown eyes that were peering appraisingly into hers.

"Mrs. Dimmer, you have the most amazing eyes I've ever seen. What's that color called?"

"Cerulean. I've been looking forward to meeting you, Mr. Drake."

As their fingers met and held, she felt a pulsating, tingling sensation. His hands were graceful, the fingers long and slim, a trait she found sexually attractive. His grip, firm and lingering, conveyed sensuality and grace under pressure.

"Are we family? I always ask," said Harry. "Most folks in this town are related."

His disarming smile, along with a slight hesitation in his tenor voice, made her wonder if she was supposed to feel at ease. But at ease was not her reaction. Her heart was thumping like a drum, and much to her dismay, she began to blush furiously, like a schoolgirl.

"Well, uh, sort of," she fumbled. *Where, oh where, was her practiced gift of gab?*

"Yes?" His eyes were roving over the curves of her body, taking them in.

"I, uh, believe my grandmother was the niece of your father's stepfather."

"Her name?"

"Sarah Bellum."

"Ho, ho. You're making that up."

"Grandpa was a mind adrift until he met his Sarah Bellum. That was my dad's line."

She joined in Drake's laughter, recovering some composure. But the way he was staring deeply into her eyes, his sensual mouth twitching humorously at the corners, made it difficult to get her lines out.

Clumsily, she burst out, "Granny's maiden name was Scattergood." Then she pulled her eyes away from his, so as to interrupt the embarrassingly loud current buzzing between them. *Surely others can hear it!*

He pursed his lips, nodding.

"A native name, like mine. There are a few others--the Brightons, of course. My grandmother married Caleb Scattergood after my grandfather died. I gather your grandmother was Caleb's niece. As for Bellum, I can't say that name rings any bells. But you certainly do."

He leaned over and kissed her with vigor on her Cupid's bow lips. "There," he said, looking her full in the eyes again. "Now we're kissing cousins."

Her earlobes were vibrating and her lips felt numb. Even more than his kiss, the intense gleam of interest in his light brown eyes was making her feel, in a room swarming with people, as if no one were there but the two of them.

Chapter Three

Once that buzz had turned into a full-blown affair, Marlena's journey into sexual submission to Drake was as prominent in her life as a flying buttress on a Gothic cathedral. Every time they made love, her mind and body revisited her entire sexual history.

As a child, she was a gawky, long-legged, big-eyed freak, painfully shy, who suffered persecution by the normal children and endured constant loneliness in silence. For solace, she retreated into the world of adult fiction she found in the local library.

She would read over and over torrid scenes where a gorgeous woman drowsily lounged, awaiting her manly lover in a silken bed draped in gauze. At the time, she was living in her grandparents' pink house, her parents largely absent, Austin working in New Gillette and in Faith's case, far off East in Saratoga, tending to her sick father.

Marlena's childhood fantasies centered on finding someone who would kindly tolerate her presence and show her the ropes, socially speaking. She invented an imaginary brother with auburn hair and grey eyes who held her hand and guided her through kindergarten.

Later, in second grade, she found a girlfriend who was unusually intelligent and saw sexual images in everything. With June, for a season, she explored a warm, tender place between her legs which her mother didn't want her to touch.

June was almost as odd as herself. Her hair was glossy black; she had freckles and startling green eyes. She wasn't pretty like the little blonde girls who were popular in class, but she had other attributes. She could multiply large numbers in her head. Her father was a medical doctor, so they had access to his books on sexual reproduction, which they pored over together, their ankles touching in the air.

Marlena's only male admirers were Typhoid Ronnie, the boy who sat behind her and gave her all the childhood illnesses, and Gareth Blood, a goony kid from down the street who ran away from home at sixteen and joined the San Francisco Opera. If they liked her, Marlena reasoned, there must be something terribly wrong with those two.

At twenty, while a graduate fellow at the University of Arizona's Drachmann School of Architecture, Marlena interned in the San Francisco office of PAD. There she met Codwell Dimmer, a sweet, balding man of twenty-five with a weak chin. He was the Chief Financial Officer, a CPA by profession but well-versed in commercial real estate.

They became best friends, then a couple to watch.

Their civil wedding ceremony was performed on June 21, 1970, on a wet afternoon in San Francisco's gold-domed City Hall. A religious ceremony for the benefit of her parents was held later at St. Boniface Church.

The first wedding night broke her hymen. *I waited for that?*

Though passion was absent, the couple lived amicably at Dimmer's house in the Marina district, on a cul-de-sac named Solid Hollow Lane. The following year, Marlena got the nod to assist the firm's senior architect with hotel construction in her home town of Alta, Wyoming.

The Dimmers celebrated with prosecco in the park, followed by a tape of "Casablanca" from Blockbusters. Marlena owned a framed photograph of Joe Cocker playing an invisible guitar at Woodstock "....for my friends," but she was all about the classics when it came to movies and books.

Two months after the ground-breaking, Bob Drummond, the senior architect, became madly infatuated with the client's wife. Lovely and dashing Lila Coffin Drake had a reputation preceding her as a devotee of free love. Soon Drummond was chasing her from one international watering hole to the next.

Realizing Drummond's dereliction of duty was an opportunity for herself, Marlena stepped up to the plate, throttled into high gear, and quietly drove the project forward to completion. There wasn't anything she wouldn't do to ensure its success, including a trek to England on a treasure hunt, though she hated long flights over water.

When she found B. L. Zebub, she wired Drake to fly in on the Concorde for a look.

Two weeks later, returning to America aboard the Queen Mary--B. L. Zebub, like King Kong, was locked up somewhere in the hold--she was surrounded by the endless immensity of ocean and overcome by a sense of déjà vu.

When she was jeered by childhood classmates for her freakish memory and Clarabelle hair color, Marlena had found peace and a universal connection in walking out on Hatter's Field to look upon vistas of empty, unusable space. Now, gazing upon the limitless expanse of the Atlantic Ocean, she felt a fateful, romantic connection as she stood together with Harry, their elbows slightly touching and the stars as their backdrop.

While remaining technically chaste, the pair seemed to be having sex as they talked business. One evening, after trading sly innuendos, Harry observed: "I've never known a Wyoming woman to have a man's dirty mind like you do. Keep it up."

"You, too," she purred throatily.

"Madam, you've just proved my point."

Harry had spent his life among rich, staid, boring Republicans; he enjoyed her hungry, consuming interest in their work and her smart, saucy banter. He also enjoyed spinning yarns for his protégé, as Marlena was socially inept and thoroughly gullible.

With impunity, he dropped names of Hollywood royalty and contemporary robber barons, omitting the fact that his wife was responsible for these connections. He'd played golf with Bing Crosby, lunched with William Vanderbilt Cecil, been recognized by a former British prime minister for his generosity in the worthy cause of refurbishing the Salisbury Cathedral.

"If I'd known he and the Archbishop were sucking each other's dicks, I wouldn't have given them quite so much!"

She laughed at his jokes and hung on his every word.

As he watched Marlena blossom, Harry felt more interest in her. The waifish young woman with the fast learning curve used her gifted memory to good effect, touching back on all he said with a thoughtful comment or insightful questions. Harry genuinely admired her acumen and was gratified by her intense focus on the project and on himself.

Fascinated by her transformation, he felt as if he were Pygmalion and she his Galatea. His wife Lila, far more sophisticated and worldly than he, wasn't nearly so much fun to talk to. Seeing himself in

Marlena's eyes, Harry's image of himself as an international bon vivant was restored.

Nor was it all about his self-esteem. Under the stars on the upper-deck lounge, Marlena sketched out impressive blueprints of what her mind had absorbed as snapshots. She was an invaluable asset.

"We steal only from the best," he said, toasting her drafting prowess. As the ship plowed its slow way across the Atlantic, the two debated the design of leather walls into the wee hours of the morning.

They disembarked in New York on a cold, rainy day in February. That afternoon, at four o'clock sharp, they convened in the lobby bar at the Algonquin Hotel, where Harry had checked them into adjoining rooms. They sat down at a small table in two red leather chairs to discuss plans for Marlena's activities in New York. From time to time, he would ring the bell for more drinks and peanuts. Five hours later, they were still there.

A week later, they remained in New York, still meeting every afternoon in the lobby bar. Marlena had learned to order gin and dubonnet cocktails.

Before these pleasant meetings were many long and grueling hours of work, requiring her to be up early and at the top of her game. In hip boots and a long camel coat, she rounded up treasures for jaded hotel guests to ogle. By day, she hunted through Soho's dustiest corners for antique clocks, scoured warehouses for Empire furniture, and selected richly patterned Moorish carpets; by night, she stayed up late sketching prototypes for the individualized décor of luxury guest suites. Meanwhile, Drake dined with former fraternity brothers at the Harvard Club.

Though she and her client often agreed, there were instances where they didn't see eye-to-eye. She soon learned to change her mind or the subject, as the case might be. Though Drake might assume humility for his public front, he was stubborn and conceited, a classic Taurus. Marlena, though willful, presented the dreamy-eyed aspect of an Aquarian. She began to ebb and flow with his preferences, submitting herself to his every whim.

Of course, as they say, opposites attract.

One night, squeezed together as they ascended at a snail's pace in the creaky cage elevator that was run manually by an elderly, uniformed employee, midway the cage jolted violently to a halt and, as if by fate, they were literally thrown into each other's arms.

It was not by chance, however, but by willful choice that they continued clutching each other as they reached the top floor.

Cheekbones burning, heart pounding, eyelids trembling, Marlena gazed bravely ahead and allowed her hand to remain in Harry's as he steered her past the operator, out the elevator, and down the narrow corridor into his room.

The door closed, and overnight, her life changed.

Oh, the incredible passion of their union! An entire world, previously unknown, suddenly hove into her view, a volcanic planet characterized by smoldering desire, the crescendo of shuddering delights, and the final, mind-blowing explosion of orgasm! Why had she not known before about this dark star, the power of illicit sex?

It's our discovery, ours alone; no one else feels this special intensity.

After that night, only one of the two bedrooms was used. The maid, experienced in such matters and confident of being rewarded, discreetly made up both rooms each day with fresh linens and sprigs of lavender.

Thus began the glory days of their affair, when every thrilling moment seemed a golden-throated harbinger for a blissful future. Lila Drake was a mere phantom on the loose as she cavorted through Europe's priciest watering holes, leaning on Bob Drummond's tanned arm. On the rare occasion when Lila flew into town, she and Harry barely spoke.

They took obvious precautions to keep the affair hidden from prying eyes. However, there is an old Arabian proverb to the effect that there are three things you cannot hide--love, smoke, and a man riding a camel.

Chapter Four

On the television set mounted on the far wall of the doctor's waiting room, Marlena watched national coverage of the Russian space walk. Astronaut Georgi Grechko from Salyut 6 EO-1 looked hot in his dazzling white Orlan spacesuit.

"In Russia," the newscaster said, "Santa Claus is known as Grandfather Frost."

"Marlena Bellum," called out the gray-haired nurse. As she got up from her seat, a commercial announcement came on the television, and in a deep voice the announcer boomed, "Choosey moms choose Jif."

Avoiding direct eye contact with the others, a young businessman and a married couple, she walked to the glass door. The businessman had constantly checked his watch and fidgeted, while the couple seemed placidly inured to waiting, the husband reading his newspaper and the wife idly leafing through a dog-eared copy of Life.

Married squares and her creepy little home town at the holidays, she thought; what a drag.

Marlena wished she were anywhere else, hanging out with her lesbian roommate in their loft in San Francisco's Castro district, getting it on with Harry in his penthouse suite at the hotel, or, the best idea yet, walking in outer space with Grechko.

Could the Russian astronaut possibly feel any weirder than she did, entering Typhoid Ronnie's examination offices?

"Date of birth?"

"February 1, 1947."

The nurse took her blood pressure and temperature, then measured her height and weighed her.

"Five feet, seven and one half inches; one hundred and fifteen pounds. Step down and follow me, please."

Following the nurse, she thought: funny, how for seven whole years she'd been shuttling between San Francisco and Wyoming with nothing odd, weird, or even mildly disturbing ever occurring.

Then she'd set up the holiday family reunion with Mama and Chloe and packed her bag for a guilt trip. Sure enough, ever since Saturday, life had taken on new dimensions.

Now here she was on a Tuesday morning, signing on as her personal physician a classmate from Teddy Roosevelt Elementary. In her life in the City, what would be the chances of such a thing happening? As likely as getting struck by lightning!

She felt loopy as a drunken sailor.

Saturday morning, on an impulsive, nostalgic visit to her grandparents' empty Victorian (she'd always fondly called it "the pink house") a chance discovery had packed the first disconcerting punch.

Along with two brown spiral notebooks lying in a wooden sea chest in a corner of the dank basement (these turned out to be her childhood journals), she'd pulled from its dusty hiding place a tiny, hardbound book by Thurston Scott Welton, M.D., F.A.C.S. It contained comprehensive instructions on the "Rhythmic Method of Birth Control." Enclosed were menstrual calendars from 1947 to 1955 and a handy plasticized device to detect safe and unsafe dates for sexual intercourse.

With the exception of two years, the calendars were marked in Faith Bellum's distinctive, round handwriting.

But, she couldn't help recalling, ever so clearly, how Mama, with her rosary beads dangling and convincing tears in her eyes, had once remarked: "It is God's will and my greatest sorrow, Lena, you didn't have a little brother or little sister."

Marlena was still digesting this information when she was caught off guard and completely blindsided Saturday afternoon in the hotel ladies' lounge. She was assailed by a barrage of foul words hurled by Letty Brown-Hawker, Alta's self-appointed witch-hunter.

"Be gone, witch! Thou art accursed! If you fail to heed my warning, there will be two deaths on your head before the bonfires are extinguished."

Surreal.

Now, a decision was needed.

Should she move from her posh hotel suite to Mill's Creek for the rest of her stay, as Chloe has urged her to do?

If she did, she would have a chance to discuss these disturbances in the field with her cousin, the world-renowned evolutionary psychiatrist. Though Chloe was older than Faith, she couldn't be more radically different, and Chloe was willing to talk about their special powers.

On the other hand, wasn't it best not to get hung up on puzzling events? Simply ignore them and forge ahead?

"Forge ahead" was Marlena's mantra. She fancied herself a futurist, even imagined she carried a crystal ball around inside her head.

But if I leave the hotel for a few days, I might feel safer.

It was even possible Letty's harangue had triggered a reoccurrence of the persecution complex she'd suffered from as a child, causing her to vomit from anxiety. For sure, the weird scene was proving hard to expunge, though she was focusing her will on dismissing it.

Alas, a talent Marlena shared with her mother and cousin--their gift of perfect recall--made forgetting even a fraction of a second of that freakish hullabaloo well nigh impossible.

Chapter Five

On Saturday afternoon, Marlena Bellum and Dr. Chloe Vye had kicked off their long delayed reunion by having a couple of drinks at B. L. Zebub's. Faith Bellum wasn't there yet; her train from Rapid City was arriving later in the evening. Marlena had ordered gin and dubonnet cocktails for them both.

"It's Queen Elizabeth's drink," she informed Chloe, "a house specialty."

Marlena then gave Chloe a behind-the-scenes hotel tour, running down the high points of their success story. Chloe's books took her on world tours and she was seldom at home, but even so, Marlena felt embarrassed she hadn't invited her older cousin to the Alta Hotel. The truth was, she had pushed her family away in recent years, assuming they wouldn't tolerate her situation. Now Chloe and Mama were all the family she had left.

As they returned to the lobby, she began to feel sick to her stomach again and quickly excused herself to go to the ladies' lounge.

When the heavy, carved wooden door swung shut behind her, a frothy mass of spittle hit her directly in the right eye, bubbling and burning as the spray found its mark.

"Be gone, witch! Thou art accursed! If you fail to heed my warning, there will be two deaths on your head before the bonfires are extinguished!"

The big woman's massive head was entirely swathed in a purple turban. There was a wilted corsage pinned to her chest, right at the level of Marlena's nose. The mingled odor of sweat and dead roses on Mrs. Brown-Hawker's heaving bosom made her feel nauseated.

Accursed? Really?

Letty shook a fat finger in her face and bellowed: "Marlena Bellum, I call you out as the reincarnation of Cassandra Vye and the devil's spawn! I invoke the hexing of Goody Brown against your evil spirit!"

As Marlena tried to get past, her antagonist ranted, "There's gambling, drinking, and fornicating going on all day in this devils' den. But you took it upon yourself to hide Mr. Drake behind your skirts and protect him from ME. Shame on you! Take care, Marlena Bellum. God rewards the innocent and punishes the wicked in this town. Remember, He punished the cold-hearted witch with the red hair whose blood courses in your veins. He will wreak vengeance on you and your paramour for opening Alta's doors to Satan!"

Marlena calmly wiped the spittle from her face. "I'm sorry, but I have no idea what or whom you're raving about, Letty. Will you please let me go by, or do I have to call for security?"

"You and Drake was laughin' at your betters, and you throwed my letter in your waste can. A God-fearing woman from my church saw you do it. You were in a hotel room together, though you're bound to others by solemn vows in church. It's known hereabouts, Satan's whore, that Cassandra's evil powers are yours. And an untimely death awaits men who make the fatal mistake of consortin' with your kind."

Then Letty repeated her opening threat. "Be gone, witch! Thou art accursed! If you fail to heed my warning, there will be two deaths on your head before the bonfires are extinguished!"

"Let me pass, please!"

There'd been a struggle, but somehow she'd got past the draped bulk of Mrs. Brown-Hawker and fled into a stall.

"A community of unforgiving souls" was how one outsider had described a cult of religious fanatics among the natives of Alta. This wasn't the first time these bigots had raised their ugly heads. Letty had been hell-bent on a mission to close them down for the past six months, ever since the fifth anniversary celebration of the hotel's opening.

The event was held on July 10, 1977, a propitious day of blazing sun and a cloudless sky colored a robin's egg blue. The festivities were carefully planned to coincide with the anniversary of the Wyoming Territory becoming the 44th state in 1890. A day of pomp and ceremony was planned on the grounds of the 200acre hotel property.

On hand were the Lieutenant Governor, the heads of the Union Pacific and Chicago, Burlington, and Quincy Railroads, the president of the Iron Workers Association (founded in 1901), and a representative of the DOE, to whom Jimmy Carter had transferred management after re-opening the rich Wyoming oil field reserves to counteract the Arab Oil Embargo of 1973-74.

The publisher of the Casper Star-Tribune was not on hand, but Drake was the biggest advertiser in the newspaper founded in 1891, and so the Star had sent instead an Overland Stage Company replica for the short parade that started off the festivities at 10 a.m.

On another horse-drawn vehicle, pageant players representing frontiersmen, trappers, prospectors, and homesteaders from the late 1880's sang songs from the Oregon Trail, interspersed with the peals of a fire bell from 1876 and tunes on a 1900 calliope. The parade ran along Sacajawea Pathway, a private two-mile stretch leading up Alta Mountain to the hotel's massive stone facade.

The parade was led off with a flourish by the Troopers, a Wyoming drum and bugle corps of national fame. Several female hotel staff were said to have swooned while watching the practice session the previous night under the lights on a local football field. It was hot, unseasonably so; the buffed lads had their shirts off and their horns held high.

Industry press was well represented, including one of the foremost food critics in the nation. Slated for the speechifying event were the head of Amoco Oil Refinery, a tribal chieftain from the Black Hills, and, of course, Harry Drake, the king of the mountain. To enthusiastic applause, the three men were splendidly carted to the front of the grandstand (which was draped in the Wyoming flag and Drake's ancestral Scottish banner) in a white carriage drawn by two Morgan houses named Indian Paintbrush and Pathetic Fallacy.

From the eagle-eyed perspective of its young director, the anniversary ceremonies went off without a hitch. Marlena felt as though her fairy godmother had waved a wand. The local dignitaries were on time and stayed sober, the microphones worked, and Harry's welcoming speech was well received. Flags flew in the sparkling sky; sleek black limousines lined the entranceway; and, after an informal winemakers' reception in the banquet hall, the food critic, well oiled by the vintage wines, went to his suite smacking his lips over the vichyssoise, Prince Edward Island mussels, potato strips fried in duck fat, thinly slivered carpaccio, and foie de gras petit fours.

In the glistening success story that would be reported in all the major travel magazines, there would be two incidents which weren't covered but which marred and soured the occasion.

The first occurred during the ceremonial aftermath. Over the objection of a small native faction, a new traffic stoplight had been installed at the intersection of Sacajawea Pathway and Hatter's Field Road, the thoroughfare angling directly into Alta proper. A souped-up Camaro driven by a young male cousin of Thom Hawker ran the red light, colliding with the horses drawing the empty white carriage. Indian Paintbrush was euthanized at the scene while his partner, Pathetic Fallacy, sadly looked on. At noon, the young man lost his leg in Alta Hospital.

The second incident carried repercussions that appeared equally serious in the minds of some religiously reborn natives who had objected, for five fruitless years, to the demonic nomenclature of the private club hidden within the bowels of Drake's glamorous hotel.

At ten p.m., dressed only in his birthday suit, a tipsy guest went out to fill his ice bucket, then wandered into the lobby to get assistance on finding his room.

His nakedness amused the front desk staff. But it elicited loud, outraged shrieks from a grim-faced knot of elder natives standing in the lobby. Led by Letty Brown-Hawker and her husband, Thomas Hawker III, they were members of a newly re-opened WCTU chapter, which had recently been referred to by a Casper newspaper columnist as "the stillborn offshoot of a dead tree."

While their cause was dead to most, these natives were very much alive and extremely vocal. They'd assembled after a four-hour sunset prayer meeting to protest once again an establishment dedicated to Satan. "Purity before Profit," they chanted with raised signs that called for a boycott of all Drake enterprises. They did so until escorted off property by security.

From Marlena's perspective, the only downside to the nudity incident was that it hadn't been perpetrated by visiting celebrity. He was merely a New York advertising executive, so the colorful mishap wouldn't be picked up by the national press.

However, for the owner-developer it was no laughing matter because a week later, Harry Drake received an indignant letter from Letty Brown-Hawker. Co-signed by ten Baptist and Pentecostal churchmen, her letter threatened a boycott of the hotel "by all decent, God-fearing souls in northeast Wyoming" unless the saloon's name was changed before the first bonfire celebration at Halloween.

"Look at this!" Harry growled, entering Marlena's suite and flinging her the letter. "It's also published in today's local paper."

"I never read that rag," she declared.

Then, taking up the letter, she pretended to read it aloud. "All persons found guilty of committing public improprieties shall be sentenced to a month's hard labor sucking the sweat off Mrs. Brown-Hawker's thighs, jowls, and double chins."

As the maid emerged from cleaning the bathroom, Marlena tossed the letter into the leather waste can under her desk. The maid glared at her, then exited, leaving them alone.

Harry tapped his chest. "It's my hide they're after now, but they'll go after yours next. Wait and see. You won't be laughing when a lynch mob shows up here."

"Phooey. These are the same Jesus freaks who see Santa as an anagram for Satan. They're nut cases. Ignore them."

He scowled at her.

"Oh, get off your high horse, darling."

Tossing her hair, she twirled and whirled, looking in her dance like a glittering cross between a gypsy queen and Rapunzel. Drake's concern with their affront to the community's moral fiber was effectively quashed by a performance that continued passionately in her bed.

During the months following the nudity incident, it seemed Marlena was right, at least from the perspective of Drake's bottom line. The Alta Hotel received a ton of positive publicity in <u>Town and Country</u>, <u>Cosmopolitan</u>, and <u>Esquire</u>. Travel writers zeroed in on B.L. Zebub's "risqué, vibrant appeal, rivaled only by Studio 54 in New York and the Monster in Key West."

Chapter Six

"Right in here, Mrs. Bellum."

"Ms. Bellum, if you don't mind," she said, following the nurse into the examination room.

"Please take off everything except your bra, Miss Bellum," said the nurse, "and put this gown on with the opening to the back."

"I never wear a bra," Marlena said. "Burned mine in '69."

"Then take everything off," said the nurse matter-of-factly. "You can sit up here on the end of the table. Dr. Huddleston will be right in."

On both coasts, she was thinking, women were cutting wide swaths through barbaric restraints that had for too long held them hostage. No fault divorce was now available, and abortion was a legal right. On the bathroom mirror, her roommate had slapped a sticker: "Out of the war, out of the home, out of the closet."

In Alta, however, the natives didn't know from Gloria Steinem, though women had got the vote in 1869 and knew how to shoot a bear. In this town, the past loomed large, immovable as Alta Mountain, and certain superstitions ran deep.

Marlena gazed at the documents framed on the wall. There were Dr. Ronald Huddleston's diploma from Stanford University Medical School and his certification of residency at a St. Louis hospital.

In the second grade, Typhoid Ronnie--so nicknamed because Ron gave her the mumps, chicken pox, measles, and finally scarlet fever-- would dip her red-gold braids into his inkwell and torment her with opinions that contradicted her upbringing. He said Catholics were ignoramuses who worshipped graven images and were over-populating Earth.

The scarlet fever she got from him kept her in quarantine while her mother successfully schemed to move her family back East, where Faith had grown up. Yet, despite Ron having been something of a bad luck charm, Marlena was looking forward to seeing him again.

Yesterday, on the pretext of picking up medication for a house-bound patient, Chloe had conned her into taking the royal tour of Ron Huddleston's offices and state-of-the-art medical equipment. She'd quickly seen her old nemesis was that rare thing, a good man and a sexy one.

Chloe had then convinced her to make an appointment. "Regardless of your iron constitution, Lena, you've been complaining of a stomach ache ever since we got here. You might have an inflamed appendix."

In the nineteenth-century novels she'd read as a girl, there was a type of man called "Beauty's Dog," a fetching title for Ron's sort. The women of Alta could do worse, it was Marlena's opinion, than trust Dr. Ron with their pap smears.

A good man is hard to find, she thought as she settled herself atop the examination table. *But a hard man will come quickly, if you just put your lips together and blow.*

She was wriggling her toes when Ron came striding through the door, his kind, grey eyes twinkling and a broad smile widening his boyish features.

"Howdy," he said, dropping his gaze to scan her chart. "Was it yesterday you and Dr. Vye came by, or was that a dream?"

"A nightmare, you mean. Now it appears you can't get rid of me."

Ron's hands and trimmed fingernails were immaculate; he was closely shaven, his sideburns long and neat; his full head of auburn hair was carefully gelled and slicked back. When he came closer, holding out his hand, she inhaled a whiff of Bay Rum, her favorite scent.

"Thanks for seeing me on short notice, Ron."

"No problem. How are you feeling today?"

"The same."

"So, the nausea you mentioned has continued for more than a week?"

"Yes."

"Any other symptoms?" With a firm, gentle touch, he began checking her throat and neck for swollen glands.

"I'm having trouble sleeping."

"Are you taking anything for it?"

"Valium and Brandy Alexanders."

She added, "That's a joke, Ron."

"I hope so. Combining alcohol and pills can be deadly." He put the stethoscope on her back and began listening to her lungs. "Now, breathe deeply for me. Once more, a deep breath." He continued to listen as she took several long breaths.

"Any cough or congestion?"

"No."

"Dizziness?"

"Some."

"Abdominal pain other than nausea?"

"Some."

"Tarry stools?"

"Making this up as you go along? Of course not."

"Exposure to school children in the past week?"

"Not on my diet."

As he listened to her heart through his stethoscope, his grey eyes were gazing steadily aside, which allowed her to examine his features. Other than the auburn hair and the pale, unusually long eyelashes, she never would have recognized this serious-looking young doctor for the boy who had sat behind her in second grade.

"Your pulse and blood pressure are normal. Your lungs sound fine. You don't have any signs of acute appendicitis or our local influenza. Your temperature is slightly below normal."

"So, other than cold feet, nothing's wrong with me?"

"Hopefully that's the case. Have you had any fainting spells?"

"Sometimes I feel dizzy when I stand up. Maybe I'm channeling the Russian astronaut."

"When was your last menstrual period?"

"I'm late, but that's not unusual."

"How late?"

"Oh, a month or so. Make that two."

"And you say that's normal for you?"

"My flow is erratic; the timing's all over the place. Usually it's heavy, but at the end of October, there was some spotting and that was all she wrote."*I can't believe I'm chatting with Typhoid Ronnie about my periods!* He was asking her another question. She asked him to repeat it.

"I said, is there a chance you might be pregnant?"

"Are you serious? Can't be. I've worn an I.U.D for five years."

"What I meant was, are you sexually active?"

"Oh, I see. Um, yes." She could feel herself blushing.

The last time was Sunday, when Harry casually strolled in. She'd been out of sorts after waiting for a day and a half. But eventually she gave up pouting and sat on his cock, which was her favorite way to orgasm. Then he'd rolled her over, spanked her, entered her, and come quickly.

But as they parted, he'd spoken to her in way that rankled. As he buckled his belt, towering over her as she lay naked on the bed, he refused to answer her questions about spending time over the holidays. He sounded like a professor delivering a lecture.

"Follow your own inclinations, for your own reasons. I can't bear on my shoulders the burden of your lonely childhood, Marlena."

Parting was always unbearable torture for her, especially when he whistled as he walked away. But after that cold message, she'd started to feel physically sick, and she'd been nauseated ever since.

"Using any other form of contraception besides the I.U.D.?" Dr. Ron asked.

"Why? It's foolproof, isn't it?"

"No form of birth control is 100% effective. Sometimes I.U.D.'s spontaneously slip or hang too low to be fully protective. Mind if I take a look?"

"You're the doctor."

He called the gray-haired nurse back in. Marlena was instructed to put her feet up in the stirrups and lie back.

"Big scoot toward me," he said. "Just a little more. Good."

After a few seconds of investigation, he said, "there are no mullerian anomalies."

"Meaning?"

"You don't have two sets of equipment--two vaginas, two cervixes, two uteruses. Sometimes they account for a pregnancy where one wouldn't otherwise be expected."

"I didn't realize there was such a thing."

"It's not that unusual. They occur in one of three thousand women."

"It must lead to some unusual conversations in the bedroom. I can think of another advantage."

"What's that?"

"A woman might claim to be a virgin when she's not, because one hymen is still intact."

"Technically speaking, she'd be right."

"That's the kind of technicality that might save a Muslim woman's life."

When the examination was concluded, Ron waited until the nurse was out of the room, then he turned and put a hand on the table. He was looking directly at her.

"What's wrong with me, doctor?" she asked sweetly. "Will I live?"

"You'll make it to Christmas. That's a joke, Lena. We'll run a chemical test to confirm it, " he said, "but I'd estimate you're about eight weeks pregnant, give or take a couple weeks."

"But what about my frigging I.U.D.?"

In her seven-year marriage to Codwell Dimmer, they'd used virtually no birth control, and yet she hadn't conceived. When Harry became her sexual Svengali, she'd chosen the I. U. D. for its invisible, highly effective protection. *There simply must be another explanation for her symptoms.*

"The I.U.D. was a low hanger, so I removed it. If the test turns out negative and you're not pregnant, you'll want to have another inserted or choose a different method, such as the birth control pill. I'll be glad to help you with any option you choose."

"*If* I'm pregnant, is it too late to, uh, get rid of it?"

"If it's the first trimester, there's no viability. We don't do the procedures here, but there's one clinic in Cheyenne, and many options in San Francisco. I'd be glad to call for you."

She was glad she'd come to see Ron. An older doctor would've hemmed and hawed, even lectured her on the abortion issue.

Not that it was anyone's fucking business what she did with her own body. My God, she thought, getting knocked up was certainly not part of the grand scheme for her and Harry. She stared at the ceiling, her hands tightly clenched on her stomach.

"Are you all right?"

"No, I'm not all right. According to you, I'm fucking pregnant."

"Then, a pregnancy at this time wouldn't be desirable?"

"On a scale of one to ten, ten being the least desirable, pregnancy would be an eleven hundred pound gorilla."

"Forgive a personal question. How would your husband feel about it?"

"Not good. We're separated."

"Oh, I'm sorry. Is there anything I can do...as an old friend, I mean?"

She managed a pale smile. "You can join me for a drink, doctor. I'm not in a mood to be drinking alone in my hotel suite."

"What a lovely idea, Lena. But it's not yet ten, and I have a roomful of patients. Here, let me give you a hand up."

"That's why we're called patients, because we need a lot of it to see you guys. My mother used to say, 'you spend your whole life waiting on some damn man.' Dad could never move fast enough for her."

"I remember your dad. He was quite a funny guy. Didn't he have a serious accident around the time you left Roosevelt?"

"Literally a ton of coal fell on his legs at New Gillette Electric. We left Wyoming and moved to Cleveland so Austin could have experimental transplant surgery. I attended Cleveland State on scholarship, then the University of Arizona for architecture school. Lucky me, PAD's biggest project happened to land in my home town."

"Dr. Vye mentioned you're a kind of social director now for the hotel?"

"I've taken on special events as a consultant, but I still do design work for PAD in San Francisco. I travel back and forth on a regular basis."

More regular than her periods were. She felt numb, but she could hear herself prattling on. "My PR gig gives me a perfect excuse to hang out at B.L. Zebub's, where everyone knows my name and what I drink."

"Would the drink offer still be good later this afternoon? My rounds are over around five."

"Faith's in town for our reunion. But if you come by B.L. Zebub's at six, I'll be sure to be there. I can stand only so much family togetherness."

Though Marlena no longer believed in guilt, a thought that brought a feeling of shame seared her heart. Years ago, she'd slammed the door shut on her parents, rejecting them both without any explanation.

"You can get dressed now. Take all the time you want. We'll call you with the test results, so be sure to leave a phone number where you can be reached."

"Okay. When may I expect them?"

"Tomorrow evening at the latest. But I may be able to pull some strings."

"You already have, doctor."

He chuckled. At the door, he turned and said: "Save me a good seat. Tell them I drink Guinness and the name is just Ron."

"Only the best seat in the house will do for Just Ron."

He gently closed the door.

The wide smile creasing her heart-shaped face gradually faded. She sat on the edge of the examining table, still wearing the blue paper gown.

But though her blue-green eyes were looking out into space, Marlena was feeling not so much spaced-out as she was feeling tuned in. She was focused on her own psyche, a place she seldom visited, much preferring to keep busy.

Chapter Seven

Marlena was taking another look at her thought processes during the past half hour. *Something was not quite right.*

When such moments of illumination arrived, cousin Chloe had taught her, she should sit perfectly still and allow her thoughts to flow where they would.

"When you're taking a walk in your inner space, nothing is unimportant."

It had started while she was on the examining table--a sensation of hyper-awareness, as though she were floating above herself and peering through a crystal skull into her working brain. Oddly, her mind seemed much younger; a seven-year-old brain was displayed for her to observe, the brain who'd been Typhoid Ronnie's sidekick.

Marlena focused on two separate reactions that had been going on inside her head during his physical examination of her.

On the one hand, she'd been thinking: *Fuck! That's Typhoid Ronnie's hand feeling me up! Let me outa here!*

On the other hand, he now was an adult doctor of medicine, a sanctioned authority figure, and she was his patient. It was her job to submit without a struggle, right?

But, why so fast? Her submissive response had come up so quickly, she'd barely registered the first impulse. This insight shed light on episodes from childhood that had been on her mind since the discovery of the two notebooks.

Had she been programmed to be sexually passive?

Marlena touched her bare feet to the floor, coming back with a thump to the present. As she pulled on her bell bottom jeans, she jerked her mind back to the ominous specter of being pregnant and ruining her dream.

Did Typhoid Ronnie continue to bring her bad luck? But Chloe had taught her that we make our own luck. As she closed the examination room door, nausea swept over her in waves. Fearing she might tip over and embarrass herself, she walked slowly down the hall.

Harry had grown colder of late and their meetings were less frequent. Would she be able to get him on board with an escape from this gossipy town, if indeed she was carrying his child?

"Distant men and far-off places," Dr. V had once observed, "often appear far more romantic than they really are."

Naturally, if she confided in Chloe, she would be pressed to answer a slew of questions she'd much prefer to ignore.

What professional damage was she doing to herself? How would the community perceive of her if they knew of the affair? What legal hot water was she in? Finally, how would it all end?

Blah, blah, blah....

Almost everyone practices amateur psychiatry these days, Marlena thought, just as they used to apply permanent waves at home.

She'd read her share of self-help books about the bad karma created by romantic egotism. But she also knew one long weekend with her lover had the power to cast off any demons of doubt and blast all well-intentioned advice to the four winds.

Damn the torpedoes--full speed ahead!

"I will never give up on Harry," she vowed silently, clenching her fists. "Never! No matter what happens, I will never give up Harry."

At the check-out desk, she fished in her purse for business cards and came up with the house key to Mill's Creek Chloe had given her yesterday. Was this a lifeline she should grab at, before Letty took another stab at driving her from town on a rail?

As she fumbled around in her purse for a pen, the purse fell off her arm and the contents spilled out onto the floor, rolling everywhere.

"Fuck!"

"Are you all right, Miss?"

"I apologize. Too much coffee," she mumbled, hurriedly gathering up her belongings. On a business card, she wrote down the phone number for Mill's Creek and handed it to the woman. "That's where I can be reached tomorrow," she said. "The doctor will have test results for me."

"Better watch yourself outside, Miss Bellum. It's icy."

She started to correct the honorific, then gave it up.

"Do you have a phone I could use?"

"Out in the hallway, dear."

Shivering in the unheated vestibule, she looked in the yellow pages for Bryce Scattergood, whom Chloe had recommended for real estate appraisal. She noted he was broker of his own company, also president of the Northeastern Wyoming Association of Realtors (NWAR).

"I've been expecting your call, Ms. Bellum," said Mr. Scattergood.

Really? Why would that be? The Bellums and the Scattergoods hadn't been on speaking terms for two generations. Was another weird revelation in store? *The deep rumble in his voice was sexy.*

They agreed to meet in his office Wednesday to discuss the market value of the Bellum house.

Now what? If she went straight to Mill's Creek, she was assured peace and quiet. Chloe kept office hours in town during the week. She could tell Faith she was assisting Annie Witherspoon, Chloe's housekeeper, with preparations for the big Christmas Fire Night Ball.

Duty was the only excuse that worked with Faith. Marlena had relied heavily on it to keep her mother at a safe distance during the past year. The last thing she'd needed was Faith showing up unannounced at her new digs in the Castro and getting a load of her lesbian roommate, the microbiologist.

Power to the sisters and their exuberant romps, which they sometimes inveigled Marlena into joining. But Faith would die if she walked into that scene, nor would she be tolerant of Kat's heavy eye makeup, multiple piercings, and tongue stud.

There was no point waiting around at the hotel for Harry. Last night had been another disappointment. He'd never shown, presumably kept longer than expected in Laramie. *Harry doesn't confide in me as he used to.*

What would Harry say when she quizzed him about the bank's low-ball offer to buy a pink Victorian house on an abandoned city street, which for decades was the Bellums' beloved home? What would he say if she turned out to be pregnant?

First stop today, she decided, would be the hotel, where she'd pack, touch base with Chloe and Faith by phone, and, most critically, leave a note for Harry that they needed to talk. Then she'd go to Mill's Creek, collapse, and attempt to recover from this latest blow to her equilibrium, not to mention her ego.

As she drove into Alta's tiny downtown district, the shopkeepers were letting in customers. Snow-blowers were out on the sidewalks, plows were clearing the streets, and school children were admiring the display through the glass windows of Harrison's Olde Timey Department Store.

She loved holidays but she felt lethargic, not at all in the spirit, as she drove under Harrison's silver banner:

Celebrating 75 Years of Lighting Local Christmas Trees
Join us Sunday for Fire Night 1977

Fuck me!

Instinctively she slammed on the brake pedal. All she had in her suitcase was a red sweater from the Horchow Collection for Faith. There were no Christmas gifts for Chloe and Annie. How could she have forgotten? *Was she losing her powers, just when she needed them most?*

As she proceeded up the mountain to the Alta Hotel's valet parking, a new agenda emerged, a shopping day with Faith. She got out from the silver BMW with less bounce than usual and in the proximity of old black Joe. The grizzled valet now worked only part-time because of rheumatic legs; he came hobbling over.

"Seen Mr. Drake today, Joe?"

"Nope. Not expectin' him neither. Will you be needin' help with any bags today, Miz Marlena?"

"Oh, no. You know me, Joe; I travel light."

"Yessum. Never seen you even once with anythin' bigger dan a knapsack. How you manage dat?"

"Traveling light is my specialty, Joe. It's a state of mind."

"My wife Dorothea don't know fum dat state. When we tooken our weekend in Vegas she brung herse'f a suitcase big as an ice-box. Woman, I ses to her, you expecks me to truck that big ol' thing up dos steps? Carry yer own big bag; you got de muscles for it. Uhn, uhn, uhn."

The last big suitcase she had trundled, Marlena told Joe, got left behind on the Queen Mary when she was bringing B. L. Zebub to

Wyoming from the Cotswolds. It took weeks to recover the suitcase and another week to iron her clothes.

Their arms were pressed lightly together as they stood at the railing of the ship's aft deck. When their eyes locked, the sensation was like wildfire through her veins.

"Do you feel it?" Harry said.

The world beyond his eyes was cloudy, as though she were being hypnotized.

"Do you feel that current?"

She hadn't answered, but did she ever! Her panties were sopping wet.

Hastily sweeping the words and images from her mind, she continued: "After that, Joe, I bought myself a travel wardrobe that wears like iron. And I carry a small bag I can easily tote."

"Yo' sho' do *look* light. Seem to ol' Joe you needs to stop hangin' around 'dis here hotel and workin' day and night."

She watched Joe slowly tighten his white gloves.

Not every native in Alta was a gossip, a prude, a bigot, or a vicious hatemonger like crazy Letty Brown-Hawker and her clan. Perhaps the good people were why Typhoid Ronnie had come back and why Chloe stuck it out here, when she could be living the high life doctoring famous people in San Francisco, New York, or even Europe.

Or could there be another reason why Chloe stayed?

During Sunday brunch with her mother, when she had delivered the torpedo-like news of her legal separation from Coddie and admitted to a relationship with Harry Drake, Faith had shot one back.

She'd revealed that Chloe and Harry had nearly eloped in 1947. Their elopement had fizzled before it started, and 1947 was so long ago, but yet--what if Chloe and Harry were more than old friends?

Marlena strode through the hotel lobby, acknowledging the perfunctory smiles of the staff as she breezed past them.

"We go way back, Harry and I," Chloe had said on that first day over drinks.

"Chloe and I go way back," Harry had said Sunday night in her hotel suite.

An image of Chloe and Harry naked in bed, getting it on, arose unbidden. Walking into the elevator, she numbly pushed the button for the sixth floor.

Which made her more jealous? Chloe as a rival for Harry's hungry lips and hard cock? Or Harry as a rival for Chloe's motherly affections?

In the annals of sexual politics, odder things had happened than one's psychiatrist stealing one's lover. All the more reason, then, to stay at Mill's Creek, where she could keep an eye on Chloe's comings and goings. *Keep your friends close and your enemies even closer.*

With her next deep breath, Marlena managed to become thoroughly ashamed of herself. She would have washed her mind out with soap if it were possible. She reached the sixth floor, ran down the hall to Suite 66, clutching her stomach, and got inside just in time to vomit in the bathroom toilet. *See, it's all stress-related, not a pregnancy.*

Then she called Chloe, to tell her she would be checking out of the hotel and moving to Mill's Creek later today.

Two decisions down. Now for the note to Harry.

At that precise moment, Marlena noticed her signed divorce petition papers were still spread out on her desk.

Fuck!

She'd intended to hide them before running out of here this morning. Harry mustn't see them. It would plant the wrong idea, a suspicion she was applying psychological pressure on him to file for divorce.

Having jammed the signed papers into the preaddressed overnight delivery envelope, she then set the envelope in her out-basket, where her assistant would pick it up before leaving and mail it for her.

Quickly she jotted on musk-scented notepaper: "Harry, urgent we connect before the holiday. Let me know when, where. Staying with Chloe. Call me. Marlena."

Ball's in your court, my love, she thought, putting the note inside its pink linen envelope. She would take this message up to his room personally, to make sure he got it.

Harry would probably assume she was fishing for her Christmas gift. The pearl-and-aquamarine bracelet he'd given her Sunday wasn't a

Christmas present, but penance for showing up days late without sending a word.

"The stones are the same color as your eyes, my love. Are you crying? No. I didn't think so. I've never seen you cry. I like that about you."

Dry-eyed, but in her heart, she was bleeding from wounds of rejection, so dismissive had her lover's words and actions become of late. She feared his seeing how much she needed him, how obsessed she was with regaining the fervor of their early years.

She'd worn the bracelet yesterday for lunch with Chloe, and when she'd said it was a gift from Harry, no frown or wrinkle had appeared on Chloe's smooth face. There was no reason, she assured herself, to fear Chloe's reaction to the affair.

Indeed, as it turned out, Chloe had already known about the affair. It had all come out over cocktails at B. L. Zebub's, after Marlena's nerves had already been shot to hell by Mrs. Brown-Hawker's threat of a curse hanging over her head.

Chapter Eight

"Chloe, it's been so long since we had a chance to hang out."

"Much too long, dear."

"The last time was between Cleveland State and grad school, when I came out on the train to spend the summer with Granny. You'd just opened the summer horse camp for girls. I signed up and immediately developed a huge crush on Jack Nelson, your blond horse handler with the rippling back muscles. But Jack didn't know I was alive."

Chloe chuckled. "I find *that* hard to believe. Jack's an older cousin of Apollo Nelson, my current ranch hand. In fact, Jack's getting married this week to his former sweetheart, a second marriage."

"Well, Jack put me on a fat-assed Spanish nag named Holy Toledo, nothing like your well-bred steeds, Dickens and Darwin. I was determined not to go anywhere on that beast. I wanted to stay near Jack. He slapped it and yelled, 'Go, Holy Toledo, go, goddammit!'

"But the horse wouldn't move an inch. I was willing it not to go. That was the first and last time I ever used my mental powers on an animal."

"Your ability to concentrate is powerful. No question of that."

"A girl at horse camp told me Jack had the hots for the barmaid at the Plush Horse. So I snuck down there one night and caught the pair doing it outside in the holly bushes. But after awhile, I could care less.

"Remember what a beautiful place the old Plush Horse used to be, back in the fifties? I couldn't keep my eyes off the old inn. I was horror-stricken by what terrible shape it was in. That night, I lay awake for hours, thinking if there was something I could do to save the life of the Plush Horse. Despite my willing it otherwise, the fire department condemned it, and it was torn down the following year."

Chloe observed, "That was a great opportunity for Harry Drake. He got his grandfather's prime property back for pennies on the dollar."

Marlena noted the pointed comment about Harry. Was Chloe testing her? If so, why?

"I felt a lot worse about the Plush Horse going down the tubes than I did about the barmaid going down on Jack Nelson."

"Perhaps that's when you found your calling, dear, to save historic buildings."

"Well, it wasn't the other," Marlena quipped. "Oral sex is hardly my favorite, unless I'm the one getting it. And--"

"Yes?"

"That wasn't the only eye-opener I received. You were volunteering at the Brighton School for Indian Girls, now corrected to Native American Girls. Remember?"

"I taught courses for them--"

"In Cultural Trends and Western Philosophy," Marlena quickly finished her cousin's sentence.

"Right."

"That was my first exposure to Ayn Rand and Objectivism. We read her introduction to the 1968 edition of <u>The Fountainhead</u>, and I became a devotee. But the philosophical H's also had a big effect. I stored it all here, alphabetically," said Marlena, knocking her knuckles on her large noggin.

"Let's see. There was Hamilton, an evolutionary psychologist who was applying Darwin to modern human behavior, like you. I dug Hegel's dialectic: one extreme precipitates the other, like a pendulum. Finally, the best of all, Heisenberg's Uncertainty Principle: when you examine a particle with an electron microscope, the nature of the particle is changed. So, the more you investigate, the more skewed the results. What's my grade, Dr. V?"

"'A' for adequate, given your talents."

In a lowered voice, Marlena said, "I remember everything I see or read, almost in the same degree of detail you can."

Chloe could quote an entire book verbatim.

"It's a rare gift. My mother had it. Yours does too. The correct term for it is an eidetic memory."

"It sometimes presents a problem."

"For whom, dear?"

"You aren't about to practice psychoanalysis in a bar, are you, cousin Chloe? So, what are your plans for the rest of the afternoon?"

"A young patient of mine has invited me to her seventh birthday party at Bottomly's Cafe. I promised I'd be there by five."

The Age of Reason.
"What is, dear?"
"Oh, did I say that aloud? HMC--that's what Daddy called Holy Mother Church--decreed that seven is the Age of Reason. Of course, Daddy would try to talk a leg off a wooden Indian. 'Marlena Mae, at your Age of Reason, you'll know it all.' I didn't realize he was putting me on."

"Your father was the most charming man I ever knew," commented Chloe agreeably. "Why don't you and Faith come over around seven thirty tomorrow night for Sunday supper? Plan to stay over if you like."

"Count on me for champagne."

"Only if you want it, dear. We've got wine."

"Oh, but I do. Bubbly and Faith, a trippy combination. Like taking mescaline and then going to church on Good Friday. Hopefully by tomorrow evening I'll have recovered from our brunch and will be able to keep something down."

Chloe scrutinized her. "Stomach's bothering you, dear?"

"I guess it's the jitters. It's been a long time since I sat down and had a heart-to-heart with the Gestapo."

Chloe choked on her wine. "Lena! Isn't that what Granny Bellum used to call Faith?"

"She did, and with good reason. On the other hand, I'm looking forward to our pajama party on the solstice without any reservations. Remember, you promised to tell me Cassandra's story Wednesday night. But I wonder what makes you think I own a pair of pajamas?"

"Would you prefer we have an evening in the raw, like they do on the New York stage these days? I'm game if you are."

There was a hint of mischief in Chloe's amber eyes. Marlena returned it, twinkle for twinkle.

"Why shut my mouth, Doctor V. Once upon a time, I was a patient of yours. What if I told on you to the state board? You could lose your license!"

"But who would believe you? You know my reputation is impeccable."

Marlena threw up her hands in mock despair. "Isn't it dull being an icon of respectability? Tell you what. I'll take you on as a project, turn you into a cougar."

Chloe shook her head.

"No? Hmmm. What else could I do to make your stainless life more exciting? You don't happen to have a secret rich boyfriend stashed away somewhere? I could try to steal him away with my mesmeric powers. That would be an exciting game to play!"

Chloe's unreadable gaze bore straight into her cousin's sparkling, blue-green eyes. There was a pregnant pause, the air suddenly growing heavy.

"What would you do with another one, dear?" asked Chloe in an even tone.

Marlena's cheeks reddened. She looked away.

"Who told you?"

Chloe's face was neutral. "It's the coconut hotline here, darling, only without the coconuts. But in fact I didn't learn your secret from anyone here. "

"Then how did you? We've been so careful!"

"A colleague at a conference in San Diego saw the two of you at a Santa Monica hotel. He knows both Harry and Lila quite well, only he didn't know who the beautiful lady on Harry's arm was. From his description, I figured out the mystery woman had to be you. So, do you want to talk about it, Lena? We go way back, Harry and I."

As the final sentence lingered in the air, Marlena's eyebrows shot up. Chloe bit her lip, as if regretting the words.

"So do Harry and I, five long years now. I'm a big girl, Dr. V. I make my own decisions." Marlena added dramatically: "Two can play at keeping secrets, you know."

Chapter Nine

Marlena picked up the phone and dialed Ho Jo's, remorse churning in her belly.

Since arriving for this reunion, she'd been second guessing Chloe's motives and putting off Faith. It was high time she did the right thing by both mother figures, get this family reunion back on track, no matter how hellishly weird the aura was getting.

"Hello?"

"Mama, it's Lena. Sorry to have been missing in action today. I slept late. Any chance you can tear yourself away from the crocheting? Turns out I've got all my Christmas shopping left to do. Great. I'll be there to pick you up in fifteen minutes."

She zipped up her small roller bag and checked her briefcase to make sure the brown notebooks were inside. Then she locked her private closet door, what Harry called "Marlena's den of iniquity."

It contained a black satin eyeshade, lingerie, a Yahtzee game, and a bong, amounting to a kit for entertaining Harry.

She took the elevator up one floor to Harry's penthouse level.

After unlocking his suite and entering, she placed her urgent message on the fireplace mantle. A man of routine, this time of year Harry always turned the gas fireplace on first thing upon coming in; he'd be sure to see the note.

"Hi, Martha," she said to the Finnish maid standing outside with her cart, waiting to enter. "Haven't seen Mr. Drake today, have you?"

"No, ma'am. Merry Christmas, Ms. Marlena."

"You too, Martha."

Twenty minutes later, as the cleaning lady left the suite, an air current was sucked in by the quick movement of her cart as it banged against the door. The current caught and rode on a draft that happened to be coming from the fireplace. Then it swirled around the pink linen envelope, caught an edge, and finally tumbled it off the fireplace mantel.

The distress signal from Marlena to her lover drifted like a snowflake, riding the air current toward the white marble floor, floating down, down, down and then entering the copper log-carrier. There it flopped over and was wedged to the side by a pile of small twigs, becoming invisible.

On such small motions may one's fate depend.

Chapter Ten

A weak ray of sunshine slanted across Hatter's Field, briefly highlighting a jagged, towering peak called the Hat, which would be the main field of action during the upcoming Christmas Fire Night bonfire.

But from the perspective of Harold Augustus Drake, fuming on the outskirts of town late Tuesday morning, it all looked like a fucking field of fucking inaction.

Negotiations in Laramie had broken down once again. Then his mobile phone battery died, and so he was rendered helpless when the front end of his black Mercedes 200SL sports car slid into a ditch at the tail-end of a mile-long pileup of stranded vehicles.

He was trying to be patient so as not to elevate his blood pressure, which his doctor in Casper had warned him about. But an hour later, when at last a county sheriff's car slowly approached with red lights flashing and tire chains grinding, Harry was out of patience and his jutting jaw line was aflame.

A round-faced deputy slowly rolled down his window and inquired laconically into his particular tale of woe. Then, when the officer saw who he was, his tune changed. Before the deputy moved on to the next vehicle, Harry was afforded the use of the officer's mobile phone to contact his secretary, Carlotta, at his office in the hotel.

As he waited for his private tow truck to show up, Harry began singing to pass the time. He had a decent tenor voice and a good memory for off-color lyrics from the wild parties of bygone fraternity days.

Smokey the bear, Smokey the bear,
Has a prick like dynamite, covered with hair.
When he plucks his magic twanger, the girls all shout with glee.
He can shoot a wad of jizzum 'cross the state of Tennessee!

He followed this up with a George Cohan medley--"Yankee Doddle Dandy," "It's a Grand Old Flag," and "Over There."

When Harry tired of the sound of his own voice, he then set about recalling the names of friends with homes in Palm Beach or the Caribbean. If this bullshit mobile phone were working, he would have been on it making arrangements to escape. That's how disgusted he was with the Laramie deal and the damned winter weather, by Mungo.

A conservative man by nature and breeding, Harry Drake was often reckless in his business deals and in his relationships with the fairer sex. Some would argue these are not mutually exclusive traits in powerful men, even into the second millennium. But, provided the status quo suited him, Harry was not one to flee from it, and this engrained trait was the source of some current conflict with his mistress.

An imperious child with a bad stutter that took years of practice and an iron will to conquer, young Harry had been adored by his older sister, Susannah, who'd gladly indulged his expressed wish that she exclaim "hail, Augustus!" whenever he entered the room.

His mother thought the sun rose and set on Harry.

His father was less sure his sulky son deserved the adulation surrounding him, but Nicholas was seldom there, and when he was at home, he was in bed reading a newspaper. Harry therefore grew up seeing himself as a superior being whom women automatically worshipped, whether from afar or close-in.

Yet he always tried to behave in a gallant way toward the weaker sex, so as not to leave himself open to complaint.

All in all, he believed there was much cause for dissatisfaction going in the other direction, however. For instance, he'd lavished all his worldly goods upon his beautiful wife, only to find her indifferent toward himself and his castle. So he'd sought attention elsewhere. But lately, he'd been getting a rash of shit from his mistress, which was an unexpected, unwanted development.

To hear her tell of it, she was a miserable bird singing alone in a gilded cage. But Marlena couldn't very well complain about her accommodations. The Alta Hotel had won a five star Michelin rating in 1976. Their affair could go on indefinitely, from his perspective, so long as they didn't have to talk about it. In the past, they'd talked about the hotel, which suited him fine.

There simply weren't enough hours in the day for a man of business to waste time conversing with women.

The single exception had been Chloe Vye, brainy, beautiful, and gracious, a triple threat. He'd ardently enjoyed her company growing up, and he wished, in retrospect, they'd managed to pull off their foiled elopement.

They would have made a great couple. Chloe was steady as a rock, comfortable with tradition, and also, like him, she'd come back after traveling the world to live and work here contentedly.

As for Lila and Marlena, they were forever and tiresomely chomping at the bit. Lila was a fag hag of the first order; she was at her happiest touring Europe with some dickless wonder.

Marlena was that anomaly, a loner who worked hard at her career and also loved sex. It was precisely that combination which had drawn him in the first place. But of late she'd developed an annoying habit of demanding more emotional attention. She sometimes behaved like a clingy schoolgirl.

It wasn't his responsibility to make the needle move for her, was it? So the more she craved his attention, the less he gave.

Harry had gone to business psychology camp at Harvard last summer, so he knew his way around terms like "X and Y management styles," "Transactional Analysis," and the "'I'm OK, You're OK' personality." He went out of his way to make Marlena feel that she was OK, even if he himself felt uncomfortable about her encroaching presence in his personal life and her off-putting harping on something she called "emotional intimacy."

What this was, he hadn't the foggiest idea. He had much more interest in new ways to get his rocks off.

At first, it had all worked satisfactorily. He had the best of two worlds--a glamorous, stay-away wife and an adoring, part-time mistress. Lila had her freedom to roam. Marlena had the run of a fairy-tale establishment.

The bloom departed the rose when Lila came home and demanded to have a child, despite her doctor's opinion that she had a deformed uterus.

His gall was still rankling over Bob Drummond, so he wasn't about to cater to Lila's whims. But, if he toured Europe with Marlena while Lila sulked at home, there'd be hell to pay. So, since the hotel had been opened, Marlena was allowed to trot on back home to Dimmer.

That, he'd thought, was the end of their affair--sad, perhaps, but inevitable. Truthfully? He'd felt a tad relieved.

Yet somehow, against all the odds, Marlena had wormed her way back in. Bottom line, she'd used the milk-toast husband as a pimp. Coddie had caught him at a weak moment, and he'd paid for her return, getting part of her time on national promotions.

At first, they were caught up in the thrill of re-igniting the flame, having sex twice a day, jetting around the world. But now there was a lot on his plate. The affordable housing deal in Laramie, which had seemed in the bag, was anything but. It was taking extra time and effort to get the interested parties to come to the table and be bought off.

Outside of an occasional day trip to Santa Monica, days or weeks would pass when she would be at the hotel, waiting. Tough shit. He was sticking to the deal.

From the outset, they'd agreed no strings were attached. Obviously, each had other obligations, even if they could be characterized as unhappy marriages. Whose marriage wasn't unhappy? Why should theirs be any different?

He felt no more obliged to be faithful to Marlena than he did to his wife, who had shown her stripes early in the marriage by running off with her personal trainer to Ibiza and thumbing her nose under the guise of "free love." Free, my ass. He paid the bills!

"If you want to cry on Dimmer's shoulder about life's problems, it's no skin off my hose," he'd said in late October, emphasizing the ticklish point he was making by scratching his cock. She'd been putting out feelers about the holidays. Would she be deprived of their mutual orgasms again, like last Christmas?

Why not shift to Dimmer this mother-fucking intimacy thing?

"It's only natural for the two of you to stay in touch," he pressed on, giving her a sidelong look of appraisal. "Dimmer's someone you can communicate with, probably better than you can with me."

That had forced a rise out of her. He was amused by how Marlena managed to feign a high-and-mighty tone, despite her hurt feelings.

"If I wanted someone who communicates better than you, my love, I'd get a cat. Anyway, I never talk to Coddie anymore."

He knew that was a lie.

The truth was, she called Dimmer almost daily, and they talked at length. He knew because her hotel phone line was bugged.

He could feel the muscles clenching under the scar along his jawline that came from a knife fight in a Soho alley in a quarrel over unpaid gambling debts twenty years ago.

Dimmer and Marlena were long-time business associates, and he didn't really think there was anything more to it than that. But, she shouldn't have lied.

Lying had been Lila's downfall, too. To be more precise, it was Lila's blatant, assertive disloyalty to a degree which was staggering that had driven Harry to crave a submissive woman. Marlena wasn't even capable of the kind of promiscuous misconduct Lila had rubbed his nose in. Moreover, he wasn't fooled by Lila's current pose of repentance. Tigers didn't change their stripes.

Marlena had always been a purely submissive partner. Granted, this was a one-way street, but in the affairs of *his* heart, a one-way route was the only one he would allow inside.

To put it in business terms, from then on, he had the two beautiful women in his life pegged as unreliable suppliers.

Strike one for Marlena.

Though Harry had intended to imply to Marlena by his encouraging her to confide in Dimmer that he was looking for less, not more, communication in their connection, she, to his mind perversely, took it the other way.

As if to convince her lover she needed no one but him, she began to reveal more and more personal things from her past, even far back into her childhood in Alta. Suddenly, by Mungo, Harry knew more than he had ever wanted to about Marlena or any other broad!

One night, while they were watching the news on television, a story was aired of a celebrity who claimed she'd been molested by her father when she was a child, leading to various dysfunctions in her emotions and behaviors as an adult. A long time had elapsed between the occurrence of the events and the histrionic star's memories.

"I have a hard time getting worked up over that kind of garbage," Harry commented. "The bitch is just trying to get attention."

"Actually, it happened to me," Marlena blurted out, then blushed furiously.

He stared at her, at a total loss as to what to say. Finally he stammered, "Are you sure? Maybe it was a dream."

From her glimmering face, he could see he was expected to go on pretending he cared about her childhood. *The past was the past; let it lie.*

"So, what happened?"

"When I was almost seven, I was confined for nearly two months with scarlet fever. As it happened, my father had been laid off from the electric plant while they did work on the boilers. My mother's father had suffered a stroke, and she was in New York. For a time, I was home schooled by Dad, in our cabin in New Gillette. That's when the stroking of my private parts began, sometimes when he was singing songs to me or I was reading books on his lap. Sometimes it happened when I was in bed. I would lie very still, pretending to be asleep. The only time I felt safe was when I was in my grandparents' pink house, here in Alta."

What was a man supposed to say? Only degenerates, Southerners, and Mormons went in for getting their jollies off children. As repulsed as he was by her story, he felt obligated to continue showing some interest. "Did you tell anyone?"

"Well, no. Whom would I tell?"

"A priest or your mother. A psychiatrist, maybe, like Chloe."

She shook her head. "I was too afraid of getting my father into trouble. It's not like he raped me or anything. I believe he did it out of excess love and frustration. I used to think I'd dreamed it, but now I know better."

The low class nature of Marlena's disclosure left a bad taste in Harry's mouth.

Strike two.

Harry sometimes wondered what the big attraction in their affair was for Marlena. Social climbing, he supposed, but that wouldn't account for her obsession.

Women were susceptible to addiction when they were brought to climax for the first time, or so he'd heard. He had no doubt he was her sexual emancipator.

It was a fact, though, that she didn't need him as much as she thought, though he wouldn't tell her so until he was ready to call it off.

If it was intimacy she craved, then she would have to get it from someone else, not him. He'd made it clear where they stood, but on this one subject, she deliberately turned a deaf ear and a blind eye, though her memory was flawless, like a steel trap.

When he was able to be with her, about once a month now, he'd always make it a point after sex to ask if she was happy. She would always say she was. Case closed. To his mind, there was nothing to fix in the relationship, even if some of the fire had gone out of it.

He couldn't help it if he wasn't one of those guys whose passion burned on unaltered. He wasn't sure if guys like that even existed outside of romance novels.

Naturally, he wouldn't ever let on to Marlena she didn't exactly do for him what she used to do. That wouldn't be civilized. He tolerated the reduced temperature in their love life, like he tolerated everything else.

So he'd been genuinely surprised when a sudden climb in temperature occurred in a quarter where the fire had long been out. The fire starter was none other than his wife. Now she'd stopped gallivanting around the globe, he was treated to an occasional grapple in bed with the sexy, black-haired temptress, often after a heated argument. Violence seemed to get them both in the mood.

One tiny concern had sliced across his linear line of thought. After all her exploits, might Lila find him a tad tame? Perhaps his wife would enjoy a threesome; he certainly would! Some charming voluptuary might be enticed into the marital bed.

The ideal candidate? Marlena.

Midnight, on the last day of October, his mind was dwelling on these erotic thoughts while in the midst of watching soft porn on one of the televisions in his 4000-square-foot, seven-room penthouse suite.

The bonfires had been lit in sequence, just as in the olden days, beginning with the big one up at the Hat. One could watch the festivities from the best rooms in the hotel.

For each of the three celebrations, in October, November, and December, Marlena would trump up a special event and build goodwill among the customers, at a minimal cost to him.

That night, the first of the Fire Night bonfires were flaming out, but his fires were raging. Marlena was giving him head in one of her sexiest get-ups. On the television set, a buxom wench in a tiny Scotsman's kilt and nothing else was going down on Johnny Cum-Lately. A second lovely, naked young thing watched and made herself useful.

Aroused on several levels, he began to concoct his own fantasy.

How would it feel, he wondered, to be in bed with his lovely black-haired wife sucking his dick and his gorgeous redheaded lover playing with Lila's breasts? His cock made an immediate standing ovation. That would be one affirmative vote, he thought.

Let's try it on the redhead.

And so, Harry wondered aloud if one day Marlena might find it interesting to be involved in a sexual adventure. Say, a three way, my love?

She drew back from him, and his cock fell.

"I find all that kinky sex stuff to be somewhat mechanical and off-putting," she said.

"Oh? I didn't know."

"Last spring I attended a Lifestyle Convention in San Diego, to check them out for our banquet business. They're all swingers. The men are a bunch of weirdoes, and the way the women look at each other in the ladies' room–or rather, the way they won't look at each other–well, it creeped me out. It's pathetic."

"I was kidding," he said. "Don't give it another thought."

But he had given the idea of a three-way considerably more thought. Now that would be a Christmas present he could get into!

Lila was staying home for the holidays to please him. A plan was forming in his head to entice Marlena to Drake's Roost on a business pretext, then to seduce them both in a feat of sexual prowess. He jerked off to this fantasy every night.

In past holidays, he'd leave a note for Marlena demanding she drop everything and meet him somewhere exotic, anywhere from Tahoe to the Italian Alps. Breathlessly, as in the old romantic movies she loved, she would fly to his side in a provocative outfit, with a bagful of lingerie and joints disguised as Salem cigarettes, and they would enjoy days of uninterrupted lovemaking.

She kept little souvenirs from these trips locked up in her private closet, a cocktail napkin, matches, or a map of the city. Pathetic, how she couldn't distinguish a roll in the sack from a dime-store novel.

He always liked their holiday escapades well enough, but he'd made a promise to his wife to stay home. No last-minute fantasy and escape-- unless Marlena could see her way clear to yodeling naked in Switzerland in a pairs act with Lila!

His resolve to stick by his wife this Christmas had been rewarded with unexpected dividends. Lila had emerged from her usual self-absorbed torpor and was responding to the holiday spirit with frenzied activity, turning their stone mansion into an elaborate Santa's castle brimming with berried garlands, scented candles, and a snow-flocked, forty-foot Christmas tree sparkling with silver and crystal ornaments.

Lila had even voiced an interest in Chloe's Christmas Ball, coinciding with the final bonfire celebration. Her sources had told her there would be a Cajun band and the best bonfire in town. Dr. Vye's books had made her an international celebrity, and so the guest list might not be too boring. Indeed, Lila had read the last one, <u>Evolving Definitions of Femininity: Natural Selection and the Whore/Madonna Archetype.</u> Impressive, she said, though not her cup of tea.

Harry had agreed they would attend the ball together. But now he was wondering: was this such a good idea? Marlena would be lurking, baiting him to meet in a dark, attic bedroom. That would be irresistible, but bad for the improved climate at Drake's Roost.

This morning, when he'd called home on leaving Laramie, Lila had been hard at work on her lists. Guests would be arriving for the weekend, people whom Harry actually liked for a change: a couple of the old guard from back East, a Montana rancher and his wife, single male members of the Union Club. This wasn't the gay crowd Lila usually invited. He'd been touched by her deference to his tastes.

He would stop briefly at the hotel, present Marlena with her gift (an Elsa Peretti gold heart necklace from Tiffany's), have one last romp in the sack with her, and that would be that. Yes, that would be best way to proceed. She wasn't expecting him today. She loved surprises. A quick fuck, and then the brush-off.

A red tow truck was approaching and passing by the other cars in the ditch. Right behind it was a black tow truck, with a row of flashing orange lights and "Cowgirl Towing" emblazoned in pink lettering on the driver's door.

The ashen-haired female driver, a cigarette dangling from her lips (or was that a roach?), waved as she drove past. In the back of her vehicle was a pink fire extinguisher, and on the back window a pink decal of a girl in a cowboy hat.

Now there was a cracker-jack native girl for you, he thought. Lorna Anderson, who worked part time at the Sheriff's office, dealt in marijuana and would even deliver a bag of pure Columbian to the hotel and go down on him while he tested the product.

Her vanity license plate read: "Pog Mo Thoin." Lorna had told him this was Celtic for Kiss My Ass. But he didn't have time for messing with Lorna today.

Thank God for his Carlotta, who'd rounded up the tow. His Mexican secretary never missed a trick. It would be nice if he could turn over the Marlena-Lila situation to Carlotta, wouldn't it? Everyone said Carlotta was a lesbian, though he himself had detected no obvious sign of her perversion.

There was distraction written on his handsome features as Harry Drake reached a gloved hand out the window and languidly waved his embossed, white linen handkerchief, signaling for the red tow truck to stop.

Inside the truck, the red-bearded man turned to the other. "Sam, what's the difference between a Mercedes and a porcupine?"

"I dunno. What?"

"The prick's inside the Mercedes."

As Harry jounced along in the passenger seat of the tow truck, he found he was thinking about Marlena's voluptuous body, her hair and eyes, the package that was so devastating in bed, a spirited woman whom only his kind of man could possibly dominate.

He checked his Philippe Patek watch. It was eleven a.m.

Marlena was a late sleeper, and he didn't doubt for a moment she would be there when he entered her suite, that she would welcome him with open arms and a wet pussy.

But he found she wasn't there. Further, she seemed to have been in the midst of packing, as her tiny suitcase was half full.

Surely she wasn't planning to stay with her mother at Ho Jo's, with the odor of fried clams!

He sniffed, as if smelling the odious grease, and then his eyes fell on some papers strewn on her desk.

He ambled over, picked one up, scanning it quickly. It was an official document, requesting the final dissolution of the marriage between Marlena Bellum and Codwell Dimmer in the county of San Francisco.

His eyebrows knitted together; his eyes grew stormy. Obviously, the papers had been left out where he would see them. It was her devious way of putting pressure on him to get a divorce.

He didn't vary his pace, but he slammed the door on his way out. He went up to his hotel suite, where there was no sign of Marlena and no message from her either, only warm ashes in the fireplace where the maid had burned the trash.

Strike three---the bitch is out!

Chapter Eleven

While her husband's car was being towed to the Alta Hotel through blizzard conditions, Lila Coffin Drake was sitting before a fire at her ornate French provincial desk, one of the few places in Drake's Roost where she felt comfortable. She was putting the finishing touches to her holiday correspondence.

Lila had a light, musical laugh that was almost girlish and quite out of character with her elegant appearance. Laughter would be her first response if she knew her husband thought of her as an "unreliable supplier."

Her second would be a bored yawn.

At 39 still slim, restless, and very glamorous, Lila saw herself as a valuable commodity indifferently used. She was certainly no fool. She knew what slut Harry was sleeping with and where they did it.

Though she despised her unfaithful husband, she had no intention of giving up her claim to the vast real estate empire of Harold Augustus Drake--HAD, as she and Bob sometimes referred to him.

Despite her firm resolution this season to behave herself, fervently and deep inside her wild nature, she longed for escape from Drake's Roost. The piteous pleas she received from poor Bob Drummond tore at her heart and made her itch to run away again. Yet she'd vowed to make herself listen to her head and not her heart.

Anyway, the sex hadn't been that good on their final escapade. She'd had better on the way home with a pretty, dimpled female masseuse at an exclusive spa in Boston.

She put her pen aside and allowed her mind to wander.

Drake was fast approaching fifty, she thought. Perhaps he'd die and she'd be off the hook. His grandfather and father had died in their mid-twenties, his mother and sister were deceased, and he had a weak heart and high blood pressure.

What if the end came soon, making her both wealthy and independent? Wouldn't she just love to scram from this outpost and travel the world for a long spell with her redheaded, green-eyed sister

Marty, a real hoot who'd just married (for a third time) a handsome Lebanese doctor in Pasadena. Marty knew how to party.

Lila sometimes thought she would scream if she had to stay in Alta one day longer. The natives, with their big families and stay-put wives, were about as hip as Attila the Hun.

Except for B. L. Zebub's, the place was empty of life. The sexual revolution had not made it to Wyoming and never would. Her particular life in this rock-pile was like inhabiting a mausoleum.

Like most men of his type, Harry was an egomaniac and completely blind to his faults and her needs. Under the male bravado, he suffered from an inferiority complex about his stature among their powerful friends in the East. He rightfully suspected they made fun of him behind his back as the proverbial BFSP--Big Frog, Small Puddle.

At least, however, he wasn't a man with a penis complex, like many of those over-sauced, febrile, Eastern pencil dicks. Harry Drake liked it on the rough side, as did she, and he had the right equipment. And it had been fun landing the big hunk; she'd give him that as well.

The critical juncture had been the party in Georgetown during the Cuban missile crisis. It was attended by none other than the distinguished, liver-spotted hedonist Senator Cockburn, whose family had held a tenacious grip on a Senate seat since the founding of the nation.

Before dinner, she'd played a parlor trick with the gentlemen's toes. It always got the party moving and the male libido charging. Harry's friend Chloe Vye, an intellectual type, was giving her the evil eye, but she knew exactly what she was doing. A longer second toe, she claimed, was a sign of virility; to a man, they'd taken their socks off.

Literally leaving her two companions in the dust, after dinner she had allowed herself to be whisked away in the great man's stretch limo. They'd proceeded as slowly as if they were in a parade toward Senator Cockburn's lovely brownstone in Georgetown.

In the foyer, Lila coolly took in the family portraits from five generations of Cockburns, also the Senator's fragile wife of sixty years, conveniently at home in the ancestral residence, several states distant.

On the Senator's bedside table lay a short leather riding stick, which he loved liberally applying to the buttocks of young women during intercourse.

Lila did not allow him to use the stick "to stretch her pleasure," as the Senator put it, but she did allow other sexual liberties, closing her eyes so as not to be overly bothered by his liver spots.

With the hook planted firmly in the great man's mouth, she used his frequent phone calls to reel in her target: 40-year-old Harry Drake, on Esquire's list as one of the nation's most elusive bachelors.

At the time, she was working in a publishing house on Beacon Street in Boston.

The enamored Cockburn would call her at work from the Senate offices. When would she return to the capital? Would she be "properly escorted"? There was nothing proper in the motives behind the Senator's questions.

She made it a point to answer the calls only when Harry was languishing in her office, pretending not to listen in.

On each occasion, she made Harry cool his heels for at least an hour while she teased Senator Cockburn into a frenzy. Then she would allow Harry to take her to lunch down the street at the Ritz and hold her hand. After six months of this callous treatment, which made Harry hard as a rock every time she subjected him to it, he capitulated and asked Lila to marry him.

Their glamorous wedding, which was covered by Town & Country, was the event of the year in Boston.

Harry would always make the point, while courting Lila, that she would be walking into a "castle fit for a queen." But Drake's Roost was no place for a woman at all, much less a queen.

Harry had built it a decade before she arrived. It was a man's cave, inside and out. Try as she might to alter the gloom, she could find no pleasure in the stone mansion or its corporate twin down the road, the Alta Hotel. To her sensibilities, they were stone cold, as was Harry.

For lovemaking, she preferred the look of one of those old hovels that had once been sheep drover's huts. Now there was a warm, earthy place where a woman might have multiple orgasms with a rough-and-tumble cowboy.

Much like other rock piles that had been built by wealthy men as a lasting memorial to themselves--Hearst's Castle in California, the Vanderbilts' Biltmore mansion in North Carolina, the Broadmoor Hotel in Colorado--Drake's twin towers stood as monuments to the owner's colossal self-regard.

In her salad days, she had been courted by descendants of the great Robber Barons and shipping magnates, and she had their number. When one's ancestor had accumulated wealth past all spending it, what was left for a descendant to do? Erection and self-glorification, in one fell swoop: a stone mansion with flags flying from the parapets, a phallic symbol bigger than the next guy's!

In a way these castles all looked alike, dreary and lightless inside, with Flemish tapestries, twisted dark wood furniture, and names from Olde England. Adapting the word "moor" was a favorite notion, to make the context as bucolic as possible, even when the landscape was about as much fun as a graveyard.

Enter, the sexual fantasy: lord and master in the guise of a shepherd cavorting amid his flock, frolicking on the green, or an angler with a tight line. At Drake's Roost, the greens were tall stands of grass, tall enough for cattle to get lost in, and there was a stocked bass pond.

Since they didn't need the money, the robber barons of the 1920's would usually call the rock-pile their "home," at least until their wives were driven stark, raving mad by the dark, cloistered interiors. Their descendants always needed the money, however, so the second or third generation would turn the "family home" into a huge tourist attraction and collect the dough in drips and drabs for perpetuity.

Drake had built Drake's Roost and then the Alta Hotel, with the help of that SWAT design team from San Francisco, within a mile of each other and on the same rugged, windswept mountainside. Taken together, hardly anyone could claim bragging rights beyond his, not even the Biltmore family. Harry had managed to have his cake and eat it too -- how like Harry!

However, she had to give the devil and his consort their due. B.L. Zebub's was priceless. If it belonged to anyone but Harry and Marlena, Lila herself would be hanging out there all the time.

Marlena Bellum (formerly known as "the Dimmer dame" before her separation) had singlehandedly conceived of and created an astonishing over-the-top watering hole. Nothing, not in Wyoming and perhaps not in all the West, could rival B. L. Zebub's as a hip oasis. Lila freely admitted it to herself: she was green-eyed with jealousy.

Outside the hotel's walls, the howling wind raged. Inside B. L. Zebub's, all was cozily aristocratic and blatantly sexy. While Lila was tooling around Europe with Marlena's boss--so Lila's inside sources relayed--the redhead had been bribing descendants of an English lord to let her take a peek at the design of a leather-dominated billiard room.

As a result, the interior walls of B. L. Zebub's were covered in squares of hand-tooled Spanish leather, the design copied from the secret sixteenth-century gentleman's enclave Marlena had visited.

Also thanks to PAD's young architect, the gleaming hardwood floors of the saloon were cushioned with rare Turkish rugs. The pool-table, hand-built in Philadelphia, featured a scarlet cloth. A music box from 1900 along with the antique humidor graced a corner. Elk and antelope balls festooned the antlers of a collection of stuffed mule deer.

Overall, the décor came off as a perfect blend of upper-crust hunting lodge and ribald drawing room. To keep the right people coming, B. L. Zebub's was guarded and open to privileged adults only. The drinks were over-sized and over-priced to keep the riff raff out.

The games played weren't entirely of a sexual variety. Local politicians had been handsomely paid off to look the other way when a high-stakes gambling game came off in a smoky back room, serviced by carefully selected staff: cup-size D waitresses and obsequious, clean-cut waiters in starched, long-sleeved black shirts and long white aprons tied neatly over smart black pants.

No tired Christmas carols in the musical mix this week, which according to her inside source featured the Staples Sisters, Peter Frampton, Phoebe Stone, Maria Muldaur, Wayne Shorter, Steely Dan, and Silver Convention. And to top it off, his red-headed love slave had seen to it that the lord and master's entrance was heralded by a round of "Hail Britannia" and a skirl of bagpipes. Harry would flash his vintage, shit-eating grin, shake hands with any notables, and boogey.

It was enough to make Lila throw up that by staying away, she missed out on all the fun to be had in these glum parts. In November, Mick Jagger and Bette Midler had been seen in B. L. Zebub's. Meanwhile Lila was at Drake's Roost, drinking alone and managing the upkeep of her husband's creepy mausoleum. Boring!

She particularly hated the guest quarters, dismal corridors of old-fashioned bedrooms bearing the names of Harry's many ancestors.

However, there was no room named after his paternal grandmother, Clare Brighton Drake. Lila supposed that was because the young woman had done the ultimate disrespect to the line after Augustus "Curly" Drake died; she had married a commoner.

Harry was an intensely competitive and unforgiving man. In this regard, he was exactly like the two Drakes that had gone before him. The most successful of the three was the mildest in personality, Harry's father Nicholas. Life-size portraits of three Drakes, Augustus "Curly" Drake, Nicholas Samuel Drake, and Harold Augustus Drake--painted by a Sargent wannabe (two posthumously)--were prominently featured in the library, along with Harry's wall-to-wall collection of fake, leather-bound books.

Harry didn't read much, and he wanted the collection to look identical.

However, there wasn't much else about Drake's Roost that was faked. The large grey stones had been quarried locally and were hand-hewn; everything dripped with imported English Ivy.

There was a heated solarium with an indoor swimming pool, stables to rival those in Kentucky, and a separate garage for Harry's eight vintage cars. An entire wing, three stories high, was dedicated to the marble clock tower. Atop it was a plumed rooster made of gold.

The house carried 41,607 square feet of stone-encased living space under the towering mansard roof. There was a formal ballroom on the fourth floor and a bowling alley in the basement. Between the formal dining room and the gigantic cook's kitchen was a pantry the size of most houses, which housed a walk-in dumb waiter.

Under the carpet in the dining room were bells Lila pressed with a tap of her toe to summon the servants. The mahogany dining table could seat thirty comfortably. Six chandeliers, each a yard wide and six feet tall, glittered along the domed ceiling's length.

Here, Lila had installed the Christmas tree, thirty-six feet tall, four less than the one at the Biltmore. She'd told Harry his was taller (he wouldn't bother to check).

After their guests oohed and ahhhed over the tree, Harry would drag them off to see his curiosities. These were scattered around the mansion, in collections and single presentations. Harry had a weakness for odds and ends--he collected colonial spinning wheels, medieval suits of armor, antique swords, and red-headed women. She wouldn't put it past him if he'd tried to score with her sister Marty at their wedding in Boston.

Once Harry saw the Napoleonic chess men at the Biltmore, he didn't rest until the obliging Marlena scoured the universe and discovered something uniquely historic. She'd found a humidor once in use by the Archbishop of Canterbury; it was displayed in B. L. Zebub's.

The front of Drake's Roost was where Lila had made her mark and counteracted the gloom. She did so in the early days of their marriage, before Harry began to show his true colors with his childishly vindictive cheating.

Where once there had been a formal entranceway, flanked with a pair of stone British lions on the outside and on the inside, a faded wall tapestry depicting a hunting scene from Merry Old England woven at a Benedictine monastery in the 17th century, there were now three arched windows soaring from the tiled floor to the vaulted ceiling.

An Alexander Calder mobile slowly rotated in the Wyoming wind that somehow managed to insinuate itself through fifty glass panels.

But the most spectacular of her innovations was a glass elevator for transporting guests up to their fourth-floor ballroom without their missing the spectacular view down the mountainside. The glass elevator had replaced not only a hideous electric chair for elderly guests but also the massively ugly, ornate, grand staircase that Lila had always feared tumbling down, ala Scarlett O'Hara.

Despite these improvements, Drake's Roost had the dank airlessness of a Gothic fortress. After the first year of marriage, Lila had patently refused to invite guests who were friends of hers to spend the night, until Harry built ranch-style Plover's Nest on the grounds of the former Plush House Inn to house them.

When one day this estate belonged to her, Lila thought, she would sell it or give it away to some worthy cause her husband would loathe. Smiling at Harry's eventual comeuppance, she drew out the piece of paper she had tucked inside her black lace bra. It was Drummond's most recent, tear-stained letter (the tears were his), begging her to visit him in California at some guru's campsite. She read it again, crumpled it up, and threw it into the stone fireplace.

Something in her gut continued to warn her the time was past when, bored to madness by Drake's Roost, she could fly to an inspiring rendezvous.

Her favorite bower of bliss with Drummond had been atop a skyscraper in San Francisco. Unluckily for them, Harry's friends belonged to the Union Club, not the Bohemian Club. When word got out, the club's founding families made it clear to Lila's lawyer they didn't approve of flagrant transgressions by a member's wife. In the end, she had chosen to heed their warnings and had sent Drummond packing.

A lot of good it had done her! Harry hadn't been so impressed by her show of repentance as she would have liked, and patient Griselda was not her best role.

However, it was only a matter of time until she prevailed in the contest.

The young woman who had masterminded B. L. Zebub's and wore a construction hat over her curls at the Grand Opening was no more than a talented fool. Slowly but surely the slut was becoming irksome to Harry; at this point, it was a waiting game between them. And though she was highly intelligent, Marlena Bellum didn't grasp the simple concept that skulking will eventually wear out a man's desire.

Lila felt sure enough of her present advantage to put it to the test. She planned to show up at the Fire Night Ball in an outfit that would rock Bellum back on her heels. Let the annoying competition prance about in hard hat and décolletage and stoke the bonfires with the boys. Let her just try to out-fox Lila Coffin.

Chapter Twelve

As a result of smooth sailing during the shopping jaunt with Faith, Marlena felt positively light of heart as she drove up to Mill's Creek-- unprecedented, actually, her feeling of high spirits. Queen came on the radio, and she began to sing along, deliberately ignoring an ominous darkening along the horizon.

But, as she reached the top of the winding, half-mile long driveway to Mill's Creek, icy rain and hail began to pelt the windshield. The stone house appeared totally deserted, with no workmen in sight.

She ran to the front door and found it was locked up tight.

Dripping wet, rummaging through her purse for the house key, her memory provided a sudden flash of where it was. She had left it on the dashboard of the rental car. Fighting her way back through the wind and drenching rain, she finally got to the car door, whereupon she beheld something truly horrifying: the car key, dangling in the ignition. *Why is this happening to me? I never forget anything!*

"Fuck! Fuck! Fuck!"

She stamped her foot, splashing rain water with each expletive. Then she ran back through the hail, wind, and rain once again and stood on the porch, wet as a mermaid, the small projection of the roof her only protection against the punishing elements.

Shivering, she called for help. She could hear her voice growing scratchy; she was losing it. She told herself to calm down, that the mishap wasn't life threatening and she was feeling more panicky than the situation actually called for.

Then, just when she was considering whether to take to the road on foot and find shelter at a neighbor's home, there arose out of the mist, the rolling thunder, and the pelting sleet the Nordic figure of a young man, tall, blue-eyed, and muscular, with white-blond hair. He was coming toward her around the side of the house at a slow run.

"Thank God you're here!" she cried out as Apollo reached her side. "I've locked all my keys inside my car!" she yelled at him through peals of thunder.

"No one's home!" he yelled back. A mixture of snow and rain was streaming down his face. "They're both in town. I don't have my key to the house. But there's shelter in the barn."

From under his arm, he pulled out two wool Indian blankets. "Here, put these around you."

She put one over her head and wrapped the other around her waist.

"Follow me, miss." He took her hand and dragged her along. The terrain seemed as treacherous under the high heels of her shoes as the surface of the moon.

She quickly got mired in the dirt path. This happened several more times, but each time she got stuck, Apollo would pull her forward. Wrapped like a papoose, she blindly followed, swaying in the howling wind, staggering and slipping through the snow. In the distance, she could make out the lighted doorway of the barn.

Finally, they were dragging themselves inside. As he closed the door behind them, she could smell the musty odor of wet hay. Her eyes were still adjusting to the low light, but she could see he was moving around.

"Watch your step," he said, leading her by the hand along the stalls, which were all empty with the exception of one at the very end. It held Pathetic Fallacy, the descendant of Chloe's Morgan horse, old Dickens. She wondered momentarily if the beast still mourned the loss of his partner, Indian Paintbrush, from the mishap six months ago. Chloe had not been in town at the time, having given her permission via telegram for the use of her horses in the parade.

But that was ridiculous; animals didn't have memories of their losses, did they? Still, looking at the sad eyes on the horse made her feel guilty, and she made a mental note to ask Chloe how the horse was faring.

"Is this where you hang out?" she asked Apollo, throwing the blankets aside and looking at him with snow-fringed eyelashes. Her voice sounded oddly hollow, as though it were coming from somewhere else. Her legs felt leaden, as though she had been walking on alien turf.

"It's my office. You can get off your feet and keep warm. I'll make us some coffee while you dry off." "How did you know to come for me?"

"I thought I heard something. Then I remembered seeing Miss Chloe put the porch light on before she left. She only does that when she's expecting someone. So I thought I'd better check."

"Good thing you did. I might have drowned at the doorstep."

She shuddered involuntarily.

"Coffee's coming right up."

"I didn't expect that storm. The timing couldn't have been worse. I locked myself out of the car just as it hit. And the key to the house was in the car. Stupid cow!"

She sat down on the chair he pulled out for her, and he patted her arm awkwardly, as if to comfort her. Then he said: "Storms come up pretty fast here. One time when I was camping I got caught out at the Hat in a terrific storm, hail big as golf balls, lightning everywhere. The storm picked up all my gear, tore the tent right out of its moorings."

"You're lucky you didn't get hit by lightning and killed."

He laughed. "Oh, lightning don't strike any of the Nelson clan, like it do some other natives around here."

"Is there a story behind that claim?"

"More than likely."

"May I have one then?"

"Well, you asked for it. Here's your coffee. Take anything in it?"

"No thanks."

Her blue lips were still chattering, but she tugged the blanket snugly around her shoulders and settled in on the dilapidated horsehair chair that constituted, along with a three-legged desk, the office furniture. It reminded her of Grandpa Bellum's chair in the basement of the pink house. He would sit and tell her tall tales of the Old West while she braided his shaggy gray hair.

Apollo cleared his throat. She could see his breath in the air. He put one muscular arm on his leg and the other on the rickety desk and leaned in, fixing his light blue eyes on Marlena's eager, upturned face.

There was nothing in the world she loved so much as being told a story.

"My old man was up in his cabin in the mountain one night, when the lightning strikes and the thunder was a-comin' at him all at the same time, hail and seventy mile-an-hour winds. Between the bangin' of the thunder and the crackin' of the lightning, he was pretty near deafened.

"He had his bird dog with him, Baldy was his name, and the bird dog was hidin' his head under his paws, he was so ascared. All of a sudden Fred--that's my old man-- hears a really loud C-R-R-A-A-C-K-K and out he jumps through the door to see what's been hit.

"It was the big juniper tree right beside the cabin that was hit, and now it's just a smolderin' piece of ash in the shape of a tree. Well, my old man stays out a minute longer to take a leak. When he tries to get back in, Baldy won't let him; he growls at him and bares his teeth, protecting his turf from whatever's out there in the storm.

"'What the hell's a matter wid you, dog?' old Fred yells at him through the door. 'Cain't you count? One out and one in.'"

"My old man told everyone his wife had shot a bear dead, which they all knew to be true. He also told 'em his dog Baldy could count, but that they refused to believe. He insisted. He told 'em he'd been out with his pals on Hatter's Field, huntin' for pheasant. Baldy went out in the bush and sniffed around; then he came back and tapped his paw three times. Sure enough, three pheasants went flyin' out of the bush.

"One day his pal Pinky said, 'Hell, Fred, that don't prove nothing. There ain't no dog that can count.'

"'Well, jus' try 'im once and see for yerself,' ses my old man.

"So Pinky and the dog goes out to the bush and the dog sniffs around. Then he starts a-humpin' on ol' Pinky's leg. Pinky gets mad and tries to shake him off, but Baldy hangs on for dear life.

"'See what I mean?' says Fred to Pinky. 'The dog's a genius.'

"'Why, this dog don't count. He was just humpin' my leg to beat the band.'

"'That's right, Pinky,' my old man ses. 'He's tryin' to tell you there's so many fuckin' birds out there he can't count 'em all!'"

Marlena laughed delightedly while the young man kept a straight poker face.

His boiled blue eyes were trained on hers, which meant he wasn't through entertaining her, as she was willing him to go on. But as she waited for him to fulfill her wish, she was also beginning to feel drowsy.

"I was out on the mountain once with Fred in an old beat up truck when one a' them lightning and hail storms struck. I never been so shit scared in my life.

"It was comin' down all around us, and we couldn't go anywhere. Our truck was mired deep in the mud from the rain, and we couldn't get out to fix it with the lightning striking.

"My old man kept on saying, 'Just don't touch anything that's metal, Apollo. Don't touch, dammit!' I was too scared to sass him, pretty near wet my pants, because I was only a little cuss, and pretty near everything on that truck was metal.

"Finally the storm was over, and somehow we had made it through. I'll never forget how beautiful everything was after that in my eyes. There was rainbows everywhere, and the smell of the ozone and the wet sagebrush---why, it was heavenly, made it almost worth the trouble, even though it took us four hours of sweatin' in the sun with boards and chains to get that truck out and running again."

Marlena opened her eyes and smiled up at Apollo. He was gently shaking her by the shoulder. She felt more rested than she had in weeks.

"What about my story? Oh my, I must have dozed off," she said, realizing what had happened.

"What time is it, Apollo?"

"Miss Annie just now pulled up the driveway. You'll be able to get into the house now. I called old Fairwell about your car; he's a cabbie who's also a locksmith. He'll be here shortly to take care of getting the lock picked for you."

She slowly untangled herself from the blankets. "You're a nice boy. I hope you've got a girl who appreciates you."

"Ain't no boy. Ain't got no girlfriend neither," he said plaintively.

"I'll remember every word, Apollo."

Because of her special powers, she knew that even the words she had heard in her sleep would remain in her memory banks. What would she do with them? She thought of her old notebooks.

Apollo rubbed his chin.

"Aw, they wasn't worth much,'" he said, but the deep blush crawling along his jaw-line belied his modest statement.

Chapter Thirteen

At half past six, Ron Huddleston was sitting at the bar chatting up one of the female bartenders, a blonde, buxom girl named Shirley.

Marlena suddenly appeared at his side, carefully hiding her slim body within the shadow of his sturdy physique.

Farther down, she had spotted Sally Honeywell holding court with three young women in heavy eye makeup and bell bottom jeans, the sum total of feminist sisterhood in these hinterlands.

The wealthy older lesbian was in Marlena's sights as a business prospect. They'd met earlier in the week. Sally and Stretch, her young, Amazonian girlfriend, were guests at the hotel. Stretch had relatives in town, the Bloods, whom they were visiting for the holidays.

Coincidentally, Sally was rehabbing a mansion in the Florida Keys and therefore hot on the track of a top-tier architect for the project.

One thing had led to another. Tonight Marlena would be dining alone with Sally, with an eye to rehabbing her 14,000 square foot Italianate mansion near the Southernmost Point in Key West. Could it be the next rung on the ladder to career success?

If so, she would have to cut the umbilical cord with PAD. Was she ready to do that? She'd spoken at length to Coddie on the subject, but then, suddenly, their conversation had gone haywire, when she made the colossal mistake of confiding her personal troubles.

Today, she reflected, had been very abnormally stressful. Would she later look back on it as a watershed in her life, or was it the beginning of the end? Ominous signs were everywhere, and the Key West mansion was perhaps a mere pipedream at the far end of the line.

"Sorry I'm late, Ron. Locked my keys in the car, had to get rescued by a cowboy."

Then she segued into storytelling mode, sharing Apollo's colorful anecdotes, word for word.

Meanwhile Ron gazed at her dopily, savoring every syllable and marveling at how she glowed in the dim lighting.

I used to take one of those red-gold curls into my hand and dip it into my inkwell, he thought.

I guess I was an ass; I wonder what she thinks of me now?

Earlier, when his gloved hand had been inside her, his mind was locked into clinical mode and she was just another patient. Now, he felt her power as a woman. It was bruisingly strong and impossible for him to resist.

On the inside, and indeed throughout the story of her mishap, Marlena had been willing him not to be the bearer of bad news. Now she gave Ron her best smile, half vixen, half girl-next-door.

"Why the serious face, Dr. Ron? Never mind. You don't have to tell me."

He seemed to be considering whether to speak, and her cerulean eyes widened with gloomy surmise.

"I ran your test before I left the office, Lena," he said finally.

"And?"

"You're sure you want to have this conversation here?"

"Fire away. No one's listening."

"You're pregnant."

She let out a long, heavy sigh.

"It hasn't been a good week. In fact, it's the worst since you gave me the scarlet fever."

"Will you tell your husband?"

"My husband? Oh, yes. Actually, I've already told him."

When she'd blurted the news she might be pregnant, Coddie hadn't taken it at all well.

"What a tangled web we weave, when first we practice to deceive," murmured Marlena.

Ron took it upon himself to break an awkward pause.

"Perhaps the pregnancy will help the two of you to make it up. I mean, get back together."

"I doubt it."

"Why is that? Because you don't want to get back together?"

"Well, yes, that's part of it. Also, I didn't like the way he reacted to the news."

"What did he say? Lena, if I'm being too nosey, just tell me to butt out."

"It's all right. I asked him what I should do, and all he said was that he didn't know, that he needed more information. He sounded like a cold fish, so I hung up on him."

She paused.

"That's the trouble with Coddie. He's smart, but he's too rigid, cold-blooded, and straight-laced. Anyway, I couldn't let him take the rap, even if he offered to."

Ron scratched his head. After awhile he said, "Oh, I get it. Your husband isn't the lucky father."

She bristled. "Not my point, and not your business. I'm still his wife. That makes him involved, doesn't it? There are men in the same circumstances who would have the chivalry not to ask questions about the paternity of their wife's baby."

"You're saying he should be one of them? In novels that might advance the plot. But in real life, you might have difficulty finding a man willing to take on another man's love child for a woman who's his wife only on paper. That is the situation he's in, isn't it?"

Marlena squirmed uneasily in her seat, thinking what she needed was a drink, and fast.

Why was the service so slow today?

Chapter Fourteen

"Ron, do you believe that the past looms larger here than it does in other places? During the last few days, I've begun to feel as if ghosts are following me. Do you ever feel that way, living here?"

As she asked these questions, Marlena had dropped her voice lower and leaned in closer. Ron inhaled the scent of jasmine from her feather-light, glinting hair. He felt thoroughly intoxicated; by way of an answer, the best he could do was shake his head.

The happy hour crowd in B. L. Zebub's was rapidly on the increase, both in numbers and raucous noise. The new bartender, a ruddy-cheeked young man with cropped dark hair, seemed overwhelmed. It was clear to Marlena he was oblivious to Ron's empty glass and her presence.

"Watch this," she said to Ron.

She cocked her head as the new bartender went barreling past them. Then, with a quick flick of her super-fine tresses, she spun into the semi-dark atmosphere a luminous mist that stopped him dead in his tracks.

Her translucent eyelids fluttering upward, she stared directly at him, the reflective pupils of her aqua eyes conveying a strong mesmeric pull. Slowly she pointed a shiny finger tip, first at Ron's empty glass and then at herself.

Julio was frozen and in a trance until she spoke.

"Another Guinness for Just Ron, Julio. I'll have an espresso. Double brandy and light cream."

Ron smiled, his mind shooting backward through the decades. He'd seen this performance done before, when Marlena was a little girl.

The ploy had never failed to amuse him, mostly because she seemed to take such childish pleasure in it. It was impossible to resist her, and impossible not to go along with the fun of pretending she was a witch, that her mesmeric powers were supernatural.

On the other hand, her reputation was no laughing matter. The natives believed her ancestor, Cassandra Vye, had been an evil witch.

HOME SCHOOLING: The Fire Night Ball

Marlena was a dead ringer for *that woman.* This phrase was how old natives referred to Cassandra, fearful the mere utterance of her name would propel her from the depths of hell back into their midst.

So far as Ron could make out, the only crime the notorious ancestor might have been guilty of was being so dead sexy she'd managed to lure the town's two most handsome, eligible bachelors into her snare.

Such a demonstration of power had been construed as downright demonic by pious native mothers with plain daughters of marriageable age.

As the story went, Cassandra Vye had been an outsider and ultimately a bounder, abandoning her saintly native husband Nicholas Brighton when she vanished into thin air on October 28, 1901, in the midst of a lightning storm on Hatter's Field. Her married friend and presumed lover, Augustus "Curly" Drake, was found dead on the spot where they'd met, struck down by lightning. He was there with the express purpose of fleeing with her but expired instead.

It was a serious issue, thought Ron, how great beauty can easily attract dangerous malice in a small town. He felt a deep concern for the safety of his childhood friend. There was a well-established pattern in the citizenry of enacting violence against unusual outsiders. Reaching far back, the natives had a reputation for holding grudges.

Meanwhile, Marlena was thinking this cocktail hour wasn't going exactly the way she'd planned. She gave Ron a frowning look.

In response to the pout, he felt an urge to kiss her, one he barely managed to resist.

"Never mind," he said, referring to his comments on Coddie. "A good marriage isn't black and white. Almost nothing is, when you examine things up close, not even penguins. King penguins in Antarctica have distinguishing marks of gold and tangerine."

Christ, I'm babbling.

"Anyway, it will all work out the way it's supposed to in the end. Perhaps your husband was just too shocked to behave in the way you wanted him to."

"Whatever. Are you a marriage counselor, too? I didn't notice a license on the wall in your office. I don't see a wedding ring on your finger. What makes you an expert on husbands?"

"To your point, I'm a bachelor, and I don't know what I'm talking about."

"Let's talk about something besides my marriage, shall we?"

"Okay, let's do."

"We can talk about the weather. Everyone else does."

Sighing, she looked away from Ron and down toward the other end of the bar, where Sally had glanced her way more than once. She waved, and they smiled at each other like co-conspirators.

If she needed to get out of town quickly, Sally would provide the escape route. There was more than one way to skin a cat.

Skin a cat? What was happening to her?

Since Faith's arrival, she had fallen into her mother's annoying habit of bandaging every complex situation with an old chestnut.

"That's better," said Ron, noting the dazzling smile, now turned his way. "I always thought you had the prettiest smile, by far, of any girl in town. Even though you were shy about showing it."

"It's a small town, Ron, but I'll take that as a compliment."

"It's the sticks, but I know where there's a great jazz combo. Interested?"

"I'd love to continue discussing penguins, but I have a dinner engagement at eight."

"Who with?"

"Ron, I think you mean 'with whom?' English grammar never was your strong suit. I had to coach you all the way. See that lady down there, the one with the mod bangs and the young women hanging on her? She's going to give me a great job in Key West, Florida, rehabbing a mansion."

"Well, that's too bad."

"What, pray tell, is bad about it?"

"I was planning to take you to dinner here, before the jazz combo."

"Here? I doubt you could afford us."

"Ouch! You *are* mad at me. What did I do?"

She laughed ruefully. "You mean, besides killing a rabbit and messing up my life--AGAIN? I haven't forgiven you yet for my scarlet fever. Anyway, Ron, I don't know how pleasant a companion I would be, under the circumstances."

"What do you mean?"

"The circumstances being, that I'm likely to vomit, or cry, or throw a tantrum. Now, at my business dinner with her down there"-- she took that opportunity to wave at Sally, and the target flapped one jeweled hand back at her--"my practiced habit of suppressing all feelings and soldiering on will come into play. Business ahead of pleasure, I always say. Unless I'm horny."

He resisted the temptation to ask if she felt horny now.

"How about the next day? And the day after that?"

"You mean, might I be horny then?"

"I mean, how will you get through each day, feeling so numbed out?"

"Well, that's my problem alone," she bristled proudly.

"Seriously, Lena, it isn't your problem alone," he said, looking into her eyes and taking her hand. She initially resisted, but then allowed it.

"You can count on me. Anything you need, you've got it."

Unconsciously, her chin came up as he began to elaborate.

"Whoever the lucky father of this baby is, if he steps up to the plate and you don't need me, I'll back off, but if he takes his foot off the bag, I've got your back."

"I had no idea, Ron, you were such a baseball fan. Seriously, I can't afford to believe you mean everything that you say. I've always had to count on myself alone."

"I do."

"Those two words are too heavy for bar talk. Anyway, why would you want to help me out?"

"Well, I'm a doctor in a small town, as you've pointed out. We stick together in these parts. You're an old friend who could use some moron support. And I've been in love with you, Lena, ever since the second grade. But just let's forget I said the last thing."

"Forgotten. My dad thought you were okay, even though he nicknamed you Typhoid Ronnie. Once upon a time, I may have been a little in love with you, too. You came to my rescue often enough."

She paused, reflecting.

"When I left, didn't we promise to write each other always and be married one day in the future? Or maybe that was just a dream I had. I have this funny kind of memory. Everything I've ever known is on this spool of thread, but where the spool comes from, I don't always know."

"That was no dream," he said quietly.

His smile was shy and genuine, and she squeezed his hand before moving hers away.

"I'm sorry to have to leave you at this juncture, Ron. But I see my date for the evening is looking my way, and it's almost eight. I'll need to kiss her ass all the way to Christmas if I want to land that gig."

"Do you really want it that much? What do you know about her?"

"She likes me, and that's about all I know, except that she's likely to be my ticket to independence. I've been letting my career slide lately, waiting on one damn man, but I've just received my wakeup call. Whatever I decide to do about--well, you know--I need both feet planted firmly on the ground. I've put my mind to landing that dream job in Key West, and land it I will."

Ron nodded. "You were always good at getting what you went after, Lena. The smartest girl in class, the most talented, and the most caring, too."

"Oh, please. We both know I'm Becky Sharp, not Jane Eyre."

Her tone was flippant, but her eyes told a different story.

"Don't say that, Lena, even jokingly. It's not true. However, I'll admit to being a little gun shy of you. You were such a brilliant student we were all afraid to talk to you."

"It's just the memory thing, like a sleight of hand, but it made me feel like a freak. I knew all the answers better than the teachers did. I was too tall and skinny, and my hair looked like Raggedy Ann's. I desperately wanted to make friends, but I didn't know how, so I made the world of books my refuge."

"A world that you could control?"

"One in which I could pretend to be the heroine, not the victim or the freak."

"Well, now you're in a position to be the heroine of your own story. The question is, who-- I mean, whom--do you take with you on the journey?"

"I'm sorry about what I said earlier, about Coddie. Truly he's a great guy, and he'd jump through hoops for me. He didn't want children as I did in the beginning. He wanted our marriage to work in a practical, career-centered way. But he also loved me, in his own style. Then Harry came along--"

"The father's name is Harry?"

"Forget I said that, will you? Harry as in Tom, Dick and…"

"It's forgotten. Go on."

"Then I fell in love with...someone else, and Coddie eventually gave up on me. The funny thing is, he gave up just as I was starting to wonder about the reality of the other relationship. If he hadn't sent separation papers, we might still be together."

"Timing's everything. How about now, when you are pregnant by Tom-Dick-and-Harry? Are you still questioning the relationship? Possibly thinking about getting back with your husband?"

"Not seriously. Isn't life a kick in the head? Timing is everything; you said it, Ron."

"Is there anyone you can talk to? A counselor or a minister, perhaps, or a family member?"

"My cousin Chloe has always been my confidante, mentor, therapist, even my surrogate mother. Faith abandoned dad and me for a couple of years. That's why I went to Teddy Roosevelt."

"I had no idea. I'm sorry. We assumed your parents were both day laborers, off working fields while your grandmother cared for you."

"Faith will disinherit me if she gets wind of the trouble that I'm in now."

"I remember your mother," said Ron. "She had jet black hair with a white streak through it, and she wore bright red lipstick. She'd come into my father's office sometimes when I was hanging out there."

"Yes, well, that would be Faith in her official dressed-up mode. She wore lipstick to go to the doctor's office and to church. Otherwise, she was Plain Jane Marine."

"Your mother was really a Marine? That sounds like a joke."

"She was a Marine all right, served to the end of World War II, and she could kick your ass. The bed had to be made just so; life under her was all barked orders and tight corners."

"And what is she like now?"

"Gray, still feisty. Her life is sad; she was left all alone after my father's death. Her family's all gone, except for me and Chloe. I know I should do a lot more for her than I do. But she'll never speak to me again if she learns of this train wreck."

"So you won't tell her?"

"Not until after I've decided what to do. Otherwise, she'll quote the Bible at me and make me crazy."

"Are you sure she won't be sympathetic?"

"Never. Women of Faith's generation weren't in charge of their own bodies. So why should we be able to pick and choose? Besides, abortion means excommunication from the Church."

She shuddered. "Young women need to guard our hard-won rights to reproductive choice. Mark my words, the old warhorses, male and female, will try to take them away."

"I'm on your side," said Ron, "all the way."

She grabbed Ron around the neck and hugged him. "You're the best," she said. "I feel better now after talking with you, really I do."

Shirley came up just then.

"Another, Marlena? Just Ron paid for your first one in advance."

"Shirley, please get Just Ron another Guinness and put it on my tab."

"So, it's gonna be that way, is it?" he asked, cocking his head at her in a puzzled way.

"Yep. You scratch my butt, I'll scratch yours."

"Deal. Well, stop by the office whenever it's convenient. I have vitamin supplements for you. Big brown ones."

"Like my mother's eyes. You don't make house calls, Dr. Ron? I thought country doctors were all over that like a cheap suit."

"Well, I might make an exception in your case, Lena."

"Please do so," she said, putting on a flippant and imperious tone of voice. "I don't relish the thought of getting pregnancy vitamins from the town pharmacist. He spreads gossip the way you used to spread germs. You're going to Chloe's Christmas Fire Night extravaganza Sunday evening, aren't you?"

"Wouldn't miss it. You'll be there?"

"Front and center, with more front in my center than there ought to be."

By way of a goodbye to her friend, Marlena kissed Ron on both cheeks and hugged him. She turned and walked off, leaving him gazing at the spectacle she made from the back.

He shook his head in admiration. Not only was she highly amusing, but the caboose was every bit as dazzling as the engine.

She had said she was going to have dinner with the white-haired lesbian who was holding court down at the end of the bar. It was the first time in his life Ron Huddleston could recall feeling envious of an older woman.

Murmurs arising from the middle of the bar, he looked down to where a black oil executive with bulging forearms, thick-framed eyeglasses, and an Afro was attempting a balancing trick with two forks. The tines were crossed over a toothpick, which in turn was balanced on another toothpick that was stuck into the hole of a silver salt shaker.

On the third try, the forks remained suspended in mid-air, slowly rotating on the topmost toothpick.

"Magic," piped up a barrel-chested woman in a harlequin vest and pleated trousers. "Third time's a charm."

"No," said the black man. "Physics."

Ron glanced around the room, sizing up the clientele, mostly "native" sons and daughters along with an assortment of travelers and refugees from family gatherings. The Easterners could be spotted by their fat ties and brand-new cowboy hats.

Even the glummest customer, an old Native American woman with grey hair tightly skinned back into a pony-tail, appeared to be having a good time; two words were printed across her bulging breasts--"Fun Uprising."

As the song "I'll Take You There" came blasting over the amplifiers, a woman seated to his right stood up on wooden platform heels and began to dance in a slow, gyrating motion, shaking her shagged top and fringed leather mini-skirt as her thin, muscular arms twisted snakily.

After a few minutes, the lady abruptly sat down.

Anne Carlisle

"I've got a tight one, " she said to her companion, an overweight man with a bulbous nose, who was wearing a Fred Flintstone tie.

He retorted, "Your pussy or your underpants?"

The man on her other side shouted: "Fire in the hole!"

Ron rolled his eyes.

Chapter Fifteen
December 21, 1977

    Marlena awoke on the morning of the winter solstice to the loud chirping of birds and the intermittent shriek of buzz saws.
    She'd stayed out late, partying into the wee hours with Sally and Stretch. They'd closed all the district bars, ending at a Bulette dive rumored to be lesbian-friendly. When they left at 2 a.m., the loudspeakers were blaring "Happy Trails" by Roy Rogers and Dale Evans.
    She'd dropped into bed with confidence that the project was hers for the taking, as well as a new life in wide-open Key West.
    In 1962, Marlena and her parents had vacationed in Key West, but the Cuban missile crisis forced a retreat. Nuclear war had seemed imminent, a near certainty. The nation held its breath.
    But Marlena was oblivious to any danger. Her fifteen-year-old brain was awash in color and form never before seen in such lush profusion.
    Her eyes were full to bursting with tall, rickety, white-washed or pastel fishermen's cottages tricked out in gingerbread cutouts, second-story widow's walks, and dark Bermuda shutters. Even the cinder block bungalows where the Cubans lived were nestled in a dense, aromatic jungle of bougainvillea, jasmine, and mangroves.
    In the central graveyard, the above-ground tombs looked like a Grecian village. The pathways had lovely street names, like "Violet" and "Palm." Adjacent to the cemetery was the so-called "writers compound" on Windsor Lane, an enclave of resident or visiting writers, among them John Ciardi, James Leo Herlihy, and William Styron.
    She'd wandered into their green cloister unawares, while her parents were viewing a Spanish poem carved on a gravestone inside the wrought iron enclosure for casualties of the Spanish-American War.
    Her nostrils flared, full of the fragrance of jasmine vines breaching a fence. She found herself joyously overwhelmed by the riotous red and purple of the bougainvillea blossoms amid the glossy green leaves of the mangrove jungle. Then she noticed she was standing close to the

screened door of a modest cottage, one like the others scattered around the pool, half hidden by lush foliage.

She slowly turned, feeling rather than seeing the man who stood just inside the screened door. He was only partly visible. But clearly he was naked from the waist down, and he was masturbating.

Recently the Windsor Lane exhibitionist had appeared in her dreams. She'd seen him again last night. His eyes had looked like dead dark holes, an image of compelling power.

Now Marlena crawled from bed and went to leaded glass window, made a hole in the fogged glass, and peered out. Her guest room overlooked the wooded portion of the property and far beyond it. Nothing could be further from the sights and smells and lambent air of Key West than the distant boundaries of this frozen landscape.

However, the immediate scene was much less bleak because of the trees. Alongside the poplars, junipers, and ponderosa pines Mills Creek was famous for, blue and Engleman spruce abounded.

She picked up an antique telescope that was sitting on the antique dresser and aimed it through a window.

Adjusting the view, she watched Chloe in her white fur coat out in the kitchen garden. She was handing out treats from a woven basket on her arm to a group of well-bundled Native American children.

Neighbors and clients of Chloe who'd been invited to help themselves were out in the woods chopping down their Christmas trees and hauling them away. Apollo Nelson was spied in a dense pine stand out beyond the juniper grove, helping neighbors with the tying of the trees they'd felled.

Apollo was accompanied by the dog, whom Annie always called "the little white devil."

Owing to the West Highland terrier's predilection for taking his time during his diurnal outings, the dog was named Pierre, after Pierre de Fermat, the French patron saint of unfinished business. As Pierre had grown old, his teeth were going bad; Annie often fed him with a fork.

Marlena was thinking about the Engleman spruce that had been cut and now graced Chloe's living room, how its knob reached the high point of the vaulted ceiling.

This afternoon it would be decorated with the help of the visiting carolers, neighbors and children from the Brighton Charter School. After the caroling, Chloe would invite them all in for cider, hot chocolate, donuts, and tree-decorating. The children would have a field day with mounds of silver tinsel and cartons of old-fashioned tin ornaments. Chloe would help the girls and boys string popcorn and berries into garlands or hang ornaments, holding up the very littlest ones so they could festoon the branches.

When Marlena was a girl of five, some of life's best moments were spent among Chloe's Christmas flock.

She put down the spyglass and rubbed the moisture from her eyes. There were chores to do, wrapping presents, helping Annie. But what she felt most like doing was spending some time outdoors.

Was there time to fit in a walk before her appointment with Bryce Scattergood? (To her surprise, Faith had asked if she would go see Scattergood alone, on both their behalves.)

Moving quickly now, she scooted into woolen underwear before putting on her jeans. Then she went down the stairs, taking two at a time, and found Annie in the kitchen.

"What's all this?" she asked, surveying the serving table, laden with toasted homemade bread, crispy bacon, and a chile relleno casserole.

"Your brunch," said Annie. "Dig in."

"Do you know what day it is today, Annie?" she asked with a full mouth.

"Wednesday."

"It's the winter solstice, the shortest day of the year. I have a hunch it's going to be a momentous one in my life, even more than yesterday, which was a doozey. Dr. V has promised to tell me a dark, secret story tonight. It's about her mother, Cassandra Vye."

"Wonderful."

"You don't sound very upbeat, Annie. What's the deal?"

"My tribal ancestors went in for storytelling circles. To my way of thinking, they did way too much peyote and storytelling, not enough hard work on the farm."

Marlena laughed. "It's been work getting this story out of Chloe. Twenty years' worth."

"Well, she's a cipher, that one. Butter don't melt in her mouth, she keeps it so chilled when she's of a mind to."

"Speaking of melting, how's it outside?"

"Well, this mornin' snow was comin' down, but suddenly it stopped. Now the sun's out and pretty near has melted the new snow. They said on the TV the roads are clear. I'm goin' to town to run some errands. You're welcome to come along."

"I have an appointment in town myself, but first I want some exercise to stretch my legs. It's been ages since I've walked out along Hatter's Field."

"Don't you get yourself lost out there. Folks do it all the time, and we have to send out Apollo a-lookin' for 'em. I have my suspicions some of them town gals get lost out there on purpose, just so he'll come runnin' after 'em."

"I don't blame them. Apollo's a fine-looking young man."

"Not all that young, Miz Marlena. You've maybe only got a few years on him."

"A few? Annie, you need new glasses. Or maybe we white-eyes all look alike to you."

"Go along with your impertinence. But, if you're of a mind to walk along Hatter's Field, you might collect me some holly branches. That was on my list of chores for today, along with washing them windows in the guest bedrooms."

"I'd be glad to, Annie. And I'll wash the windows when I come back from town after I check on the guys fixing the mill wheel."

"Don't you touch them windows, Miz Marlena. I'll find you a nice woven basket to carry the holly branches. Do you remember where the patch is? It's near if you drive."

"Couldn't forget it. I collected them every Christmas with Granny."

Suddenly she was hit by a wave of nausea.

"Be right back, Annie."

She got up from her chair and moved at a sprightly pace to the front hallway.

"I'll put the basket for the holly by the front door," Annie called up to her as she sprinted up the central staircase, then ran into the bathroom adjacent to her bedroom..

When she was through vomiting her breakfast, Marlena turned on the radio in her room to catch the local news.

The lead story was of the bituminous coal strike by the UMWA, the national contract having expired on December 6. That strike was likely to be a long one and would affect a lot of the people here.

Not good news for the holiday, she was thinking as she got dressed, putting on her fur boots and hat, then throwing a full length raccoon coat over everything.

She recalled the conversation she'd had with an old school mate, Lorna Anderson, about joblessness.

She owed her classmate a favor. During Letty's diatribe, Lorna had providentially shown up in the ladies' lounge, scaring off the old hag.

Lorna had asked if she would intercede with Harry for a job at the hotel for Lorna's twin brother, who was out of work.

She made a mental note to swing by the sheriff's office where Lorna worked and personally deliver an invitation to the twins for Sunday evening's ball. That way, Larry could meet Harry in a social setting, perhaps paving the way for employment.

Outdoors, the air felt crisp and light, just the way she liked it, with a light, steady wind. The recent snows had left a glittering mass of billowy whiteness as far as the eye could see, as though clouds had alighted on the ground for humans to play on.

In the distance, she saw a figure of man standing by a grove of trees, watching her as she moved toward the pond.

Impulsively, she lay down on her back by the pond and made angel's wings by sweeping her arms up and down. When she got up, there was no one in view. *Odd, but it wasn't the first time she'd sensed a spectral presence, sometimes a man and other times a woman.*

After brushing herself off, she trudged through the snow to the garage and her car.

The special places in Hatter's Field were indelible in her mind, and she soon came to a stop at a spot where she recalled holly bushes had thrived when she was a child. Leaving the engine running, she got out of the car. The fumes from the exhaust created what appeared to be smoke signals curling above her head.

Stomping through the snow along the path to the circle of trees where she recalled the holly bushes used to be tucked inside, she gloried in her isolation, the illusion that all this beauty belonged to her alone.

After several minutes of carefully picking her way through the snow-covered stubble, she stopped and turned aside, as she thought she'd heard the snorting of a horse and the jingle of leather harnessing.

Looking back, she saw a man on horseback in the distance, galloping towards her along the road that led from Mill's Creek.

That idiot has an awkward mount, was her thought; he must not be a native. But at least he appeared to be flesh and blood!

Then her line of sight was distracted by a blaze of red ahead of her--the holly bushes! Picking up the pace, she moved into the grove.

Chapter Sixteen

Clipping off the branches most heavily dotted with glossy red berries was hard work, but fruitful. Soon, her basket was half full and weighing down her arm.

"Marlena! Where are you? Marlena!"

The basket dangling heavily, she came out from behind the holly bushes. The man on the horse was approaching at a wild trot--he was none other than her estranged husband!

The light snow had laid a thin dusting of white flakes onto Coddie's bald, uncovered head. She couldn't help but giggle. Then she saw the clenched jaws, the creased forehead.

"Whatever are you doing here, Dimmer?" she asked lightly.

"It's a free country." His tone was defiant.

Marlena ceased her attempt at a smile. She watched as Coddie awkwardly got down off his horse and tied the rope to a nearby tree stump. In a departure from his usual European styling, he was wearing a full-length leather coat, a wool scarf, leather chaps, and thick boots.

"Let me do that for you," she said. "You're doing it all wrong."

Coddie stepped aside. While she retied the rope and patted the horse's nose, he launched into his explanation.

"I got this sudden urge for a white Christmas. So I jumped on a plane yesterday and checked into the hotel last night. The front desk said you'd moved out. I got this steed from a livery stables near here-- you know, when in Rome--they told me this is the road to Mill's Creek."

"It is, but I'm just leaving. You've caught me with tons to do, on the year's shortest day."

"Miniscule. Like what's left of our marriage."

Coddie was wearing sun goggles so she couldn't see his eyes, but she sensed he was surveying her. Instinctively, she put a gloved hand on her abdomen.

He broke the silence by gesturing at Hatter's Field. "What are you doing out here in this snowy wilderness? Shouldn't you be in your room, resting?"

"I'm not an invalid. And by our standards, city slicker, this isn't much of a snow, not enough to stop me from doing my chores. I'm collecting holly branches as decorations for the party."

She pointed to where she'd been. "Over there."

"So we'll do it together. Okay by you?"

"As you please," she said. Then she allowed him to take the basket in one arm and her arm in the other as they moved into the bushes.

Just then the sun came out, and the snow stopped falling. After a half hour of constant physical labor crushed against brambles, choosing the best branches, then snapping or cutting them off, they were both sweating in their winter clothing.

"Do you think this is enough? The basket's full," Coddie said, taking off his goggles and wiping his eyes. Marlena looked over at him and laughed aloud.

"Too much for you, Slick? You should try hay raking some time if you really want a workout."

"Are there people in this place to do it?" He gestured toward the rocky wilderness surrounding them. "Or any trees?"

"Not many people. A few trees, but quite far between."

"I guess Wyoming's an acquired taste."

"Some would say you have to be a native to appreciate it."

"Native, huh? You mean, like savages?"

They were walking slowly around the holly bushes. From their vantage point, the car and the horse appeared to be having a sportive standoff, silently confronting each other.

"You really don't know much about this part of the West, do you, Mr. New School of San Francisco? Of course, Native Americans are the true natives, but the homesteaders used the term to differentiate themselves from the wanderers. They still do, in some older neighborhoods."

When Marlena uttered the word "homesteaders," there was a proud thrill in her voice that registered on Coddie. He looked at her with a grudging curiosity as to unknown events in her past. Evidently, something here besides Harry made her tick.

"Some stayed only because they were too exhausted to go further; others, because they loved the land and wanted to settle on it."

"Well, color me one of the exhausted ones," said Coddie with a sigh of defeat.

She had plunked down yet another load of entangled holly branches on top of the others in the basket he was holding.

"I'll take that as an 'uncle.' I'm sure that's enough hollies. Let's put them in the trunk of my car."

As they trudged along, Marlena easily picked her way, while Coddie couldn't keep his eyes off her curvy backside in her tight jeans, which hindered him from walking gracefully through the snow drifts. There were several near mishaps when he came close to upending himself and the heavy basket of hollies.

Finally, they reached the horse and the car. He wiped his brow and sighed heavily after heaving the contents of the basket into the trunk.

"I'd invite you up to Mill's Creek," said Marlena, "but I'm going downtown for an appointment with a local realtor--as you suggested."

"I don't suppose you could carve out some time in your busy schedule today," said Coddie glumly.

His sour tone and quivering chin set Marlena's nerves jangling.

"Not in the cards today. Tomorrow would be better."

"I'll just go back to the hotel, then, after I tame this stallion."

"He's a gelding."

"You should know. You're the expert at cutting off balls."

"I'm sorry I'm busy, but we're getting Chloe's mill wheel functional again, and I'm decorating it. And then there's the hotel business."

He coughed nervously. "Chloe's invitation arrived at the office a month ago, to us both. I plan to come."

"I don't know why you'd want to. You won't know anyone well enough to talk to, except for me."

"There's always Harry. I assume he's coming."

"Yes."

"With or without the wife?"

The thought of the inevitable confrontation with Lila at the Christmas Fire Night Ball filled her with a tumult of dread, resentment, and excitement.

She said haughtily: "I don't waste my time thinking about her."

"Ha!" He laughed harshly. "That doesn't mean she's not thinking about you. Better watch your back. She could sue you for alienation of affection, you know."

"I never was one to retreat."

"Yes, you're bold. To the point of foolhardiness."

Marlena was opening the door to the driver's side of the silver BMW. He started to open the door on the passenger side to get in and continue the conversation.

"Coddie, don't do that!"

He stopped and stared at her. "Why on earth not?"

"Speaking of foolhardy, everyone knows not to open the two car doors at the same time in Wyoming."

"Bad luck?"

"No, city boy. The wind forms a funnel, like a tornado, and whips everything out of the car. It's gone for good, unless you can run at sixty miles an hour and catch it."

He shook his head in disbelief. "You don't say."

"The force of the wind can even rip the car door off. I've seen it happen. Cross my heart and hope to die."

Marlena was swiftly getting in while he stood outside the passenger door. Realizing he was looking foolish standing there holding the door handle, Coddie had no choice but to go over to his horse and pull himself up by the bridle.

"Easy there. Whoa. Easy, fella."

The horse reared before he could get on, throwing Coddie onto the wet ground.

Rolling down her window as he picked himself up, Marlena called out, "You okay? Need help?"

He shook his head. As he scrambled back on to the house, cursing, off she went with a wave of her hand.

He reflected angrily that he hadn't even managed to tell her what he came to say--that he was hoping to convince her to destroy the signed papers and try their marriage again.

He viciously kicked the horse's sides with his cowboy boots. The new boots pinched his feet; he'd bought them at Saks in a hurry before flying yesterday.

Chapter Seventeen

Bryce Scattergood's clear-sighted blue eyes, forthright nature, and manly, sculpted physique made the single father of three boys a spitting image of his famous Alta ancestor from the turn of the century, Caleb Scattergood.

Caleb had been a coal miner before he started his own ice harvesting business. He was also an early Native-American rights activist. Thanks to Caleb and Caleb's uncle, Ian Scattergood, a California financier, Bryce Scattergood had been blessed by considerable holdings in Wyoming and California, all held in trust for the Scattergood descendants.

Marlena's grandmother, Sarah Bellum, was Caleb Scattergood's niece. She acknowledged this when Bryce told her so, meanwhile wondering what he was driving at. It was already clear he was better versed in her family's history than she was.

Raised and educated in Colorado, Bryce had returned to his roots in Alta ten years ago, initially taking on an accounts manager position for Wells Fargo.

"Primarily," he told Marlena as he served her a steaming cup of green tea, "because I was sick and tired of watching developers clear cut every damn acre to build shitty little frame houses with plastic siding."

In a Houston subdivision, he'd watched his spindly, toothless neighbor take down a majestic live oak and pave his yard. The next week, Bryce sold his ranch house and moved to Wyoming.

He was ambitious, eager to learn the ropes, and also a self-described, unapologetic "tree-hugger."

Within the decade, Bryce had lost his wife to cancer, raised his boys alone, opened his own real estate brokerage firm, and garnered as much detailed knowledge of the territory and its homesteading families as any man alive.

Along the way, he'd collected as many unique physical remainders of the past as his house and office could hold.

The office building he owned and occupied in downtown Alta was an original brick schoolhouse, the first one in the territory. It was packed like a museum with Wyoming paraphernalia, ancestral memorabilia, Native American artifacts, and enough books to rival the public library's archives of the history of the West.

Among them were first editions of the entire collection authored by Nicholas Brighton, teacher, philosopher, and the area's first and foremost civil rights agitator.

"Last winter," Bryce said, "I had a meeting with our foundation board in San Francisco, and I stopped by the PAD offices in San Francisco in hopes of speaking with you. Then your husband told me you spend about half your time right here in Alta. Afterward, I learned you are the brains of Drake's hotel operation, the power behind the throne. I felt pretty stupid that I didn't even realize you were here."

He felt pretty stupid as well about the tumescence he was feeling now, but he couldn't help himself. The young woman gazing at him with eyes the color of aquamarines had a waspish waist and voluptuous curves, long legs and slim ankles, and gorgeous Titian hair rippling down to the rounded line of her ass.

A goddess, much too good for old Drake.

Bryce added: "I assume Mr. Dimmer told you about our meeting."

Marlena nodded at him in a neutral fashion, though Coddie had not done so.

"Do you mind terribly going over it all again with me?" She batted her long eyelashes, then added a lie on Coddie's behalf: "My memory is not what it should be."

Bryce told her that when her grandmother married John Bellum, she voluntarily waived all rights of inheritance to Scattergood trust properties. She even created a binding legal document that carried forward to all descendants.

"Apparently she acted out of emotional spite. I hope you don't mind my saying so."

Sarah's family had posed strong objections to her marriage to John Bellum, who was a Presbyterian, even though he promised to change his religion to accommodate the wishes of his bride's Catholic family.

Sarah never forgave them their harshness; she split from the family, never speaking to them again.

"Granny was a flinty pioneer woman," Marlena admitted. "When she lost her twin infant girls to diphtheria, she threw her rosary across the room, and she never forgave God. Please, go on."

Bryce said Sarah's exclusion of her descendants from any interest in the amassed Scattergood properties, though it might be legal, represented to him an ethical problem. He didn't like to think his good fortune was at someone else's expense.

Ultimately he had decided to do something about it, which was why he'd sought her out in San Francisco.

He went on to say the northern California real estate holdings of Ian Scattergood had long ago been parceled out to various charities. But, there were several historic Alta properties remaining in the trust which were about to be put on the market for a price much below market value. Investors were eagerly hovering, and in anticipation of this pre-arranged sale, Bryce had been called into San Francisco for his necessary consent.

He'd told the bank officers he felt it was his moral obligation to offer Sarah Bellum's grand-daughter first right of refusal, even though her acting on the option would effectively block the large development deal. Reluctantly, they had drawn up papers that put the offer to her in writing.

"When I gave your husband the document, as he requested, I also told him the land under your grandparents' home--or the Fairwell house, as it's historically known--is the only hindrance to West Third Street being developed."

"By that you mean, what?"

"They will raze the buildings, clear cut the trees, and erect cheap, coyote ugly condominiums."

Hearing received no contact after his visit, Bryce had assumed there was no interest on her part. Now, he was being pressured to ink his consent to the pre-arranged sale.

"Are the investors local?" she asked.

"Local and powerful. I guess you know that means Harry Drake. But," he added, looking her squarely in the eye, "it's not too late for you to change the game back to square one."

Marlena had followed his briefing closely, clenching an embroidered linen handkerchief Annie had pressed upon her as she left the house.

Was Scattergood motivated by a desire other than altruism? He came from a long line of naturalists and environmentalists who were also savvy businessmen. Was he casting about for a likeminded partner to help him beat the developers at their own game?

What about Coddie's role in the play action? Had he forgotten about Bryce's visit and the tendered offer? *Was there another reason he had kept the information from her?*

"I very much appreciate your giving me another chance."

Bryce looked at her keenly. She'd said "me," not "us," and she'd introduced herself by her maiden, not her married, name.

He said, "I'd buy it myself if I wasn't so over-invested. I've been holding the wolves at the door for some time. Oh, I'm sorry, ma'am. It occurs to me Harry Drake is your employer."

Marlena could feel the blood rushing into her face.

What was behind Harry's involvement? He might have inside information, possibly about the interminably delayed northeast freeway, bringing a population surge to the district and a bonanza for developers with cheap land at their disposal.

Harry may have counted on the bad blood between the Bellums and Scattergoods to keep me out of the loop regarding the value of our property.

"So, do you think the bank's interest in the Bellum house is connected to the development deal?"

"It smells like it."

"What would you advise us to do?"

"I would strongly advise holding tight. They're eager to push the deal through before the situation changes. There's money coming into the area, not only from investors who see potential for a quick buck, but also from a different kind of investor, those working with government agencies to restore historic architecture in America's small towns."

He told her rehabilitation projects were springing up all over the country. Ordinary citizens were saving old houses and building historic replications in vacant lots.

"It's exciting for someone like myself, or anyone who values our storied past. In your case, you have the right background and the opportunity to make a difference and save a community's history."

So that was the pitch.

She knew what Harry would think of it. Outside of his twin castles, Harry was all for throwing up crap and reaping quick profits. Some charged he'd lavished money on circumventing common land regulations, to develop untitled property for his own purposes.

She didn't mind that Harry's home and hotel were monuments to himself, but she didn't like his shoddy time shares. And she minded very much if her heritage was to be sacrificed on the altar of monopoly.

Marlena's eyes blazed. "I hate what's happening in our country. Unbridled development is draining the life's blood from our small towns."

Scattergood sat up straighter.

"It needs to be stopped, before there isn't a small town in America that hasn't been malled to death, without a shred of identity or vitality left in the original downtown."

In the sixties, instead of agitating against the war, Marlena had put her energies into attempting to defeat the forces that were toppling beloved old buildings. She'd traveled to New York in 1963 to protest the demolition of Pennsylvania station, a nine-acre building of glass and steel with a soaring 450-foot ceiling that had captured the modern spirit and stood as the landmark for New York City since 1910.

Sadly, the building was sacrificed and replaced by a boxing ring and a subway station, but the long fight was credited with sparking the architectural preservation movement and the National Register of Historic Places.

"I see I have an able ally," observed Bryce. "I'll continue to hold off the wolves as long as possible. But you can help in the short run by not selling your historic house to those Rotarians at the bank. They'd as soon swing a wrecking ball at it as a golf club."

"And they'd hang you at their sunrise meeting for tattling, Mr. Scattergood. Or bite your leg off with their big false teeth."

"Call me Bry."

"Call me Lena. I've never seen a condo development that I didn't want to tear down--including Top Hat."

"That's what I hoped to hear."

They were both thinking of Hatter's Field.

In olden days, when Hatter's Field was viewed as unusable commons not worth stealing from the Indians, Hatter's Field and its highest point, a thumb-like landmark known as the Hat, were un-gated. The Hat bore a resemblance to Devils Tower, thirty four miles distant, though it was much smaller; both overlooked the Belle Fourche River.

Now, the Hatter's Field wilderness was enclosed by security fencing that bore the stamp of Drake Enterprises. The iconic Hat was brimmed by the ugly sprawl of Drake's new time-share project, Top Hat, adjacent to the Alta Hotel. The sight of it made Marlena feel physically sick. No true native, she thought, would be caught dead owning a "time share" on Hatter's Field.

"I'll take my chances with the bankers and the developers," Bryce was saying. "And if they start showin' teeth, I'll wear my leather breeches. Now we both know where the wind lies. I'll wait for your call as to when we should meet again."

"I'll get back to you very soon, probably right after Christmas."

"Good. Well, is there anything else I can help you with today?"

"I'd like to use your bathroom, if I may, and then your telephone."

"The bathroom is down the hall, to the left of the moose head. The office is yours as long as you like. I'll leave you to it, as I've got a showing down the street. Just lock the front door behind you when you leave."

"Thanks, Bry. I'll think carefully about your offer."

After fiddling with something on his desk, Bryce wound a muffler around his neck, shook hands warmly, and went out the door.

Chapter Eighteen

From her perch on the wooden toilet seat, Marlena found she was gazing squarely at a poster of Charlie's Angels. It was good to know her ally was no Bible-toting jackass. Scattergood probably jerked off while he was sitting here.

Any woman might be happy to have those stout arms around her. Why didn't she fall for guys like Bryce, the upright, protective type? What was it about Harry that drew her to him so obsessively?

She forced her mind back to Scattergood.

He had made her see Alta in a new light. Right here in her home town was a cause very dear to her heart, the rescue of historic buildings. It could be combined with saving her own heritage, about which, she was beginning to realize, she knew very little.

Tomorrow, however, would be another story. Her head would be swimming with family history, the naughty story of old cousin Cassandra that had been forbidden fruit for over twenty years.

As she returned to the office, she resolved to check out further what Scattergood had implied about Drake Enterprises and the detrimental effect of corporate greed on the community.

While she lingered in the leather desk chair, enjoying the aroma of pipe smoke and the pleasant afterglow of their enlightening conversation, her eyes fell on a scrapbook. It was placed so she could scarcely help from being drawn to it.

Had Bryce Scattergood left it there on purpose?

She felt a queasy lurch of disloyalty, but kept on turning page after page of yellowed newspaper clippings. Each revealed a new shenanigan in the region's development. One headline in particular caught her eye: "Prince of Darkness Uncloaked as Spy for Feds in Native American Land Scandal."

"Prince of Darkness" referred to Princeton Negrah, a man she knew to be one of Drake's secret, powerful partners.

The story behind the headline was an eye-popping thriller, a tale of political payoffs and scamming that had occurred back in the late 1960's when Negrah had got the permitting necessary for building "affordable housing" on vacant land near Laramie that had once been occupied by a Native American tribe, now dwindled to three families.

When bribery stopped working, Negrah resorted to a genetics scam, claiming he was twenty percent Cherokee; he had the forged DNA tests to prove it. Therefore, he was legally exempt from the land protection laws applicable to non-native Americans.

A sidebar told the story of Princeton Negrah, who was neither East Indian nor Native-American Indian. Born a dairy hand's son in Wyoming as plain Richard Miller, he changed his name in the early 60's and set out in a turban to develop wildernesses. The first of the young man's holdings was a dirt parking lot in Laramie, offered in lieu of cash for a variety of nefarious services that earned him a nickname among associates as "the Prince of Darkness."

The parking lot had been transformed into a real estate empire by 1965, encompassing huge tracts of vacant land, the ownership of which had been previously untested in the courts. All transactions took place behind closed doors.

In 1969, a fraudulent scheme to take over a huge tract of unclaimed Native American property in Wyoming was uncovered by a Laramie reporter. It promised to be as big as the Teapot Dome Scandal of the 1920's. The land-grab scheme took down a hapless mayor and county attorney who were implicated in the payoff pipeline. The attorney was disbarred and the mayor got out of his fix the hard way. He died of a heart attack on the tarmac of the Casper Airport as he was preparing to fly to Brazil, in a desperate move to head off arraignment on federal charges.

Princeton Negrah, however, remained untouched by the scandal. In this instance, he had been working for the Feds, wearing a wire in his Brooks Brothers boxer shorts. His silent partner Harold Drake then stepped in to parlay the land negotiations, more openly playing the role of Satan to Negrah's Prince of Darkness. The deal had been stalled by environmentalists for years, but it was now nearing completion.

Chapter Nineteen

Marlena dialed her mother's room number at Ho Jo's. After seven rings, Faith answered the phone.

"Mama? It's Lena."

"Oh, hi, Lena."

"You sound distracted."

"What? It's just that the maid is in here again."

Marlena laughed. "You're keeping an eye on your fries."

"Fries? What nonsense are you talking, Lena? It's way past lunch time."

"Nothing, Mama. It's an expression. Listen, I'm here at Bryce Scattergood's office. He gave me an earful about the local real estate picture. His advice is the same as Coddie's. He says we shouldn't jump at any offers on the house. How much is the mortgage on it?"

"It's $25,000 and change, not exactly chicken feed."

"That's what I thought. Well, Bryce says the boys at the bank are trying to pull a fast one on us and get the house on the cheap. It sits in the middle of a REIT's big development project."

She swallowed hard, feeling the lurch of conflicting loyalties. *It was Harry's project, his REIT.*

"Well, I have no idea who this guy Reed is. He could be the devil himself for all I know. You and your husband have the background for this sort of thing. You deal with Reed."

"Speaking of the devil, Mama, Coddie's in Alta."

"Glory be! When did that happen?"

"I ran into him yesterday out on Hatter's Field, while I was collecting holly. He's staying at the hotel."

"Well, it's no surprise to me he couldn't stay away from you during the holidays. Your marriage can and will be saved."

"Sure, sure, whatever you say, Mama. Anyway, Mr. Scattergood has some really good news for us about the value of the house. He also says there's money available from the feds for a residence restoration project downtown."

"You don't say."

"What we have is a gem, Mama. We have a chance to fight the bad guys, right here in my home town. What do you think about that?"

She neglected to mention who the bad guys might be.

Faith at times could be intuitive. She had easily divined what Marlena was driving at. "You can climb down off your high horse now, Marlena Mae. If you want to do something with the property yourself, all you have to do is say so."

"Really? Well, now you mention it, Mama, I might think about your take on it. The house would make a great restoration project. With the help of someone like Scattergood, I could do it for us both, as an investment."

"Your husband could help us--"

"Oh, no," Marlena interjected. "Coddie's not to get his hands on this deal. If I take it on, I do so for us girls."

Faith sighed. "I was only going to say, Lena, that Coddie might be able to help get us financing. It would take at least forty five grand, am I right?"

"Yes, but I have an idea of how I might come up with money elsewhere. And Bryce said he would help me to find other investors."

"Well, have it your way, Lena. You always do."

"Mama, I do appreciate the vote of confidence."

So, the pressure was mounting in Faith's campaign for Marlena to save her marriage. She'd think about that later, for she'd just won a major victory: the pink house could be hers, if she wanted it.

How would Harry react? Would they be at cross purposes? Or would he behave like a loving partner and be supportive of her efforts?

Faith could hear quick breathing over the phone. She became concerned. "Lena, what's wrong? Lena, are you all right? Lena, can you hear me? Talk to me!"

"I'm still here, Ma," Marlena murmured weakly.

"Lena! Lena!"

"It was just a dizzy spell. It happens sometimes when my thoughts run too fast. Don't worry. I'm fine now."

"So, what did the doctor say about your symptoms? You did hear from him?"

"Doctor? Oh, yes, I did." She paused while concocting her story. "And just as I expected, it's an iron deficiency. Dr. Ron---do you remember Typhoid Ronnie, Mama?"

"I can't say that I do. 'Typhoid Ronnie' doesn't sound like a fitting name for a doctor."

"He was my classmate in second grade. Dad used to call him that because he infected me with everything. Now Ron's a local doctor, a very good one."

Faith sighed. "If you say so, Lena. I wouldn't put too much stock in any doctor in these parts."

"Mama, there's no need to drag me off to the Cleveland Clinic. All I need are some B12 shots."

"Are you sure, Lena, that's all that's wrong?"

"Yes, Mama. Hey, congratulate me."

"On what?"

"Remember what I told you at brunch, about our fifth anniversary year at B. L. Zebub's, and how we were targeting some pretty big numbers? Well, I heard today that we're almost sure to exceed our numbers for 1977. Isn't that great? I'm about to go over there and celebrate with the staff."

"I suppose this means I don't get to see you until tomorrow. I have my crocheting and my prayers, and a little television to watch in the afternoons. The food at the counter isn't too bad. Don't worry about me."

"Mama, spare me the Ma Perkins routine. That's not all I have on my plate. Later tonight, Chloe has promised to tell me Cassandra's story."

"Wonderful," Faith said sourly.

"That's what Annie said. Well, today's a busy day for me, no doubt about it, but tomorrow, first thing, I want you to come over and stay at Chloe's. Please do come for the rest of your stay, Mama. It's really beautiful here and very festive. We can spend some quiet time together. What do you say to that?"

Faith thought her heart would burst. It was the overture she'd been waiting on for three years.

"Chloe asked me to come, but I didn't want to interfere."

"How could you be interfering? Jeez, I'm inviting you, Mama. Just show up tomorrow, but not too early, since I'll be sleeping in. I take it Cassandra's story will be a long one."

"Cassandra came out to Wyoming in 1899 when she was nineteen, and when she died in San Francisco she was almost a hundred. How she made it that far, I'll never know. Of course the people here think it was because she was a witch. Why you want to dig up those old bones, Lena, is a mystery to me."

"So you'll come to Mill's Creek?"

"You've asked me, Lena, and I'll come. You can tell Chloe I'll be there tomorrow afternoon, with bells on."

After putting down the phone, Faith went straight down to the front office and cancelled the remaining days of her stay.

"If anyone calls for me, though I can't think why anyone should, I'll be at my cousin Chloe Vye's house, out there at Mill's Creek."

When the desk clerk asked her why she was departing early, Faith looked her straight in the eye.

"I'll be on God's business," she said. "I have to save my daughter from making the worst mistake of her life."

Chapter Twenty

She would be there "with bells on," Faith had said. She was one to quote the Scriptures, but never in Marlena's hearing had she used that phrase before. *Was it possible Mama loved her?*

A child too often left alone, Marlena had always sincerely doubted her mother wanted to have her in the first place, and she felt she wasn't unconditionally loved.

But she tamed the flutter in her heart and set the comment aside, as something to discuss later on with Chloe. Her focus now must be on the 1977 numbers and the staff holiday gathering at Zebub's. Long hours and hard work had paid off. Hooray!

As for her gnawing personal concerns, hopefully it was only a matter of hours before she would hear from Harry about when they could meet. Possibly she would even see Harry when she got to the hotel, as he sometimes would show up at staff parties.

Afterward, she'd lure him upstairs, in his suite or hers. Her sexual hunger for him was like a wound in her heart.

She was envisioning his cock, how she would flick it with her tongue until it was standing straight up at attention. And then, after riding him hard and getting herself off, she'd go back down on him and make him come in her mouth.

That was Harry's favorite part, though she could take it or leave it. His eyes would cross with pleasure, he'd grunt, and then she'd be swallowing his juices. She'd read somewhere that ejaculate was good for the mouth lining.

Perhaps a change of scenery would be good for their sex life. If she landed Sally Honeywell as a private client, she'd be exchanging the West's cold mountains for the balmy, open atmosphere of Key West. It would be fun hanging out with the sisters, indulging in cuddly lesbian sex for awhile until Harry managed to get there. *Harry would surely follow in pursuit of her, wouldn't he? He couldn't resist.*

In the crystal ball she carried around inside her head, Marlena envisioned a future of starlit nights when she and Harry would emerge from their thatched cottage and walk hand-in-hand along the Gulf shores. On a rock in the middle of the Gulfstream, the bonfires of their early passion would be rekindled.

Yep, this week was shaping up great after all. She was clear now on the road ahead of her. It was almost possible to convince herself the hexing hadn't happened. She'd always been an optimist as well as a futurist; she believed there was no problem that couldn't be fixed if she put her mind to it and shoved hard against anyone or anything in her way. And Letty was one impediment richly deserving of a shove.

As for that other problem, the one she was carrying in her belly, it couldn't be willed away. She'd get a quick abortion in San Francisco, then fly down to Key West. She'd helped Harry achieve his dream of building a Xanadu in their home town. Would he step up to the plate and make her dream of a life with him come true?

She allowed herself to continue the luxury of daydreaming. The crystal ball in her head was steamy with images of a blissful future life, starting all over again in Key West with Harry.

Oh, how she missed that end-of-the line hangout, was her thought.

The Bellums had driven south in a used Dodge sedan with pink and white fenders. She'd loved it. Unfortunately, after several forced stops for repairs, Faith declared the Dodge to be a "lemon" and traded it in at a Miami car-lot for a four-door Chevy sedan, a big disappointment.

She had also been disappointed when their open-ended stay in Key West was curtailed by the explosive international situation in Cuba. She'd felt happier in Key West than she had since 1952, when she'd been forced to leave her grandparents' home in the mountains.

She was building an elaborate sandcastle on Smathers Beach when the Cuban missile crisis broke out, and they were told they must evacuate. Her last vision was of sand bags on the beach and sailors brawling on the streets. And forever after she could see in her mind, in exact detail, a banyan tree on Whitehead Street. It was sprawling and shamanistic, its gnarled branches thick as a man's arm, large yet still inviting, something out of a Hollywood movie set.

She would climb up and sit on its thickest branch, her long legs dangling and her mind wandering far afield, as she used to do on Hatter's Field.

The tree jutted out in all directions, up, down, and sideways, with exposed roots that were taller than she was. It drew nurture from the soil and extended over her a rich canopy of spiritual and physical gifts, transforming her view of the universe and all the possible connections among humankind, God, and nature.

It was mysterious as a boat of singing ravens, inspirational as a cathedral.

For ten years, HMC and Faith had been the mainstay of her belief system, but all that was changed as she sat on the banyan tree, reading a book from the Key West library.

On a rain-swept day early in their stay, she had boldly ventured into the library on Fleming Street. She had been inside many libraries but had never seen one like this before. Low slung and stuccoed, much like a house in a Bahamian neighborhood, it was painted a pepto bismal shade of pink.

In her humdrum life in Ohio, the public libraries were towering concrete mausoleums, endowed by the Carnegie foundation during the old robber baron days. She had spent hour upon hour in the echoing corridors of one such repository of wisdom, volunteering her help over the summer in shelving books under the surveillance of a sour, elderly librarian.

The Key West librarian looked like a character out of Dickens; his black hair cascaded in corkscrew curls, and he wore round, wire-rimmed eye-glasses. She politely asked for his recommendation of reading to keep her occupied while her mother shopped.

"Where are you from, young lady?"

"I'm a native of the wilds of Wyoming, but I was taken by force to Ohio. I have my library card with me, sir. May I have one of yours if I show it to you?"

He looked at her skeptically. Then, as she beamed her eyes into his, he promptly relented. "I guess we could arrange that."

"I've been reading the philosophers in alphabetical order. I'm through the C's. Would you pick something from the D's for me, please, sir?"

In a few minutes he was back at the desk with a hardbound copy of Darwin's <u>Origin of Species</u>.

The day was brilliant, with a scalding sun and the sky the same color as her eyes. Hidden high up in the arms of the banyan tree, speed reading her way through Darwin, Marlena had a kind of epiphany.

It came to her then that the venerable authorities of science and religion actually offer two sides of the same human imperative, which goes something like this: "adapt/do as we say, and you have a chance to live forever." But she preferred to think that God was in the banyan tree--and in her--exactly as she and the tree existed, not in some project of science or zealot's delusion.

The name of the church she and her parents attended in Key West was Mary, Star of the Sea. As usual, Austin trailed behind her and Faith, leaning on his cane and with a hidden flask in his pocket. She had never heard a more beautiful name for a church. Nor had she ever seen so many dark-skinned people at mass. Were they like the poor African-Americans who lived in the slums of Cleveland?

Her mother told her these people were Cubans and that Cuba was only eighty miles away; a ferry went there every day from Key West, though the present situation would no doubt end all that.

Chapter Twenty One

As Christmas week was traditionally the deadest time of the year for B. L. Zebub's, Marlena had won Harry's grudging approval to close the bar for two hours this afternoon so the staff could enjoy a private Christmas party. At noon, guests would be given a last-drink signal. At two, a special punch would be concocted, which she had named the Bonfire of the Competition, in honor of the year's unprecedented numbers. Favors would be laid out for each staff member, who were the heads of the various departments from Front Desk to Laundry. The party would then commence, and at five the bar would be reopened to guests.

The favors were bronze replicas of the new bonfire sculpture created by a world-famous Denver artiste and roustabout who was a popular customer at the saloon. The dazzling piece had been unveiled amid much fanfare at the outset of the holiday season. Flanked by pristine Western landscaping, its location was at the corner of the sculpture garden nearest the arching windows of the hotel restaurant, so dining guests could enjoy the newest addition to Drake's art collection.

The sculpture was cleverly made of metal and ponderosa strips. It closely resembled the historic bonfire that would be burned up at the Hat on Christmas evening. But the bonfire sculpture, because of the ponderosa and metal composition, would not burn.

As Marlena approached the hotel, the first sign of trouble was a dark plume of smoke hovering over the sculpture garden and two fire trucks parked on the lawn. Beside them were two empty squad cars with their red lights swirling.

She got out of the car and ran to the nearest person she saw, who was old Joe.

He told her that in the dark of night, unknown persons had embedded kerosene-soaked pine strips into the sculpture, additions which had gone undetected.

Then at noon, the sculpture had been torched, again by unknown persons and in full view of the annual solstice luncheon attended by members of POT (Pioneers of the Territory).

Though the sculpture itself hadn't burned, it had been enveloped in flames, along with two stick figures that had been placed there by the vandals. These effigies and their conflagration were large enough to be seen through the windows, where the diners witnessed the unplanned event first hand.

Joe reported the burning figures had spectacular devil's eyes, red horsehair, and metallic neckbands crudely carved with the initials MB and CV. She could readily see for herself that the manicured grounds were badly scorched, an ugly sight. The firemen were still on the scene, hosing it down. All other vehicles had been removed from the parking lot.

It was only after she drilled her eyes into the security guard's and repeated her insistence that she be allowed to go inside the building that she was escorted inside. Access had been disallowed until it was known if the vandals were still around.

As she entered the lobby, the acrid smell of smoke hung in the air. She hurried past the front desk clerks, who were standing in a group, whispering.

She found the secret door to B. L. Zebub's was wide open. Where was the guard? Typically he was there at all hours. As she proceeded down the narrow hallway at a fast pace, a dead quiet was eerily present. The only sound to be heard was the thud-thud of her platform heels on the wood floor, which matched the loudness of the beating of her heart. Usually there were clusters of customers hanging out in the entranceway, which was a calculated part of the pleasure. Newcomers would stop to observe and admire Drake's collection of classic erotic art.

As a patron had once observed, the entrance to the West's only eerie pub was "part of the fun, much like having sex with a cowboy who has a groovy way of getting on and getting off."

But no one seemed to be up for having fun today. For once the hallway was empty, and it echoed like a tomb.

Odder still, the bar itself was empty as she entered it. Despite the plans for the staff holiday party, the entire room was deserted; she could see the bronze favors laid out on the table were untouched.

She put her hands on her hips and looked around. No one was tending the bar. No one was sitting in the saddle bar seats. Not a living soul was present.

"What in hell is going on?" she wondered aloud. "Where is everybody? Did we get raided by the DEA?"

Then she noticed the entire mirrored back wall of the bar was shrouded in huge pieces of purple velvet drapery, like the statues on Good Friday in a Catholic church. That was certainly peculiar.

She called out. "Hello! Anyone here?"

The blind eyes of a stuffed mule deer hanging on the leather wall seemed to be staring at her reproachfully.

"What're you looking at?" she muttered. "You're creeping me out."

It was then she heard a familiar whistle--Harry's--and she smiled widely with relief while she watched him stroll into the bar at his usual sauntering pace, as if nothing were going on. But from his pallor and a clenching at his jaw-line, she knew something serious was up.

Behind Harry lurked Lorna Anderson, her old schoolmate. Marlena was surprised to see her, and Lorna wasn't looking her in the eye.

"Oh, hi, Lorna," she said politely, though what was on her mind to say was "What in the hell are you doing here?"

"We've got a hell of a situation," said Harry laconically.

"Yes?"

"We've been vandalized. The central mirror on the bar wall is shattered. Someone threw a javelin at it."

"What century are we in? Who throws a javelin at a bar mirror?"

"Well, apparently someone who doesn't like you very much."

"What do you mean?"

"You were burned in effigy out in the sculpture garden, where they torched the bonfire. Two stick figures with red hair, one named Cassandra, the other, Marlena. They were burned to the ground in the sight of alarmed guests. Another message was left for you in here."

"I don't believe it."

"Take a look for yourself." He gestured toward the back of the bar, which was heavily draped.

Marlena quickly ducked under the bar's flap door and then moved toward the drapery. She took a strong yank at it, pulling off the middle drape.

She gasped, "Oh my God."

By some mechanism, the mirror on the gigantic central panel had been warped beyond recognition. It now resembled the mirror in a carnival, and her image appeared grotesquely distorted. At the center of the mirror was a large gaping crater, the size of a manhole cover. A javelin, fashioned like an oversized Indian arrow, lay where it had fallen on the hard wood floor after doing its damage.

It was as she gazed at the floor that she began to notice the creeping worms and snakes. The whole place was infested with the slimy things! She shook her head in disgust, reaching her hand back to Harry. He had followed her to the mirrors and drawn near her. But instead of taking her extended hand, he stepped away from her. She shuddered.

"Who did all this?" she asked.

"You tell me. You've missed the best part."

He walked to the left panel of the mirrored walls and flung back a second velvet drape, revealing three lines of writing scrawled in a childishly rounded hand, all in red crayon.

"Behold: the handiwork of Marlena Bellum, who has invited Satan into our midst.

"Harry Drake, this is your final warning: stand against the forces of evil!

"Smite the hellish snakes from the red head of Satan's whore, or your eyes will be turned to stone."

She stared at her lover, her eyes round and her cheeks ashen.

"Someone thinks you need a haircut," he said.

Their eyes met, and she shivered. The pin-point pupils in his pale brown eyes were cold, hard, and angry. The sensation in her stomach was the painful, terrifying lurch of falling from a very high place.

"It's Letty and her legions," she said in a whisper.

"How do you know that? More to the point, how would she get in here?" he demanded.

Harry's scornful eyes were boring into hers, resisting her power. To counteract his cold stare, she was envisioning the last time they had climaxed together.

He had teased her with his cock, putting it in and then pulling it out, until she was in a frenzy. Then he'd mounted her, ruthlessly pushing his entire member into her. They had cried out in mutual orgasm, the sweat from their bodies spurting from their chests, draining into their eyes, nostrils, and open mouths.

She willed him to remember it; she poured her eyes into his. It was no use; his eyes were stone cold, blocking her power.

"I don't know," she said in a whisper. "Somehow she did."

Think on it, Marlena; worms and mirrors.

Worms and mirrors, she thought. An odd combination, wasn't it? The words and images resonated with her in such a particular, peculiar way. Suddenly her eidetic memory had it, her brain having culled the database and pulled up a solitary entry in the first of her two brown notebooks.

Worms and mirrors were iconic images from an old wives' tale told to her by Granny Bellum.

Having noticed Marlena spent hours staring into the mirror, Granny Bellum had impressed a stern, superstitious warning on her granddaughter: "If you look at yourself too much in the mirror, Lena, you'll get worms."

Had someone gone through her journals and fiendishly devised this particular punishment, just to freak her out?

The notebooks had been locked in her private closet for a couple of days. It was possible one of Letty's spies had a key to the closet. If so, her most personal memories and childhood secrets were now ammunition in the enemy's camp. *How to fight back?*

She forced herself to focus.

Harry said stonily, "You're on leave from your official duties here, as of now."

"You don't think I had anything to do with this?"

"I don't know what to think."

Marlena pressed her fingers to her temples. This couldn't be happening to her. Just an hour ago, the way ahead had seemed clear.

She was looking forward to a celebration of 1977's numbers, followed by an afternoon of lovemaking with Harry.

Now their icon of success was smashed, littered in broken glass and infested with worms. And he was looking at her as though she were a stranger, or worse.

"I don't pretend to know what's on your mind, Marlena, but my mind is on the money. It's a holiday week, and I can't afford to keep this bar closed because of whatever spook is out to get you."

Harry sneered as he uttered "whatever spook is out to get you."

She had special gifts, but she could not see what was going through her lover's mind.

What was gnawing in Harry's gut was a suspicion that Marlena herself had master-minded this travesty to elicit his sympathy, that it was part of a relentless campaign to push him toward marrying her.

First, she'd purposely left out her divorce papers for him to see; then, she'd fled to her cousin's house without a word; now, she'd staged a gruesome show for his benefit. Apparently she would stop at nothing to convince him to make an honest woman of her.

For years, she had made a mockery of his good name and reputation in his native town.

When some citizens voiced concerns with "B. L. Zebub's," she'd defied them, running advertisements touting the bar's lurid history.

Before Thanksgiving, historically a slow week for business, she'd hired an Elvis impersonator to spice things up, greeting guests in a rhinestone-studded white suit, red cloak, and pointy horns. When he'd objected--"for God sakes, Marlena, the hillbilly's barely cold in his grave"--she'd laughed and called him a square.

The message had come through loud and clear. Like <u>Playboy</u> said, B. L. Zebub's was where the possessed went to get fucked up.

It's the last straw, thought Harry, and I'll let the hellcat fry. I'll shake loose from these nails she's dug into me, even if it kills me. *No more, bitch. Take a hike, baby.*

"Love to love you baby..." sang Donna Summer over the loudspeaker.

"Will someone please turn that damn thing off?" snapped Harry.

By Mungo, he was going to make changes, pronto. Along with cleaning up the mess, he was going to sanitize the property's image.

In future, he'd also be checking the color of crotch hairs, to make sure he wasn't dipping his wick into a redheaded witch's brew. Fuck vixens, wiccans, feminists, and drag queens. These deranged female types had an insatiable, morbid desire for attention.

He'd take a simple, pot-smoking cowgirl like Lorna Anderson any day, despite her acne and fake boobs.

Marlena was the first to drop her eyes. She felt lethargic and defeated. The nausea was rising in her throat.

"I agree," she said in a dead voice. "We have to keep the bar open, if only to prove we aren't intimidated."

"Intimidated? I'm not intimidated. I'm fucking furious! Do you know what it's going to cost me to replace that mirror? God knows how they bowed it, took a blow torch to it, maybe. Those crawlers will have to be exterminated. I'll be back in business tomorrow. But make no mistake about it, Marlena. I don't want you here. Clear out your things. I'm changing the lock on your suite."

"I'm not staying here. But you already knew that."

He grabbed her by the arm. "What do you mean, I knew it?"

"Harry, you're hurting me."

He let her go, shifted the knot of his red silk tie, and cleared his throat.

As her world crashed around her, Marlena had to use every ounce of her will to keep from falling down on her knees before him.

She opened her mouth. She was about to ask about the note she'd left in his suite yesterday, requesting a private meeting. Hadn't he got it?

But before she could speak, the central mirror panel cracked in a thousand places, exploding shards everywhere. The three people in the bar bolted under the shower of glass and ran for their lives.

Once she was safely outside, Marlena looked for Harry, desperate to convince him Letty had wreaked the damage.

He was already inside the police car, talking with an officer. Lorna was nowhere to be seen.

Chapter Twenty Two

As more than one citizen reported Mrs. Letty Brown-Hawker had been spreading rumors and claiming Marlena was a dangerous witch, the police investigated the couple at their home. But they appeared to have an air-tight alibi. When the vandalism occurred, they'd been front and center at the WCTU monthly chapter meeting.

Meanwhile, Letty's repeated predictions of two deaths resulting from Marlena's taint was spreading like poison through a body after an adder's bite. Circulars were being secretly stuffed in mailboxes, warning of the dire consequences of citizens' countenancing the face of deadly evil. The message was that whether sin presented itself brazenly or in the guise of beauty and art, it remained a direct defiance of God's will.

By sunset, the violence at B. L. Zebub's at high noon had been chewed over and was widely regarded as a fitting comeuppance for the nefarious Drake and his proud, red-headed minion, who was clearly *that woman* reincarnated. More than one claimed to have suspected as much since Marlena's return to her native town seven years before, considering how her stunning appearance was highly unusual for a supposed native.

At the stammtisch table in Bottomly's Cafe, shunning of the pair was advocated, ala Ingrid Bergman. Public nudity, satanic eroticism, and unabashed adultery just weren't done in Alta, and perhaps Drake's sponsorship of his whore's shenanigans was in itself satanic.

Whether her hexing was based on Letty's jealousy or a natural result of the ancestral curse, they couldn't say, but all agreed Marlena Bellum should beat a retreat, purifying the village for Christmas.

A séance was staged that evening, with Letty functioning as medium and channeling an Indian named Red Cloud, who was plenty pissed off at Drake's real estate shenanigans and lax morality.

Letty held her audiences spellbound with whispered tales of special powers Marlena had inherited from *that woman*. There was no saying what evils might be unleashed on an innocent populace, Letty warned, even beyond the two deaths predicted.

One could hope the axe would fall on the sinning couple, but there was no knowing how God might choose to punish this community for harboring Satan's whore. The continued presence of the witch was not only an affront to morality but also a public danger, and the penalty for those who would attempt to protect her might well be death..

Hunkered down at Mill's Creek and therefore unaware of the poison swirling around her name, Marlena spent the remainder of the afternoon mulling over every detail of what Harry had said to her.

There must be a way to get to him and convince him of her case against Letty. If he continued to balk her, she would prefer to die.

When would she taste his salt again? Brush the curly chest hair with her fingertips? See his eyes glaze over as he surrendered to orgasm?

Initially she considered waiting a day before showing her face again out in public, but she soon decided against a coward's strategy of fleeing, which was what her enemies hoped for. Nor would she take on the role of martyr, dress in a sack cloth, and beat her breast.

The latter was what she thought Harry was expecting she would do. Harry no doubt blamed her for the burst of his bubble. Many guests had checked out early; no new guests had checked in as word spread. Though her belief was that the ghost story would only enhance the hotel's image in the future, admittedly the bottom line on this holiday season might be adversely affected.

If she wasn't part of the solution, she must be part of the problem– so Harry's linear reasoning would go. Therefore, she must figure out a way to pre-empt any further strikes by the fanatics against the hotel.

To that end, she decided she would invite the Brown-Hawkers to the ball. She would draw the enemy from their lair into her territory, Hatter's Field, for a final showdown. Let Harry see the bigots for what they actually were. She wasn't afraid to face them head on.

That evening, after a glorious sunset, Marlena listened spellbound to Chloe's nine-hour version of her mother's story, which went, briefly, as follows:

On October 28, 1900, Cassandra Vye was hexed in Alta's Methodist church by Goody Brown, Letty Brown-Hawker's ancestor.

Goody was obsessed with the idea that the beautiful outsider possessed a malevolent power. Her evidence was a tall tale told by Cassandra's grandfather and the observation that she had turned the innkeeper, Augustus "Curly" Drake, into a lecherous swine willing to abandon his wife on their wedding night.

But Cassandra gave up her possession of Drake in order to garner the attention of Alta's favorite native son, Nicholas Brighton, in the false hope that he would take her back with him to San Francisco.

Subsequently Cassandra was unfairly blamed for two deaths in the village. The first was that of her widowed mother-in-law. The second was the spectacular demise on Hatter's Field of Harry's grandfather. Curly Drake's reason for being there was to help her escape, as Cassandra could no longer bear the town's and her husband's low opinion of her; afterward, their adultery was falsely assumed.

With the help of the Scattergood men, Cassandra made it to San Francisco and as time passed, became a highly successful film writer and actress. On the brink of WWI, she conceived a child by a soldier. The soldier died before reaching the front. Despite excellent parentage of her daughter Chloe and her many anonymous good works, Cassandra remained in Alta a legend associated with evil. She herself believed in the curse laid upon her by Goody Brown, fearing its impact on her female descendants and their lovers.

Chapter Twenty Three
December 22, 1977

By morning, Marlena saw her world from a radically adjusted angle.

For the first time, being slavishly devoted to a powerful man and defying all convention seemed unwise and immature to her.

Her eyes were opened as well to the possibility she had been behaving like an automaton in a world of connection, so enthralled with being a love slave that nothing else held any reality; her obsession covered her like a shield.

Only one person might pierce that armor.

Ron, my friend, might you be my future lover? Dare I seek passion in the arms of a good man and true?

Many questions remained unanswered, but for the first time, Marlena was beginning to sense what she must do.

Her old brown notebooks had been banded together and put at the bottom of her suitcase when she left the hotel. In the dark of night, she had lifted them out. These journals were about the first seven years of her life, composed when she was ten. They had been a labor of love, a blessing bestowed by her special gift of perfect recall.

By the crack of dawn, she had read them through, cover to cover. Then she opened up a blank composition book and at the top of the page wrote two words: Home Schooling.

As she raced from Mill's Creek to the Alta Hotel through steadily falling snow, late for a noon appointment at the hotel with Sally Honeywell, she was still endlessly sorting out in her brain the implications of the ancestral story.

On the car radio, "Wasting Away in Margaritaville" was blaring, the song holding steady in 1977's top ten charts. The country couldn't get enough of Jimmy Buffet's tasty cocktail and shaker of salt.

With every syllable, the song lyrics seemed to be urging her toward the geographical cure as a temporary solution for her problems.

In light of her own relationships now resembling a pileup in a stock car crash, Cassandra's choice to flee held great appeal.

"Escape," counseled the wind, "escape to Key West. Waste away in Margaritaville."

As if Harry's abrupt dismissal of her wasn't enough to convince her that hopes of a happily-ever-after with him were ill-founded, Cassandra's story had cast a heavy funereal pall over her long cherished hopes and dreams. If she were to grant any credence to the tendency of history to repeat itself in a small town, their affair was pre-destined to crash and burn rather than reaching the social and romantic pinnacle she'd fondly envisioned.

What were the chances of a man leaving his wife for his mistress? Slim. What were the chances of an I.U.D. malfunctioning? She'd looked it up--about the same as getting hit by lightning.

At this juncture, carrying Harry's child seemed cataclysmic enough to qualify as an event masterminded by invisible forces.

The Curse?

Loving her husband and her mother though she did, Marlena fervently wished that neither of them was so close at hand. If she truly had magic powers, she would have banished them both from this highly disturbed field. It seemed the harder she tried to move straight ahead to her goals, the more mired she got in the past.

As her tires spun on the ice and the BMW pulled sideways, she honked her horn in sheer exasperation.

When she pulled up to the hotel and got out, her eyes were misted over and her shoulders were sagging.

Old Joe shambled forward and gave her a big hug. She could have kissed his boots, she was so grateful for his unswerving courtesy.

At the same moment Marlena honked her horn, Faith Bellum was arriving at Mill's Creek by cab.

The window shades were drawn, and there was no sign of anyone, neither out in the field nor visible near the barn, the garage, or the house.

However, it had been anything but silent in the car.

The cabbie had introduced himself as Fred Fairwell. Fairwell never stopped talking as he drove Faith up the mountain. He seemed to feel duty-bound to tell her everything ever said in this town about Mill Creek's current and former mistresses.

The heater was on full blast, and the temperature inside the cab verged on tropical, but he wore an old red woolen hat with the flaps tied down. As he was deaf, Fairwell spoke at the top of his lungs.

His roots in Alta went back to the cobbler and Sunday barber, who'd inhabited in 1900 a house on West Street that later became John Bellum's residence on West Third. Faith didn't mention she was planning to sell it.

In olden days, he shouted, Mill's Creek was a Sodom and Gomorrah--but he pronounced it "soddit and gonorrhea."

"They say *that woman* was Satan's spawn, the town's only witch. Goody Brown warned everyone ag'in her, but no one listened. She worked her black magic on the young studs in town and killed the Widder Brighton too. So, watch yerself, is all I got to say. Them's that knows, says there's still evil lurking hereabouts. *That woman* flew into the sky durin' a lightnin' storm on Hatter's Field and disappeared, never was heard of ag'in. Now there's a story you don't git on the Huntley-Brinkley Report."

Fairwell glanced at Faith in the mirror, but his passenger remained stonily silent. He switched on the radio. "I'm dreaming of a white Christmas..."

Faith knew from personal experience what it was to be the focus of suspicion by the Alta natives. After she arrived as a newlywed, her pregnancy had become quickly apparent, and the old women at church were visibly counting the days.

Luckily, Marlena dallied long enough *in utero* so that Faith's pregnancy squeaked into a tenth month. No one suspected the baby's father was a man from the East with startling blue-green eyes, who was Faith's lost love Gordon.

If there was gossip about Marlena, then the bankers, all solid pillars of the historic Methodist church, would turn a deaf ear to her request for a loan. Her high-paying job at PAD might be sacrificed, as a divorced couple wouldn't be permitted to work in the same office. Her final move would be to throw herself on the mercy of her lover.

What if Drake rejected her?

Faith wrung her hands inside her thick cotton gloves. At the same time, she was very angry. How could a smart Catholic girl who'd always been gifted and forward-thinking have put herself into such a position?

She'd said she was desperately in love, and for the first time.

If she loved Drake, Faith thought, then she was snake bit.

The bottom line was the divorce must be stopped before the affair became common knowledge. Marlena must be made to see the wisdom of returning to her husband, no matter how she felt about Drake.

"That'll be five and a quarter, ma'am, gas prices bein' up. Will you be needin' a ride back into town?"

"I'll call if I do," she said curtly.

Into the man's gloved hand that was missing two fingers--"LOST AT A SAW MILL," he'd shouted--she pressed a five dollar bill and a fifty cent piece. Then she opened the door, got out of the cab, and marched off while Fairwell glared at her back.

The frigid air stung her lungs. She gasped for breath as she made her way toward the silent house, her plastic boots crunching in the drifted snow along the terraced walkway.

Why would Chloe, who could live anywhere in the world, stick in this one-horse town? When Faith reached the door, she found it unlocked. There was a folded note tacked to it and "Welcome Faith!" marked with a red glitter pen on the outside.

"Annie is running errands and I'm at the office. We'll be back by 4 p.m. Make yourself at home. Herself is asleep on the living room couch. Shhhh. XO Chloe."

Faith had to smile despite her dislike of Chloe. In the old days, they'd all referred to baby Lena as "Herself," fussing over the Bellums' only grandchild as though she were royalty.

When they were both young girls, Faith had been jealous of Chloe's many accomplishments, jealous enough to have said "yes" to Austin Bellum's impulsive marriage proposal on the eve of his deployment overseas, only hours after they met. When she said yes, initially it was to impress Chloe, who had introduced them.

As a young and very nervous mother, Faith had felt a disconnection from Austin's family, her cousin Chloe, and even her child. It was partly because she knew her pregnancy had cost her a last chance at winning Gordon back, partly because she feared what would happen if any family member ever found out about Marlena's real paternity.

Yet she must admit that over the years, Chloe had been consistently loyal, kind, and helpful to her.

Faith shook her head over the foibles of youth. *She'd cut off her nose to spite her face.* Gordon eventually might have married her in the Church, if she'd held out. But he wouldn't marry her in haste, which she needed him to do to hide their terrible mortal sin.

And so, after a lot of prayer, she'd made her choice. Austin had never known Marlena wasn't his. It was a secret she'd always intended to carry to her grave. *Was God punishing her now, through Marlena?*

Maybe Chloe could use hypnosis on the kid and make her forget Harry Drake. Folks quit smoking and drinking that way, went into a trance and lost their taste for sinning. She'd seen it done on the Johnny Carson show.

She put down her battered suitcase in the entranceway, took off the plastic boots and her shoes, and placed all her belongings next to the door.

She was hoping Chloe didn't have expect her to sleep on one of those newfangled waterbeds she'd been reading about in <u>Good Housekeeping</u>. She wouldn't get a wink of sleep on a mattress that bounced her around. What a nutty idea!

Moving quietly, she entered the reception hall to the right of the winding staircase. Here Chloe would receive her throng of guests on Christmas night. Coming back to the foyer, Faith went to the left and tiptoed into the formal parlor, expecting to see Marlena stretched out, sleeping on the couch.

Marlena wasn't there, however, only an indentation of where she'd been. Freed from the restraint of not awakening her daughter, Faith put on her shoes and resumed her wanderings through the stone house.

Truth be told, she thought, ever since Marlena had uttered the word "Gordon," she had not felt like herself.

Of course she'd never believed paranormal powers resided in her daughter, as the Zanellis had feared when she grew up looking so much like Cassandra.

Could her utterance of her real father's name be God's way of telling His loyal servant Faith it was time to come clean?

Sometimes out of the mouths of babes come God's marching orders.

Now she was entering the bright, airy kitchen which everyone raved about. She could see for herself, though she was no architect, that it afforded space and intimacy in equal proportion, with its soaring vaulted ceiling, solar panels that let the sun come pouring in, and colorful Southwestern touches. Marlena had done a good job.

Stainless steel appliances, industrial stove, butcher block worktable, and a display of chili ristras and copper pans dangling from a low beam made it appear professional, yet homey.

Thinking of her own dark, cramped kitchen back in Parma, Faith felt a jealous pang. But how was she going to square things with Him if she kept stepping on her own flat feet? *God, forgive my weaknesses.*

In a cozy dining ell, a second note addressed to her was propped against a vase of red carnations on an oak table. She was invited to partake of the refreshments laid out under a silver dome--a glass of cider, a russet apple, and a plate of warm gingersnap cookies. Even in her absence, Chloe's gracious spirit of hospitality was evident.

Refreshed after her snack, Faith set about accomplishing her goal of spying on Marlena.

God had provided Faith a golden opportunity for surveillance, cleverly arranging it through Marlena's own invitation.

She sallied forth, marching up the grand central staircase into the guest bedroom wing. She had a hunch her daughter had revealed only the tip of the iceberg when she announced her separation and admitted to being involved with her married client.

The first room Faith peeked into she knew to have been Cassandra's old bedroom. It was small but had a breathtaking view. Her daughter's clothing, shoes, and papers were strewn about. The bed was sloppily made. On the bed were a couple of old brown notebooks. Frowning, she shook her head.

So this out of the many guest rooms available was the one Marlena had chosen for herself. That said a mouthful! Nothing good could come out of her daughter's identification with a heartless fiend.

A more thoughtful guest would keep her room neat and tidy. It was the least Marlena could do; her messiness reflected badly on Faith.

The next door was locked when she tried it. An old instinct led her to stop and retrace her steps. Moving quickly, she went through Marlena's room to get into the attached room, which turned out to be a large bathroom, with a claw-footed tub and vanity.

Here was where she would begin her search in earnest. After crossing herself and thanking God for His many blessings, Faith began methodically picking up and examining every item, beginning with Marlena's silver-backed hairbrush.

By the end of her search, she had discovered only that Marlena was shedding more hair than usual and was taking paregoric, Pepto Bismal, valium, codeine, diuretics, and sleeping pills.

None of these items being particularly suspicious, Faith stopped and thought: what exactly was she looking for? She wouldn't know a an illegal drug or a birth control pill if one bit her, but she knew these would be items worth knowing about.

She re-opened the medicine cabinet and stared again at its lone contents, a large, brown plastic bottle. It was opened, so presumably was in use. It appeared to contain vitamins, but they were huge, larger than any she'd ever seen before.

So, Lena was taking mega-doses of vitamins to counter her iron deficiency, and this bottle was physical proof she hadn't lied. However, her sense of relief was short-lived as Faith further considered that Lena's was the LSD generation, and she did live in California. Marlena might be a drug fiend. Drugs were everywhere these days.

Fumbling in her purse, Faith came up with a pencil and paper. She then carefully printed the content descriptions and tucked the note into her purse. Back East, it was after working hours. First thing in the morning, she would call her Polish doctor friend and check on these medications to make sure everything was on the up and up.

Satisfied with her reconnaissance mission, Faith quickly located the guest room reserved for her, a large, lovely suite containing a four-poster bed, a claw-footed tub in the bathroom, and, in the adjoining sitting room, a bouquet of roses on the desk.

Thankful for the peace and quiet cousin Chloe's home afforded, she closed the door. It was two thirty when her head hit the pillow, and she was out like a light.

Chapter Twenty Four

Marlena, Stretch, and Sally were tucked inside a booth at B.L. Zebub's. The bar was open to hotel guests only, and they were the only customers.

Though much remained to be done, overnight the exterminators had resolved the snake and worm infestation. Workmen were up on high ladders, reinstalling mirrored glass.

But already the saloon looked neutered, a shadow of its former erotic glory. The art lining the entrance hallway was gone. The shattered mirror was still partly shrouded in the somber purple drapery, which contrasted oddly with the bar's intricate filigree of fat, smiling cherubs, fauns sporting with wood nymphs, and a bulbous-bellied Egyptian female bearing an entire column on her head.

Marlena could feel the degree of loss in her pained emotions.

Of course she wasn't supposed to be on premises, but no one knew that except Harry, and she was daring Harry to do his worst.

He wouldn't have the balls to throw her out in the presence of her friends, who were paying guests.

Sally and Stretch were sucking down raw oysters and Bloody Mary's. Marlena was wearing sunglasses to cover up the damage to her eyes from last night's tale-a-thon.

Her portfolio of work sat beside her in a burnt orange leather case a yard wide. It had been a gift from Coddie. Oversized and hand-stitched, it could accommodate architectural drawings and blueprints.

Marlena opened the case, and Sally began flipping through copies of architectural plans, drawings, photographs, and press clippings on finished projects, also letters of recommendation.

She gave an occasional grunt of approval. Her mod eyelashes were much too young for her, Marlena thought, but her pink Dior scarf and silver Cartier bracelets were lovely.

Sally had already put her first card on the table. When Marlena mentioned a hiatus from her hotel responsibilities, she'd suggested Marlena accompany her back to Key West for a look-see at the Shell Mansion.

They'd been joined at one thirty by Stretch, marching in on her long, stick legs that made her look like a stork. She sat down beside Marlena, who immediately ordered another round of drinks.

Stretch hadn't jelled her hair, so her purplish spikes were now streaks. She was outfitted in pink leather chaps, a nose ring, and a fake Cheetah suit-coat. A jewelry artist who liked to wear her art upon her person, she had on earrings that were iron crosses. From her fringed leather belt dangled a glinting, jeweled dagger she'd designed and welded herself.

She could see the others were immersed in the employment dance; hopefully they were nearing the end of the courtship phase, as she was feeling bored and jealous.

"You won't find a better place to hang out and make interesting new friends," purred Sally, brushing Marlena's forearm. "Key West is wide open."

Marlena drew back an inch. "It's one of several places in the world where I want to spend quality time."

"What's holding you back?" asked Stretch. It was the first time she'd opened her mouth. "You've got bread; you can travel the world."

Sally frowned at her partner.

Marlena sighed. "If I were a man, I could roam the world from one watering hole to the next, no questions asked, sampling all the delights of the bazaar without being confined to one."

"Ain't nothin' much to being a man," opined Stretch.

"I wonder if you've heard of penis envy?" asked Marlena.

Stretch guffawed. "Ain't no such thing."

"Oh, yes there is, according to Freud."

"Who's he?"

"Sigmund Freud was an Austrian Jew who wrote several ground-breaking psychology books in the nineteenth century."

"So?"

"So, among other provocative theories, he postulated that women unconsciously desire to have a penis, like men."

Marlena looked pointedly at the gemmed dagger Stretch wore at her hip.

Now it was Sally's turn to guffaw, while Stretch frowned darkly.

"On the other hand," added Marlena, "most liberated women think penis envy is only a metaphor."

"I'll bet the motherfucker had a pencil dick," said Stretch stoutly. "He only wished women envied it."

"All men are wishful when it comes to women," drawled Sally. "Jewish, Christian, breeder, homosexual, or what-have-you, they all want something from us. They either want to nail us, if they're straight, or outshine us, if they're gay."

"Sally, I see your point. I'll give you that one," purred Marlena.

Stretch wasn't finished with the topic, having recalled ammunition from a field in which she had hands-on experience.

"There are plenty of artists who wanna be women. Take Mike Langelo, for example, and his Mona Lisa. The eyes of the lady line up with Mike Langelo's self-portrait, exactly. They even have the same initials: M.L."

Marlena repressed a smile. "Excuse me, but wasn't it Leonardo da Vinci who painted the Mona Lisa?"

"Oh yeah. I get them dead Eye-talians mixed up."

"So, Leonardo was projecting his feminine side on canvas," mused Marlena.

"Mona Lisa is Leonardo in drag," affirmed Sally languidly.

Stretch crowed triumphantly. "The fag wanted to be a woman!"

"It's also possible Mona Lisa was the daughter Leonardo never had," offered Marlena, "but wished for."

"Ahhhh," groaned Sally, blowing smoke through her nostrils. "That would be a breeder's way of looking at it."

Stretch gave Marlena an appraising look. "Hon, I don't see you as a breeder chick."

Instinctively, Marlena put a hand over her belly, to see if it was still flat.

"Or perhaps our new friend is a mixed breed," drawled Sally.

She took a drag on her cigarette through a long black holder. Someone had once told Sally she looked like Audrey Hepburn in Breakfast at Tiffany's, and she was still playing that card to the hilt.

Stretch guffawed. "You mean you wish she was."

Marlena checked her watch.

It was two thirty, and still no sign of Harry, no message being brought to her. She was beginning to feel extremely anxious. What more could she do to command his attention?

Then she looked up and saw Coddie striding toward her from across the room.

"Excuse me," she said. "I have to go see a man about a horse."

"Don't you mean, about a penis?" scoffed Stretch.

The two women watched as Marlena approached the tall, thin, bald man and greeted him with a perfunctory kiss, then steered him toward a booth at the far corner of the room.

"Must be the long-suffering husband," said Stretch. "Whaddya wanna bet?"

"It could be the lover."

"Naw. He's got a weak chin. Anyway, her lover's the lord of this cockamamie castle. If it was him who walked in here, that barmaid with the cleavage would already have her nose up his ass."

Sally looked at Shirley, who was lounging and chatting with the back bar runner.

"You're right," said Sally. "It's the husband."

"Look, he's pulling a wad of papers from his pocket. He's waving them in her face. I bet she don't like that too much."

Marlena was thinking she didn't like the wild look in Coddie's eyes; she couldn't remember ever seeing her stolid ex-husband appear so frantic before.

"Calm down. Don't make a spectacle, please. Remember I work here."

"This isn't our first rodeo! How about the time you cried all over your meatloaf while I was trying to pitch Boeing?"

She blushed. During a hiatus in her affair with Harry, a song had come on the jukebox, "When Will I See You Again," and she'd lost it.

"Do you know what I've got right here?"

"Those are the papers I sent back to you."

"Bingo! And do you know what I intend to do with these papers?"

His agitation was infectious. Her temper flared responsively.

"You can stick them up your ass, Coddie, for all I care."

He glared at her wordlessly. She glared right back.

"I intend to tear them into a million pieces, and then maybe, just maybe, I'll consider taking you back as well."

His voice was low, but he spit as he said the words, so belligerently were they uttered.

Marlena wiped the spittle from her face. She was unpleasantly reminded of Letty Brown-Hawker's assault.

Try to think what he's feeling, Marlena. While he made a show of belligerence, perhaps inside he was crying and saying something very different: "My pride is hurt, and I need you back. Don't you see that?"

She felt terrible about his pain, but she also saw clearly it was too late and even too dangerous for Coddie if she went back to him.

"Are you unhappy with our agreement? If so, why did you send the finalizing papers to me? I don't get it. Am I missing something here?"

He waggled a finger in her face. "Marlena, I don't have to take any crap from you. I made you what you are. Everything you know, the way you look, the way you design a house all comes from me."

"Oh, so you're Pygmalion and I'm Galatea now. Is that it?"

It was almost comical how each man in her life assumed she was his creature.

"Ha! Yes, that's it exactly. You're my creature."

She wasn't surprised when Coddie echoed the word that had crossed her mind. It often happened to someone she was focused on.

She hardened her heart, though it hurt her to do so. To protect him from the curse, she had to push him away.

Coldly she said, "Then you're mistaken. And drunk, worse than I've ever seen you. You must have quite a bar tally going up in your room."

"Cleaned out the f-f-fridge," he said, slurring as though he had marbles in his mouth, but Marlena believed he was only pretending to be drunk.

She drawled, "Well, the management appreciates the business, but it's not terribly becoming. Coddie, I'd love to continue this scintillating conversation, but I've got a prospective client I really need to get back to. We're about to close on a deal."

"For PAD?"

"For me."

As she started to get up, he reached out and shoved her back into the booth. The motion was large enough to be spotted by her friends across the room.

"Whaddya suppose is going on over there?" said Sally.

"I don't like to see any dame get pushed around, even that screwball." Stretch made a fist and punched it into the palm of her other hand; she was ready for action.

"Oh, pipe down," drawled Sally. "Let's see how Bellum handles herself."

"Look! Bellum's getting up and leaving. He's just sitting there, crying. What a dick," said Stretch.

Sally yawned. "Hetero fights are so boring."

"He didn't even slap her. I'm sure she deserves that much."

Chapter Twenty Five

After downing the last bottle of Courvoisier from the stocked refrigerator in his suite, Coddie was pacing the floor. His weak chin was trembling with repressed rage, and he felt like bursting into tears.

All his wife had to do to get back into his good graces was to apologize and come to him as a woman. But so far, Marlena hadn't made a move in his direction. It wasn't working the way he'd planned.

Too late now; he was here and the final battle was on.

Maybe it was her pride that wouldn't let her approach him and abjectly apologize--the same damned pride that had led her grandmother to cut off her nose to spite her face and lose out on millions of dollars worth of property that might have come her way.

He hadn't told Marlena about that visit from the guy who wanted to sell a gold mine to her at a low price. He wanted Marlena with him in San Francisco, not fighting a development war in fucking Wyoming.

Then she'd dropped the bombshell, blurting the news she was pregnant.

Checking out his own equipment would never, in other circumstances, have crossed his mind. But he had to know if there was even the slightest possibility the child might be his.

At Thanksgiving, after a late supper at Solid Hollow Lane and several bottles of wine, they'd done the deed. He was sure Marlena wasn't even aware they had done it, she was so drunk.

Now he wished he'd never gone to the doctor. It would've been better not to know he was shooting blanks.

The young urologist at the clinic said there was no chance he might have fathered a child during a single encounter. "A low sperm count isn't the end of the world," the doctor commented. "There's always a sperm bank."

Foreign sperm had already landed on his domain, and it was all his own doing.

That incident he'd referred to earlier, when Marlena had wept inconsolably over her blue plate special before a client, was the first signal that something had gone terribly wrong with the marriage.

It turned out he was very late in realizing it by 1974.

With the construction project wrapped up and the hotel established as a big success, Marlena was then back in San Francisco full time, but he rarely saw anything of her. She'd taken up with a coterie of gay friends in the Castro. They stayed out half the night drinking and disco dancing, gyrating under a silver disco ball. One night he went out with them.

Staring at her in action, a stranger whispered to Coddie, "Is she a professional dancer?"

In her platform heels and three-piece baby-blue polyester disco suit, the plunging neckline contrasting oddly with a lace handkerchief tucked in a chest pocket, Marlena appeared to her husband to be deranged.

"Just high spirited," he said glumly. Marlena was surrounded by a circle of pretty boys. She was shaking her opulent breasts and writhing like a bobcat in a burlap sack.

However, for a time he remained ignorant of the cause of his wife's true malady, which was the delusion she must have Harry Drake back in her life or she would die.

Coddie racked his brain for ways to remedy what appeared to be a lapse of propriety in his formerly circumspect partner. On the practical side, her wild behavior might be bad for their reputation in a very competitive profession. Personally, he couldn't stand much more Soul Train and disco nights.

One night, after she and her friends had closed all the bars in the Castro, he waited up for her, said they needed to talk.

He said he could see she was dreadfully unhappy. Was there anything he could do?

She shrugged tipsily, evading his gaze. Then she slumped forward, her head hanging low.

Finally she muttered, oh yes, there was one thing he could do that would help. He could see about drumming up more work for her in Wyoming. Perhaps she could find herself again in the mountains.

"Or," she said, dramatically widening her eyes and drilling them into his, "you could contact the Neptune Society and help arrange a final exit. I wouldn't blame you if you wanted me out of your hair."

Alarmed, her husband pondered what she had said for days on end. Could there be someone else? She had always been so passive about sex, so disinterested, that it seemed impossible.

One day Harry Drake phoned him at the office and in the course of the conversation, for no apparent reason, casually asked about Marlena.

Afterward, a light bulb went on. Coddie suddenly recalled that in a moment of drunken camaraderie, he had suggested over a pool game at the Alta Hotel that Drake might want to fuck his wife.

Harry was singing Marlena's praises, saying what an asset she was.

Coddie observed, "She's smart as a tack, but inexperienced in bed. I can see she's attracted to you. Go for it, old man. Everyone's doing it. I don't care. I'm not the possessive sort."

He had gone even further, gone so far as to imply that as a modern, freethinking man, he owed his friend this favor, that he himself was dallying outside the marriage (which was a lie). He had merely been boasting, convinced of his wife's frigidity, if not her loyalty. Afterward, he had forgotten all about it.

Evidently, his pal had taken him up on his offer. Powerful Harry Drake had done his meek friend the ultimate favor of screwing his wife. So did that mean that he was obliged to extend the privilege, now his wife was hooked on Harry?

It was crystal clear what was going on. Marlena was going through the stages of grief over a lost affair.

Should that be his problem?

It didn't make it any easier for this pilgrim slogging through the Slough of Despond that his sole companion on the journey was a wolfhound named Sexual Jealousy. He recovered from shock and went into a period of bitterness. He was damned if he would put up with this nonsense any longer. His wife was now more of a liability than an asset. Shouldn't that burden rightfully be shifted onto the responsible party's shoulders? Out of spite, if nothing else? in her deranged state of mind, Harry would soon tire of her, and that would be that.

Drake, I'm sending Marlena and the disco ball over to your side of the net. Let's see if you can field them with your usual finesse!

So his next move had been fatal. He had literally thrown his wife to the wolves. Sometime later, in a short business conversation, there had arisen an opportunity for a broad hint and he had taken it.

In passing, Drake mentioned a mountain of unanswered mail accumulating in his office, all directed at Mrs. Dimmer, many wondering when she was coming back.

"I know just what you mean," Coddie quickly echoed. "At the office, there's a huge pile of invitations to Marlena for events at your hotel. It's her call, of course, but I'd be glad to encourage an arrangement with PAD for some of her time."

How could I have been so blind and stupid?

Now knowing he was infertile made it all worse, too much to bear at a distance. He was fit to be tied, off his rocker, and out of patience. He must go to her and make one last desperate attempt to get her back.

Five years ago, the marital ship was steaming along so well, and then along came the iceberg, Harry Drake and his overpowering ego, and the ship was sunk.

Harry already had so much; why did he have to make Marlena fall in love with him?

And yet, all Marlena had to do was come back. He was even willing to suck it up and raise the bastard as his own. It was the only easy way out for her--surely she could see that. But when he'd seen her in the field, the towering rage pent up for so long had overcome him, making him speechless as to his true feelings. *Like the lame cuckold he was.*

Of course, she could elect to have an abortion, but Marlena wasn't one to miss a beat. If that's what she really wanted, she would already have done it. In some hidden part of her infuriating, genius brain, he thought, Marlena wanted this child.

They weren't as yet finally divorced. If she rejected his overtures for reconciliation and persisted in forging ahead with Harry, he would make them both pay dearly. He would sue his wife's lover for alienation of affection and make it stick. Harry hated bad publicity, even more than he despised cheap cigars. That would fix Harry's wagon, but good!

It would also spell the end of Coddie's relationships, personal and business, with Marlena.

Groaning, he threw himself onto the king-sized bed.

Still, he thought, he was only beginning to fight. There was always the possibility of a covert attack on the third leg of the love triangle.

He bolted upright. Why hadn't he thought of that before? Seek Harry out, man to man, and make his feelings known!

Harry was an Ivy League guy, and he had many other women at his disposal. If the demand was put the right way to him, he would surely give her up, and then Marlena would have no choice but to come home to her husband once again.

Coddie got up from the bed, clicked his fingers twice, and began to stride back and forth across the room. Yes, that was the ticket. A ghastly smile came over his face as a new stratagem unfolded in his feverish brain.

He would face off with the cad. He'd remind Drake of a certain moment, early in the game, when the rules had been set up while they'd smoked Drake's Cuban cigars, drunk as lords, and sparred on Drake's damned red pool table:

After broaching his spurious offer, Coddie had placed his left hand on the scarlet cloth. With the other he pointed a finger at Drake to underline his magnanimous proposal. He believed he had just masterminded a pre-emptive strike.

"Drake, as I said, I can shee there's an attraction between you and my wife. I have a stake in this game, so there are two r-rules I'm putting down on this table. Don't fall in love with her, my friend, and don't get her pregnant. Two rules only. Promish, on your word of honor as a genulman, you won't do either of those two things."

Harry bent over the table and aimed his handcrafted pool stick at the eight ball, the cigar jutting out from between his teeth.

"On my honor, I will not."

Aha! The bastard had violated both rules, reneged on his promise as a gentleman! All Coddie had to do was call him out on it.

He ground his teeth. He shouted out words, not caring who heard them.

"I'll get her back, even if I have to kill them both!"

Chapter Twenty Six

Marlena was pulling on her gloves, waiting for her car to be pulled up. She was feeling a myriad of emotions, not least among them remorse for having treated her sweet, longsuffering Coddie so coldly.

But honestly, she felt it was what she needed to do to protect him from the curse. It was also what he deserved for behaving like a lunatic. *Was everyone going crazy this Christmas? Dear Santa, please bring me sanity and a clear path out of this mess.*

The field was vastly changed and much disturbed. She felt a renewed respect for her husband, for his taking a stand on behalf of their marriage, even if he hadn't articulated it well.

On the other hand, now he'd earned her respect, there was another reason to reject him: he was too good for her! *There was a lie she could live with for awhile.*

She must dally no longer, waiting for Harry to divine her distress and come riding to her rescue. Harry must be told of her pregnancy, pronto. Together, they would decide what to do.

Carlotta had said Harry wasn't coming in today, that he was working from home while Lila was out of town.

"Sugar, have you seen how the workmen have performed a minor miracle in restoring B. L. Zebub's to a useable condition over night? Carlotta had looked at her. "How are you holding up, Sugar?"

Marlena was thinking about how the police had told her the investigation was bogged down as Letty Brown-Hawker's many followers were interviewed.

"I don't even let myself think about it," Marlena murmured.

What must be thought of was getting herself in a room with Harry.

Well, if Drake's Roost was where Harry was to be found today, there she must go.

Energized by the proactive decision, she said goodbye to Carlotta and hurried to her rented BMW.

Drake Village was an area of current development between the Alta Hotel and Drake's Roost. A few model homes, a shopping center, and a nondescript corner-bar had all sprung up in the past year.

Marlena hated Drake Village, but as the bar came into view, she decided to stop for a drink. She needed time to consider how to excuse an uninvited appearance at her employer's home.

While she was gulping down a Bloody Mary, plotting her strategy, Harry Drake was emerging from his black Mercedes at the rear of the Alta Hotel.

He unlocked the back service door and let himself into the hotel, ascending the service elevator to the seventh floor.

Last night, he and Lila had engaged in fairly routine sex, so he'd been unpleasantly surprised this morning when she volunteered to stay home, rather than jetting off to a Palm Springs spa as she'd planned.

She'd also reminded him of their agreement to "go on the wagon" and "see where they were with the relationship."

They both knew what that meant: no more straying from the marital bed, for either of them, until after the holidays were over.

This was a tall order for a man of libidinous inclination, and the thought of going cold turkey in regard to Marlena made his lust for her spontaneously ignite.

Perversely, his promise to Lila had the exact effect of pushing Harry into the arms of his mistress. Using the excuse of papers left at the office, he'd raced toward the hotel in his black Mercedes.

The only thing on his mind was a raging desire to fuck Marlena, whom he had no doubt was still hanging around, despite being dismissed.

The first place he'd check for her was in his own suite.

She would be lying in wait for him, stark naked on the massive sleigh bed.

But there was no sign of her.

Next he checked Marlena's room. No one there either, and her suitcase was gone.

He then remembered the puzzling claim she'd made, about checking out of the hotel. He took the Beefeater's gin and vermouth from her private closet and poured himself a martini while he considered the chances of her not being at the hotel.

No way, he thought, she's here somewhere. She's downstairs in the bar right now, to show me she's not afraid of anything. That's the ploy.

He was chuckling as he descended in the main elevator. The elevator stopped at the third floor, and the doors opened. There was Codwell Dimmer standing at the Coke machine, throwing quarters into the coin slot.

The apparition rattled Harry to the core. He instantly hit the door-close button so Dimmer wouldn't spot him.

Had Marlena in fact fled from the hotel, because her husband was in hot pursuit?

He felt his ardor diminishing. Too bad, because he hadn't had such a raging hard-on for his mistress in many a month.

Frowning, he walked into the bar, irritated by the strains of "Hail Britannia" that came on over the sound system.

That gambit had also been Marlena's idea, and it had gotten old. Yes, just as Lila had said, it was high time he took a break from this thing he had going with Marlena.

She wasn't in the bar either, and he felt a lurch of disappointment, until....*hold the line*. There was a young woman at the far end of the bar, not bad looking, even though she had a nose-ring and purplish hair. She was very thin and about twenty feet tall.

Damn, he'd never seen such a tall woman before, with slim legs that went all the way up!

Harry nodded at Shirley, indicating the lone customer's next drink would be on him. She poured his usual, a club soda with lime.

"What are you drinking?" he asked the Amazonian, zeroing in on her.

"Chevas and soda," she said.

"And whom do I have the pleasure of meeting?"

"Keep it in your pants, buster. I play for the other team. Just the same, I'll take the free drink. The name's Stretch, like a limo. What's yours?"

"Harry Drake." He smiled ingratiatingly. "What brings you to our fair city, Stretch?"

"Ain't that fair so far. I'm here seeing' relatives. What's your excuse?"

"Well, actually, I own this place." He tried peering into her eyes and offering a trademark smile, but her face remained unfriendly.

"No shit. Then you'd be acquainted with a friend of a friend of mine."

"And who might that be?"

"Mr. Drake, you need anything more?" asked Shirley.

He waved a hand, and Shirley disappeared into the background like a shade.

"Let's see," Stretch pondered. "Name sounds like an old-time actress. Marlena Dietrich. Yep, that's it. Marlena is her name. Big nipples, great cleavage, frizzy strawberry blonde hair, lots of it. A-mazing eyes."

"Oh yes," he said noncommittally. Stretch was staring down at him from her great height; he felt very uncomfortable in this position. "Marlena works for us."

Stretch didn't say any more, just drank down her Chevas and soda in three big gulps. Then she belched loudly.

"As a matter of fact, I was just looking for Marlena."

"Oh? Too bad. Elvis has left the building. Takes more than a lunatic to scare that broad. She's gone off somewhere. She was just here, shootin' the breeze with us."

"Us?"

"Me and my girlfriend, Sally. Mister, here's a hot tip. Sally's hiring Marlena away from this outpost to do a big project in Key West, Florida. Authentic architectural restoration. Don't know what that means, exactly, but looks like you're shit out a luck."

She put two fingers in her mouth and whistled, bringing Shirley at a run.

"I'll have another, hon."

Drake cleared his throat. "Please extend my best wishes to Marlena in her future endeavor."

Then, with a bow to Stretch--it was a difficult move, since she towered above him--he began to walk away from the bar.

He didn't move quickly; he made it a point not to. The fastest Harry ever moved was a slow stroll. And therefore, he didn't avoid the unwanted encounter with Codwell Dimmer, who was coming toward him at a fast clip.

"Thought that was you, Drake," Coddie said with a forced smile and an outstretched hand.

"Why, Mr. Dimmer. Whatever brings you from San Francisco to our cold clime?"

"Oh, relatives, the holidays," said Coddie. "Marlena's cousin always throws a big bash on Christmas day. Her mother is in town. You may have heard."

"Yes, I've heard," said Harry with cold geniality. "Well, I was just leaving. Nice seeing you again, old man."

"Oh, please don't leave me hanging," said Coddie ingratiatingly. "The women are Christmas shopping. I was hoping to buy you a drink and beat you at a game of pool. Like the old days. Remember?"

"Seems to me I was the victor."

"Righto. You owe me a sporting chance to even the score, ha, ha."

"What are you drinking, Dimmer?"

"Whisky, straight."

"Your money is no good here, old sport. Shirley, get Mr. Dimmer the whiskey we keep downstairs." Turning back to Coddie, he said, with a cold gleam in his eye, "If you have a mind to bet, name the amount."

"Five hundred is all I have on me."

"We can make it a thou. I'm sure you're good for the rest."

"A thou it is then."

"I'm a bit rusty," said Harry conversationally, as he racked the balls. "When I was in college, though, I wasn't too bad at this game. Fairly routinely, I used to run the table."

After he said the words "run the table," he did the deed, like clockwork, across the scarlet cloth.

Coddie was very gracious about the quick loss, forking over the cash he had with him. He said he would bring the remaining half to Chloe's Sunday night, when they'd meet again. There was a pool table at Mill's Creek, he told Harry, though not so grand as this one.

Harry shrugged. "Shoot yourself. I'm in no hurry."

"Perhaps next time we can play for something more interesting."

"Such as?"

"My wife, of course, in exchange for my silence."

"Your silence? About what?"

Harry was lighting a Cuban cigar, which Shirley had brought him along with the bottle of whiskey

"I could raise a stink if I wanted to. You went back on your word of honor, pal."

"Sorry, I'm not following. My word on what?"

"You promised if I allowed Marlena to come over here on this trumped up 'job,' you'd follow two rules I set down."

"I don't vaguely recall it, but, okay, I'll bite. So what were the two rules, Dimmer?"

"Not to fall in love with her and not to knock her up."

Harry laughed unpleasantly. "I can assure you, old sport, those rules haven't been broken."

"I assure you, old sport, that at least one of them has been broken, and your honor is forfeit."

Harry clapped him on the shoulder. "See here, Dimmer, I don't mean to be rude, but frankly, I'm not in love with your wife. You can have her back, if that's what's bothering you."

"Didn't think you were, Harry. Didn't think you had it in you. Now listen up. I'll say it again, loud and clear. You've broken one of the rules."

Harry had been fiddling with his personally designed pool cue, taking it apart, telescoping it, and putting it back inside its leather case. His back was turned when Coddie said the last words. When he turned around, his expression was strained.

"Explain what you mean, Dimmer."

"You got the message all right. You've knocked her up. She's pregnant."

"That's a boldfaced, despicable lie!"

"Try selling that story to the local doctor who ran the test."

Harry shut his gaping mouth and strolled over to the side wall. He stood with head bowed before a display of historic pool sticks, including one belonging to his grandfather, Augustus "Curly" Drake. Marlena had dug it up somewhere and presented it to him on his last birthday.

"Th-th-th-th-th-that b-b-b-b-b-bitch!"

Coddie came up behind him. "What did you say?"

"N-n-nothing."

"Oh dear. It appears the bitch hasn't told you. I'm sorry, old sport. Well, perhaps I was hasty in assuming you're the father. At any rate, you're on the hook. I hold you accountable, as will the world. The great event has happened on your watch, not mine."

"And what, may I ask," spoke Drake brutally, "does *your wife* intend to do about it?"

"Well, I suppose you'd better ask her yourself. You'll see her Christmas night at Mill's Creek. As I said, we'll play for keeps, and I suggest you throw the game and give me back my wife. Or else, I'll make your life a living hell. I'll take you for everything you've got."

This time, it was Coddie who strolled away from the field of play with a smirk on his face, while Drake stared at the floor, ruminating.

Even for Marlena, this was way off the chart.

First, the bitch leaves her divorce papers out like a billboard sign. Then, she ruins his bar to get his sympathy, with techniques out of the fucking Middle Ages. And now, she sends her terrier to worry him with a trumped-up pregnancy claim!

What was the next game up her sleeve – murder?

Chapter Twenty Seven

On the road, Marlena stopped twice more before arriving at Drake's Roost. Once was to vomit at the side of the road. Her second stop was at a party supply shop.

She turned into a gravel parking spot just past a signboard along the road that said "Costumes For Any Occasion."

Her idea for a ruse had come straight from Cassandra's story.

Cassandra had taken her Indian maid's place at a Thanksgiving Day pageant staged in 1900. She'd attended in disguise after applying brown makeup, donning buckskin clothing, and covering her red-gold hair with a braided black wig. She wanted to get into the Brighton ranch, where she wasn't welcome, having been vying with Miss Brighton over Curly Drake. All this, to sneak a peek at Nicholas Brighton, the returned native son who'd made a name for himself in San Francisco.

Taking a page from her talented ancestor's exploits, Marlena figured to get through the door at Drake's Roost disguised as a hotel employee, Jane Dovetail, the Native-American housekeeping manager.

Swooshing her hair under the wig and pulling down the braids of the wig in back, Marlena asked the shop clerk if there was makeup to go with the costume.

"Oh, yes, right here," he said. "Sacajawea is a favorite with the schoolgirls at the Brighton Charter School. They present a Christmas pageant every year. Ma'am, are you going to wear it now?" He looked at her curiously.

"Oh, yes. I'm the entertainment at my daughter's seventh birthday party."

The next thing she had to do was get past the butler. She drove up the long driveway to Drake's Roost with her wig on straight and her heart in her mouth. Anticipating Harry's amusement when he got a load of her costume, she giggled.

This bold gambit might be my best move ever.

"Your name, pleath, Mith?" asked the rotund butler with the shaved head, giving her a leisurely once-over. A white turban was perched atop his shaved head and a red sash was loosely wound around his white caftan, which bulged over his paunch. Diamond studs much larger than her own glittered in both ears. "Jonas" was tattooed on his forearm.

Name? Her mind swirled through its database.

"Nevada Carson," she said promptly. Nevada Carson was Cassandra Vye's stage name in California. With it, she'd amassed a personal fortune, then given it all away in her dead husband's name.

"It's a matter of some urgency that I see Mr. Drake. There's a serious problem at the hotel," she added briskly.

"Oh my," sighed the butler. "Wait here. I'll thee what *her* wants to do."

Her?

For the first time since pouncing on this bold, creative idea, Marlena felt a wave of panic, breaking out into a cold sweat. She hadn't counted on Lila being at home. Carlotta had plainly said Lila was flying to Palm Springs for a pre-holiday spa treatment.

Before she had time to gather her wits and flee, there was Lila herself, floating down the long hallway, a white, diaphanous gown trailing behind her. She wore her glossy black hair in a long coil down her back. On her neck was an Elsa Peretti heart necklace.

Marlena blanched, recognizing the necklace as the same piece she and Harry had looked at together at South Coast Plaza. She felt lightheaded, as though the marble floor had been jerked out from under her.

But setting Marlena even more off balance, was Lila's stunning appearance. She had never set eyes on her before, and Harry carried no pictures of her. Why, his wife was a knockout, with a magnetism immediately felt. Here was a fact even more dazzling and peculiar: Lila was a dead ringer for an elegant, half-nude lady in a painting Marlena had spent many hours gazing upon as a child.

Lila might have been the model for Grandpa Bellum's controversial possession, a framed painting he'd stubbornly insisted on hanging in the parlor, right over his couch, when he came home from the Italian campaign after WWI. The likeness made Marlena feel weak in the knees.

Family lore had it that upon the lady's first appearance in their home, Granny had declared one of them must exit, permanently. But

Grandpa had prevailed in the disagreement by saying the lady was the image of Granny when she was a "young slip of a thing."

Marlena herself had not been able to see a resemblance, other than the hair length. Granny's was also very long, down to her waist, but she pinned it up every morning into a steel-grey bun.

But Faith judged the painting as being neither decent nor allowable in a good Catholic home. She'd told Marlena it was a mortal sin even to look at it. Therefore Marlena looked at it every chance she got.

The gilding had worn away from the frame, leaving black paint exposed on the border, with the remaining gold flecked and scant. The tall, willowy lady was in profile and wore a long, trailing gown, diaphanous as a cobweb over the breasts, so one rosy nipple was visible. She was standing on tiptoe, her arms stretched out and holding aloft an ornate bowl filled with white roses. Her glossy black hair cascaded from the back of her head in a long coil that almost touched the marble floor. She posed, chin up, as though making an offering -- perhaps to a far-off deity, or, more likely, Marlena thought, a lazy courtier lounging behind the draperies that bounded the icy room. The coldness of the surroundings was underlined by a sinister mountainous landscape beyond three curved casement windows. The final touch of exoticism--a pair of snow leopards– crouched on the pearly marble floor, inches away from the lady's delicate, bare toes....

"What's this all about, Miss Carson?" said Lila.

Marlena was feeling dazed and confused, not only because of the subterfuge but also because her memory made it impossible to control her erotic reactions to Lila.

"Sorry to disturb, m-m-ma'am," Marlena stuttered. "There's an emergency at the hotel. I was sent with a message for Mr. Drake by Mr. Simmons. May I see him, please?"

There, finally, she'd spit it out.

Lila regarded her curiously. "Doesn't Mr. Simmons know how to use a phone?"

"The phone lines are down. I mean, they've been cut."

"Really? That's odd, because I was just on the phone with Carlotta, not a half hour ago. Harry's not here. So you've wasted your trek up our treacherous hill, I'm afraid."

A wave of nausea swept over her, and Marlena feared she might fall down.

"So, what's the trouble this time?" Lila yawned. "Did a customer cut off a finger and leave it in the custard to set up a lawsuit?"

"Oh no, ma'am. Nothing like that. Four girls under my charge have staged a sit-down over wages."

"Oh, is that all?" Lila sniffed. "Sitting down on the job. Well, that's what they're good at, isn't it? Isn't sitting a way of life for you people?"

Marlena felt a flash of anger on behalf of the underpaid Native-American employees, all dishwashers and maids. Now she regretted not having come up with a different story, one that wouldn't have made the hardworking women targets of this spoiled woman's scorn.

Then an amazing thing happened. Lila burst into tinkling laughter. Marlena was suddenly reminded of her little friend June, who had thought everything painful in life was funny. June also thought everything oblong on the teacher's blackboard looked like a penis.

"Why, you should see your face, hon. I was only pulling your chain. Fact is, I'm on the side of those girls. Harry treats his employees like shit. Serves him right if they close him down at the holidays. Power to the people!"

She was gazing at Marlena with ever-increasing curiosity. And once again, Marlena was being dragged into the past, willy-nilly, by her eidetic memory.

The lips that spoke the words were pouty, as June's had been, and like June's, they were begging to be kissed. However, June's were pink rosebuds, while Lila's lips were stained darkly scarlet. Marlena's childhood friend June Thompson had taught her the pleasure to be had from stroking the soft place between her legs. Like Lila, June had pale skin and long, glossy black hair. They'd shocked the teacher by composing an illustrated story about a school employee they had a hopeless crush on; it was entitled "The Janitor's Thing."

Lila was staring at Marlena. It was impossible for Marlena not to stare back at her, though doing so was totally out of character.

"It's been a hard week for Harry, hasn't it? First the weird thing at the bar and now a labor dispute."

"May I ask when Mr. Drake is expected back home?" asked the formerly intrepid intruder in a meek voice.

That gold heart, she thought miserably, was like a signboard of Lila's ownership rights to Harry. For the first time in their long affair, Marlena felt the baseness in her position; she tingled with shame.

"Why, I believe he was only picking up some papers. I'm expecting him back home shortly. But if what you say is true, then he probably won't show up for hours."

Lila came closer to Marlena and peered at her intently. Marlena dropped her eyes.

"So, you've made your trip through the ice for nothing, hon. You probably passed him on the road. What a shame."

"Well then, I'll be going back. Sorry to disturb."

"You know, you have the most amazing eyes I've ever seen on a Native American. What's your name, again, girlie?"

"Nevada Carson."

"Pretty name, too. I've been meaning to hire some of your people to entertain my guests. Ritual dancing, that sort of thing. Do you know of anyone I could contact?"

"No, I don't, ma'am. I've never lived on the reservation."

"Yes, well, you don't have the look of them, that's for sure. You remind me of my sister."

Again, her eyes swept over Marlena's face and figure. A look of suspicion crossed her eyes, but then they glazed over again, and Lila resumed her air of supreme indifference.

What she had to do was hold on tight, Marlena thought fervently.

Just hold on tight and get the hell out of here.

The butler now came forward. He opened the door with a flourish. Simultaneously, the Wyoming wind hit him, almost bowling him over. In trying to right himself, he stumbled against Marlena, who was already pushing her way out.

"Oh God, mith, I'm tho thorry!"

A flashy ring on one of Alexander's plump fingers had got entangled in one of Marlena's long fake braids. When he pulled away, attempting to extricate the ring, the wig came off the right side of her head.

Out tumbled long, floating feathers of red-gold hair. They seemed to hover in the air. Marlena gasped. Then she cowered, trying to hide behind the butler's bulk.

Lila Drake stood akimbo, frowning, hands on hips. "Let's cut through the crap. I know who you are. What in hell are you doing here, Marlena Bellum?"

What dignified recovery was possible? Marlena laughed ruefully and pulled off the wig entirely, tossing back her curls.

"I came to talk to Harry. That's all."

"Must be important. Seems like you were willing to make quite the fool of yourself to get to him."

Lila was pacing along the foyer in rapid strides. Reluctantly, Marlena had to admire the power and grace in every step. She looked like a movie queen of old, with the litheness of a Joan Crawford and the sultriness of a Bette Davis. *She could pass easily for my age. She's delectable.*

Lila whirled around to face Marlena, whose cheeks were burning hot.

"Not as Johnny on the spot as he used to be, is he?"

Marlena's eyes flashed, dropped away, then came back up. They stared at each other. Finally, Lila broke the silence.

"Where do we go from here?"

"I'll take my leave now. My apologies, Mrs. Drake. Most embarrassing. Goodbye."

"Not so fast," said Lila. "What were you coming to tell Harry? Why the getup?"

Marlena held out the wig as though it were a piece of evidence in a court of law.

"This," she whispered with all the strength she could muster, "is a costume for a party I'm going to. I'm sorry to be...I know it looks...weird."

Lila shook her head. "Couldn't be anything at the hotel would be so important to undertake anything so daring. What possessed you? Must be personal."

Marlena's mind was racing; her heart was pounding in her throat. What to say?

After a second of silence, she came up with a dodge.

"Isn't everything personal?"

Lila shrugged.

"My mother's in town, and there's family business we must attend to. When you came out instead of Harry, I panicked. In point of fact, there's no labor trouble at the hotel, and the phone lines aren't cut. It's just that ...well, there are some important events in the community I won't be covering for Harry as I....I usually do. I wanted to ask him personally for an extended leave of absence."

She was barely aware of what she'd said by way of an excuse. From the expression on Lila's face, it didn't appear to be passing muster. In her own head, though, something she'd just said was ringing true.

Yes, she did want an extended leave of absence from her duties at the hotel, where all she did was wait for Harry!

"Yeah, you cover for him all right." Lila laughed. "You've made yourself into quite the little love slave. But it hasn't done you one bit of good, has it? What do you have to show for it, girlie?"

"I prefer not to discuss my private life. It has nothing to do with you."

"Ha! That's a good one!" Lila swept back her glossy black hair from one side of her face. The motion pulled up onto her delicate neck-bones the gold necklace that was supposed to have been Marlena's. Again she felt its talismanic power, and she felt her heart sink lower.

"So, what's with the getup? Is this supposed to be trick or treat? Now, tell the truth, Bellum."

At that moment, Marlena felt an urge to confess all, but overpowering her urge was an automatic gag reflex.

She tossed her cookies in a jerky stream of pure, projectile vomiting, directly onto the Oriental carpet, six inches from Lila's feet.

Fuck!

She spit.

There was a long silence. The only sound was the butler talking to himself as he scrambled down the hallway enroute to the kitchen for a mop.

"You'd better sit down for a minute, hon," said Lila quietly. "You don't look so good."

She put an arm around Marlena's shoulders, which were shaking hard, as though she were in shock.

"I'm fine...I do apologize. Do you have a rag? Let me clean this up before I go." She was wiping furiously at her chin with a trembling hand.

"Please, don't look at me!" Marlena moaned.

"Alexander will be back in a minute, and he'll take care of everything. Just sit."

"Oh, I wouldn't want him to...."

"No sweat. He used to be a nurse."

"Please, just let me go."

Marlena made it to the door, but she wasn't strong enough to prevail against the wind. She got it open only halfway, and then collapsed. Lila sprang forward and helped her up.

"Take it easy. What's the rush? I'm not gonna bite. Follow me, this way."

Lila was supporting Marlena with one arm and leading her into the largest reception room she'd ever seen.

Under its domed ceiling of painted cherubs, there were two white grand pianos, surrounded by plush seating. At one end of the cavernous room was an alabaster bar that rivaled B.L.Zebub in size, though not in character.

Pushing Marlena into an armchair, Lila gingerly removed her guest's jacket, which was covered with vomit. She tossed it onto a table.

"There, that's better. I have to say it. You totally remind me of my kid sister. She's got that long, frizzy mop of reddish-gold hair like you do, only Marty's eyes aren't colored that mermaid shade you've got-- hers are boiled green. She's a wiccan, so she claims. One Halloween she dressed up as Lady Godiva and rode through Harvard Square. God, how I miss her."

Lila sighed.

"I miss everything, living in this godforsaken place. Why do I stay? Why do you? Is it because of Harry? I heard you have a good job in San Francisco and used to have a perfectly good husband."

Marlena tried to stand.

"Sit down," Lila commanded. "Listen, kid, I'm not your enemy. Let's say we call a truce. After today, if you want, we can go back to ignoring each other. But you're not leaving here today until I'm sure you won't die on the road."

Marlena slumped back in the chair. "Is that what passes for noblesse oblige in your set, Mrs. Drake?"

Lila brushed off the remark. "You grew up here, didn't you? I heard your grandmother was one of the Scattergoods."

Marlena nodded, too weary to resist her antagonist's questioning.

"When I was eight, we moved East, where my mother's family lived," she said drowsily.

"Pity you didn't stay in the East. Oh, I don't mean because of Harry. If it hadn't of been you, it would have been someone else. All I meant was, a girl with so much on the ball like yourself, your talents are wasted here. There's so much more to do in Boston, New York, or Miami, the theater and the ballet, all the parties before and after."

"I never saw the ballet," said Marlena. "We lived in the suburbs of Cleveland, in Parma."

"Oh, dear, how terrible for you." Lila laughed again, but it was without malice. "Poor baby. And then the big, bad wolf came along, smiling with all his big white teeth. Harry made it seem the world was his oyster, and you bit."

Marlena was wiped her face; she was silent, but she was listening.

"Honey, I've got news for you. There are no pearls to be found in this mausoleum. Let me tell you a few other things. Those fancy connections, the partnerships with moguls of industry? They came through my family, not his. Harry's your classic big fish in a small pond, BFSP, and a snake."

Marlena glared at Lila helplessly, but it was impossible to come to her lover's defense.

"I hope you don't imagine you've been the only one he's consoled himself with, hon, when I couldn't stand it and went off to do my own thing. There were three before you came along. Two others that I know of in the past six months. But you've hung in there like snot; I'll give you that much."

"May I go now please?"

She felt indignant and dizzy. *And also turned on by the enemy.*
"Are you feeling any better?"
"I feel fine. Truly I do."
"Then you may go."
"I'll see my way out."
"Oh, Marlena."
"Yes?"
"Harry and I have agreed to go cold turkey on the extra-curricular activities over the holidays. I'd appreciate it if you'd back off while we give peace a chance."

Lila smiled at her rival's numb look. "However, don't despair. Between us girls, I'm looking for a way out of this rock-pile without losing everything I put into it, which is a lot. Harry is better at taking than at giving. It will take some doing for me to get rid of him. He's no prince charming, hon, but if you want him that bad, well, maybe we can work something out between the two of us. Capiche?"

"Goodbye, Mrs. Drake."

"Good luck, kid. Alexander will see you to the door."

She pulled a silk cord at the side of the room, and a few moments later, Alexander appeared and escorted Marlena out.

Once she was alone, Lila paced up and down, going over in her head every detail of what had just happened. Finally, she picked up the house phone on the wall.

"Alexander, what's the name of that woman who applied for the housekeeping position here, the one who used Dr. Huddleston's office as a reference? She cleans there. Oh yes, Rosa Brown. Find her phone number, will you, in my rolodex. Then get her on the phone for me. Wait, Alex. Let's do it this way. Tell her you think there's a job in it for her, if she's willing to do me a small favor. If she goes for it, then put her on the line with me. I'll take it from there. Got it? Good."

Five minutes later, Alexander appeared at the door.

"Rosa Brown's on the line, ma'am, and completely at your thervith."

The one who gets to the lawyer first in a divorce usually wins. Based on her past exploits, Harry could probably discard her and take her money. That would be if the circumstances were normal.

But if what she suspected proved to be true, that he'd managed to knock up Marlena Bellum, then truly, the circumstances were anything but normal. Tagged with an illegitimate baby, Harry couldn't play the righteous husband in a divorce court. She might have old Harry over a barrel, thanks to the redheaded kid!

However, all in all, she'd kind of liked the kid. Imagine, showing up in a wig and pretending to be one of Harry's Injun employees! She'd be a lot of fun to hang around with in this dullsville. Too bad she couldn't see more of her.

Chapter Twenty Eight

After her humiliating, confusing ordeal, Marlena was so numb she could hardly feel her fingers as she gripped the wheel.

What had just happened in there? Was Lila in denial, or was Lila in the driver's seat?

And what was up with that pull of attraction she'd felt for Lila?

Lila's resemblance to the beautiful woman in the painting had been dazzling, knocking her for a loop, and then, when Lila laughed, she'd sounded just like June.

Tinkling laughter, tickling fingers, and soft cunts.

It was difficult to think of Harry in the same resplendent light after looking at him through the lens of his wife's poor opinion. Lila didn't even respect Harry as much as Marlena did Coddie!

Clearly, in Lila's eyes, their divorce would be a pole cat fight over status and real estate. Gross! And then it hit her. If Lila managed to find out about the illicit pregnancy, she'd take Harry for everything.

No more secret dallying for the sake of a pipedream. For Harry's sake, she must end the pregnancy quickly, before Lila figured it out. Chloe and Dr. Ron would know where to go and what to do. That was the new plan, and they'd be her support team going forward.

When Marlena got to Mill's Creek, she found a team of local men finishing work on the antique mill wheel by the pond, making it operational for the Fire Night Ball. Marlena brought out cookies and cider, hoping the activity would lighten the gloom in her soul.

"What more needs to be done?" she asked the foreman.

"Pump needs to be primed. Hey, you over there, hold this rope for me, will you? We had a time getting the rope out of the pond; it fell in and got tangled up on the bottom. It's attached to the fly wheel under the housing. Hey, you, hold this rope so the wheel don't move!"

"I'll hold the rope," she said. "They're busy."

He shrugged. "You're the boss. Just don't let go."

Holding the rope didn't require any exertion, but after a minute, beads of sweat began forming on her forehead; she felt as though she were about to vomit. The queasiness made her weak in the knees, and she felt her grip on the rope slipping.

"Over here!" she called out. "Help me, please."

No one heard her, and the mill wheel was slowly beginning to turn as her fingers were weakening and slipping off the rope that was holding it still. Just then a young man in leather chaps came out of nowhere at a run. He grabbed the rope from her and twisted it around his own hand, stopping the motion of the wheel.

"You seem always to be saving me," she said to Apollo, who blushed in response.

The wave of nausea had passed, but she remained standing there for some time, staring into the water.

Was this the end for her and Harry? *Was she at the end of her rope?*

On her way into the house, she was stopped by Chloe, who noted her drawn face and vacant eyes with concern.

"Getting some exercise out of doors, dear?"

Several times she'd noticed Marlena standing by the pond, staring into the dark waters as if mesmerized by an image below.

"I was holding a rope for the foreman. I almost got pulled into the water."

Omigod. The very thing that had happened to Cassandra, as she clung to a rope over her grandfather's well and flirted with Nicholas Brighton! There was that odd feeling again, as though a ghost was hovering and directing her actions. Mustn't tell Chloe, though. It would worry her.

"Are you all right?" Chloe gently examined Marlena's scraped hands.

"That pond has deep, still waters," muttered Marlena. "Perfect for a watery grave."

Then she shook her head, seemingly coming out of a trance. "I'm fine. Got to go wash some windows," she said brightly, "before Annie beats me to it."

Alarmed, Chloe searched Marlena's face. She seemed unaware she'd spoken of the pond being a grave.

Marlena abruptly excused herself and went up to her room. However, she was dragging her feet. She was thoroughly disheartened about her prospects for happiness.

After washing the windows and before retiring for the day, she put a sign on her door: "No Molestar Marlena."

Annie tiptoed in at seven o'clock and put a tray of food on the table by her bed, but it remained untouched.

During the evening, the phone rang five times. Four times Annie answered: "Mill's Creek. Merry Christmas." They were hang-ups. Coddie, on the other end of the line, was too drunk to speak.

The fifth call Chloe answered, as Annie was in bed. Dr. Ron said he was calling to check on his patient. Chloe confided her worry about Marlena's state of mind, and Ron said he would make it a point to stop by in the morning.

"Please do," Chloe said. She'd noticed the mention of his name brought Marlena out of the doldrums.

After falling asleep, Marlena dreamed she was on a voyage in the Mediterranean with an older man. At times he seemed to be Harry and at other times her father, but the man's most disturbing trait was his dark dead eyes.

To escape him, she dove in and set off swimming toward an inviting pink beach, but slightly offshore, she began to falter. There was a small wooden boat coming toward her, and the man at the helm had eyes the same shade as hers. She floundered and began to drown.

Her throat convulsing, she struggled desperately to awaken herself. Then she bolted upright in bed, gasping; her hand was at her throat, her heart wildly pounding.

This sleep apnea is getting worse, she thought. It's so terrifying, it could literally frighten a person to death.

On the other hand, she thought drowsily, death would be the ultimate escape from defeat and despair.

Chapter Twenty Nine
December 23, 1977

Faith wasted no time in calling her old doctor friend in Parma first thing in the morning. When she read aloud the contents and strengths of the big brown pills, he readily recognized Faith's daughter was taking vitamins prescribed for pregnant women.

"Congratulations. You're a babcia," said the Polish doctor.

"Thank you," said Faith doubtfully. "What's that?"

"A grand-mama. Was there anything else?"

"That's plenty."

She felt panicked by this new development. If Marlena's heart was hardened toward the Church, as it appeared to be from their earlier conversation, getting her to see a priest in this crisis didn't have a snowball's chance in hell.

The only help close at hand was Chloe, who'd probably cured worse cases of head problems than Marlena's.

Not being one to delay for a minute the execution of a difficult resolve, Faith marched into Chloe's study.

"Knock, knock. You busy?"

Chloe promptly set aside the white paper she was working on for an upcoming symposium in Los Angeles.

"Never too busy for you, dear. What's on your mind?"

"Marlena, of course. Do we ever talk about anything else?"

Chloe laughed. "It takes a village to raise one like that."

"Well, now she's gone and done it. She's produced something the village will never let us live down."

When she told Chloe that Marlena was pregnant and how she knew, Chloe repressed a smile. She was amused by how Faith had managed to uncover Marlena's secret. It wasn't news to her, as Dr. Ron had called her in as a confidential adviser

"Dear, the C.I.A. could use you to unearth the secrets of foreign nations."

"This is no laughing matter, Chloe. And speaking of unearthing secrets, now I'm going to tell you something I meant to carry to my grave."

Faith blurted it out rapidly: "I know all about the affair between you and Austin in San Diego, before he and I got engaged."

Chloe's face was a cipher, unreadable, the face she was trained to present, no matter what.

"I know you two got pregnant and that you had an abortion, and that's why you've never had any children. There, I've said it. I'm sorry, but I had to because of Marlena's pregnancy." She took another big breath that came out like a hiccup.

Chloe reached a hand across her desk toward Faith, who remained stiffly immobile.

"My God, Faith, how awful for you to have carried that knowledge alone for all these years. I wish you'd come to me decades ago. It wasn't an affair, only a single incident, the result of a lot of drinking and our sleeping it off in my car. It just happened."

"So, water over the dam for you, I suppose. What's to be done to prevent Marlena from getting rid of her baby and losing her immortal soul? I've come to ask if you will tell her the abortion part of your story, so she won't be tempted in that direction."

With difficulty, Chloe maintained her composure. Not even her mother had known about the abortion; it was the only event in her life she'd kept a secret, for fear Cassandra would connect it to the curse she believed was hovering over them. Based on Faith's behavior toward her over the years, she supposed she should have suspected that Faith knew. She struggled in the deepest part of her consciousness to come up with a positive slant.

Now that closed door was open, good consequences might yet come of the past's most terrible episode.

"I thought of the same strategy, Faith. I freely admit I've hung back partly because of my own cowardice. I was also afraid of confusing or distracting Marlena. But if she asks me about an abortion, I won't hesitate to tell her of my horrendous experience, if that's what you're asking of me."

"We're in agreement then."

"No, I don't believe we are. An abortive procedure is much safer than childbirth. Given her circumstances, it's probably the right thing for Marlena to do. If she arrives at that decision, I'll support her, unreservedly. I'll even go with her."

"You couldn't! Not after what happened to you!"

"What happened to me was an accidental pregnancy followed by medical malpractice. A simple procedure that should have been my right was available only by dark of night and at an insane risk. Thankfully, women don't face that terrible choice anymore."

"Lena will lose her immortal soul if she kills that child. How can anything be more terrible than that?"

"It's a fetus, Faith, not a viable being, medically speaking. There's no killing involved in scraping a few cells away. D& C's are done every day."

Faith shook her head in dismay. "You make it sound like removing a hang-nail."

"Medically, perhaps. Emotionally and morally, there are deep conflicting feelings around abortion. Marlena is entitled to her view."

"God views it as a soul. It belongs to Him."

"And from where I sit, Marlena's body belongs to her, and she has a legal and moral right to terminate a pregnancy. Nothing good can come from bringing an unwanted child into the world, Faith. After decades of counseling people in that fix, I'll vouch for that, even if it means you and I can't agree."

"So, you'll stand by and watch my daughter's immortal soul go to hell and my grandchild's to limbo?"

Chloe sighed.

"Faith, you'll just have to trust me. Marlena has come a long way, though she doesn't yet know it. She'll make the right choice."

"How do you know?"

"She connected in a profound way with my morality tale last night. She learned about how a selfish adventuress can redeem herself, how a frightful, tragic tale can have a happy ending. I'm hoping she'll follow Cassandra's example and turn her life around."

"Ha! Nothing good can ever come of that woman's life, Chloe. I'm sorry to say it, as she was your mother. But she brought disrespect onto the family and a vindictive curse, one that promised to haunt her descendants."

"We'll have to agree to disagree on Cassandra's influence on the situation, Faith. Was there anything else?"

"No, thank you!"

Faith stomped off to her room and her rosary beads.

Afterward, Chloe meditated on an irony. Acting sensibly on everyone's behalf, she had aborted her pregnancy at risk to herself and was left with nothing. Her cousin had delivered a child she didn't want only because of her fear of God, and now she had a brilliant daughter she cared deeply for.

On that self-pitying note, thought Chloe, I might need to see a psychiatrist or priest myself, before this is all sorted out.

Chapter Thirty

The phone was ringing off the hook.

"Mill's Creek," said Marlena. "Merry Christmas."

There was silence on the line.

"Hello? Harry, is that you? Harry, please don't hang up."

Click.

She remained in bed most of the morning, paralyzed in her mind as to what to do.

Should she have an abortion to save Harry's neck? Keep the child and hope for Harry's cooperation, betting on her deepest longings? What about the pink house? Stay put and fight for her heritage, saving her ancestral home from destruction? Or fuck them all and flee to the Keys with the lesbians?

When she emerged at noon, she went straight to Chloe, who was in her study.

"What's up?"

"Everything. I need your help," she said. "May I intrude?"

"You're never an intruder. Would you like to sit or lie down?"

Marlena took a deep breath and sat down in a chair.

Then she told Chloe what had led to this juncture, beginning with the start of her relationship with Harry at the Algonquin to finding out she was pregnant on December 20.

"It seems I've become a public disgrace. I need to fix it. Tell me what to do."

"The choice needs to be yours," said Chloe. "It's an important one. Don't look at just one angle. Primarily, you need to decide what you can manage and what you can't."

"Have you ever known anyone who had an abortion, Chloe?"

Her cousin swallowed hard. "I was hoping you wouldn't ask me that. I myself had one, when I was a young woman. It ended badly, but that's because it was the back street version."

"Omigod. Was it Harry's?" blurted out Marlena, before she could think.

"Heaven's no! Whatever put that idea into your head?"

"Well, Faith said you and Harry, when you were younger, almost ran off together. I put two and two together...."

"And came up with the wrong answer," Chloe said flatly.

Marlena felt a surge of gratitude, and this gave her a sudden ray of hope, that Chloe was the one who could pull her out of the quagmire of indecision.

"What would you do? Oh, please, just tell me what to do!"

"I can't," said Chloe.

"Sorry," Marlena said miserably. "So much for self reliance and forging ahead. It's embarrassing how frantic I am for a rescue."

"Ask yourself some thoughtful questions. What do you want your life to look like a year from now? Can you make room in your life for a child? What would parenting add or take away? There's no guarantee Harry won't fall into the category of low male parental involvement."

Then Chloe repeated what she'd told Faith, that whatever choice Marlena made, she would help her carry it out.

"That helps," said Marlena. "Dr. Ron has been very kind to me as well. He's offered to help no matter—well, you know."

"There's someone else who'd like to be on your team, who's waiting in the wings."

"Really? Who?"

"Your mother, dear."

Her eyes widened. "You mean…Faith knows?"

"Yes, she does."

"How? Who told her?" Marlena glared suspiciously at Chloe.

"She figured it out for herself, after finding pregnancy vitamin pills in your bathroom. I told her she should get a job with the C.I.A. It runs in the family, you know."

Marlena was confused. "What does?"

"Decoding messages, outwitting the bad guys. Cassandra volunteered for the civilian corps during World War II. Because of her facility with the English language, she was trained to be a decoder. She looked for hidden enemy messages in the American press."

"Huh. Daddy and I used to play games where he'd leave coded messages for me. He'd write upside down and backwards on a mirror, and I figured out that if I held up another mirror, I could read the message."

"I wish I had your facility with words. Or Faith's. Or Cassandra's. I struggle writing my books."

"That's surprising, Chloe. I've never heard a better oral storyteller than you are. I would really like to have the full story on why you never married. May I hear it one day? You never know when we'll be together like this again."

"Why? Are you planning to leave us soon?"

That evening, the four women enjoyed Annie's supper of corned beef and cabbage with boiled potatoes and carrots. They talked about the upcoming party as they dined casually in Annie's nook, which is what Chloe called the kitchen ell.

Then they took their coffee into the parlor. It was as if a seemingly impregnable wall erected by decades of misunderstanding and resentment had finally been knocked down and the three kinswomen saw each other clearly for the first time.

Faith was the first to plead weariness. After she'd toddled off upstairs to bed, Marlena turned to Chloe.

"Cousin, you've accomplished a minor miracle with your ancestral voices. I've bought into the connection between my own dilemma and Cassandra's, hook, line and stinker--the stinker being moi."

"You're no stinker."

"I have been. But I know now a happy ending is more likely if one isn't intent on being selfish. I do have a question. Were Cassandra and her lovers truly accursed? Or is that an old wives' tale? It does seem as though every man she made love to ended up in an early grave."

"That was coincidence. Unfortunately, it played into the hands of rank superstition. I think of Cassandra's life as a story of growth and redemption through increasing connectedness. That word may resonate with you now you've heard the truth about her. As for the curse and the witch-hunt, well, those practices are unfortunately common among those who are compelled to heave the first stone. Truly, they are poor in spirit and not God's emissaries, as they believe."

"I get it. Ultimately Cassandra triumphed over adversity and a community of unforgiving souls. She sure made herself a tough act to follow, even for an upwardly mobile sinner like me."

Chapter Thirty One
December 24, 1977

Marlena had set her alarm clock on its radio setting. She awoke to the voices of Alan Alda and Marlo Thomas on a NPR Christmas Eve show, telling the tale of Atalanta for young listeners--Atalanta being a fleet-footed princess from Greek mythology who roamed the entire world. The message was that girls needn't stay put because of their gender.

About fucking time.

Still, she didn't approve of re-crafting traditional myths to promote a modern belief system, feminist or otherwise. She'd take her Grimm tales unfiltered and bloodcurdling, thank you. Meddling with the classics was against her religion.

Then a thought, willy-nilly, popped into her head. *If my baby's a girl, Atalanta would be a cool name.*

Marlena, she told herself, don't be perverse and, for God's (or Goddess's) sake, don't get bloody sentimental over the little intruder, especially when her father doesn't yet know of her existence. *Get a grip!*

She took out her list and wrote two sentences: "Call Cheyenne abortion clinic today and ask questions. Find Harry!!"

Would Harry come with her and hold her hand while she got the uninvited lump of cells vacuumed out of her? No way, never in a million years. She would have to rely on Chloe for that unpleasant task.

Was an abortion her get-out-of-jail-free card? Afterward, she could roam the world like Atalanta. *Why did Lila Drake come to mind at that moment?*

While Marlena was dressing to go out, Annie knocked, then poked her head through the door and told her Dr. Ron Huddleston was downstairs, waiting on her.

"Ron is here for me? Seriously?"

"He don't seem to be in any hurry. I invited him in for coffee."

"Perfetto. Where's Chloe?"

"Making her rounds at the hospital."

"Seeing patients who are having the holiday jitters, I suppose. Poor suicidal slobs. Tell Ron I'll be down in a jiffy."
"I'll put another pot on. And then I'll make myself scarce."
"You're a dear."
Ron smiled as Marlena swept in, provocative in a laced blouse and Capri slacks.
"I didn't know doctors still made house calls."
"As I told you, your case is special."
She poured them both a cup of coffee, enjoying the strong aroma, one of the few that didn't cause an acute wave of nausea. She added cream to hers.
"Good," he said. "I like to see that calcium alongside the caffeine."
"It must be hard being a doctor and seeing all the awful things people do to their bodies."
"Sometimes it's hard." *It's hard right now.* Ron coughed into his hand. "You raise an interesting point, though."
"Which is?"
"We should be spending more time on prevention. Fixing problems is a job best done by specialists, but too many GP's let their egos rule their practices."
"How do you prevent people from getting diseases in the first place?"
"Many are preventable, like colon and lung cancer. Early detection and quitting smoking are key. But how many GP's insist on their patients getting colonoscopies? How many don't blink an eye when their patients continue to smoke?"
"My father died of a preventable disease."
"What was that?"
"Alcoholism."
"Yes, that's a big one. By the way, that leads me to one thing I came to talk to you about."
"Alcoholism?"
"Every drop you drink goes into the fetus. There's a lot of new evidence that suggests a connection between fetal abnormalities and alcohol consumption by the mother."

"So you're saying I need to go on the wagon or else have a baby with two heads."

"Hate to be a wet blanket before the big party, but I'm hoping you'll limit yourself to a glass of wine and chase it with soda water. I felt guilty afterwards about leading you down the wrong path by meeting you for a drink. Very selfish of me."

"What if I don't intend having this two-headed baby?"

"Then of course you only have yourself and your own liver to worry about. So has that been the final decision between you and the father?"

"The father hasn't weighed in yet. In fact, he doesn't yet know he's the father."

"Lena, please don't take offense at this question. Is there an issue about paternity?"

"Oh, no. There isn't a mystery. I know who he is, all right. He just doesn't know I'm that way."

"But why the delay in discussing it with him?"

"It's a case of bad luck and crossed signals. I haven't heard from him, and I haven't been able to connect with him, though I've tried." She sighed. "How I've tried."

Ron looked into her eyes.

"Let me do it."

"What?"

"I told you I'd help. I'll track him down and deliver him to you, with a gun to his back if necessary. We have our ways, here in the Old West."

She laughed ruefully. "Well, hopefully nothing that draconian is required. I forget you're a cowboy at heart, Ronnie."

"Just say the word and this cowboy will lasso him for you, Lena."

"You would really traipse around town? In this weather? For me?"

"Of course. There's no way I'm going to let you to walk around on that ice, not in your condition."

She looked into his steady, grey eyes. "Why, I believe you really mean that, Ron."

"I do, Lena. Try me."

She took a deep breath.

"All right. I'll tell you who he is. But I must swear you to secrecy. A lot rides on keeping this quiet. And I don't want any morality lectures from you. The man is married and he's local. Do you swear?"

"I so swear," Ron said solemnly. "I'm not one to deliver lectures on morality. That's not my area. So, who's the lucky guy?"

"The father is Harry Drake, as you may have suspected."

"I didn't. Never met him, in fact, though I've heard of him."

She scanned his face for disapproval, but could detect none.

"I'll go over to the hotel this afternoon, after rounds. Shouldn't take long, man to man. I'll make sure Drake shows up or calls you, whichever you want."

"My sources say he's taken the rest of the week off and is at his home with his wife at Drake's Roost. I've already tried once to find him there. I flopped, miserably."

Ron shook his head, his lips compressed. It was the first time she'd seen anger on his face since he caught a fellow classmate heckling her on the playground and promptly thrashed the big bully.

"My God, Lena," he muttered. "You shouldn't have had to go through that."

"I left him a message to call me, days ago. He knows where I am. But so far he hasn't tried to phone me here, as asked. I'm stumped."

"Perhaps when he calls here, someone else answers and then he hangs up. Chicken shit thing to do. Sorry, Lena. I can see from your face you don't like it when I say anything against him, so I'll cool it."

"You're right, though, Ron. What we need is a signal system, so he knows it's safe to call me. How about this? I'll stay by the phone at one o'clock. He should ring me for three times, then hang up. When he rings the second time, I'll know it's him, and I'll immediately answer."

"I'll call him at home today and tell him the signal system."

Fleetingly, it flashed on Marlena's mind that a system of signaling had existed between Cassandra Vye and Curly Drake, involving pebbles thrown into a pond or against a window.

Their secret system had ended up costing Drake his life when they got their signals crossed one fateful night in 1901, and he misinterpreted a holiday bonfire as her signal light.

But before Marlena had a chance to tell Ron to forget the whole thing, that it was too dangerous for him to get involved in, he was buttoning his coat, hot to trot.

On the other hand, she thought, if fate was stepping in, there was no way of knowing what random series of events would trigger either disaster or victory. Fate, after all, was inexorable as well as random. Ron had volunteered for this mission, and she needed the help. Shrugging off an intuition of disaster, she decided she would let matters take their own course and not try to second-guess her destiny.

"Thanks a million, Ronnie."

"Suddenly I feel like Dolly Levi."

The young doctor had put on his galoshes. Marlena assumed he was in a hurry to head for the hospital. In fact, his sense of urgency was directed at carrying out a mission for the woman he loved.

"Ron, come here for a second," she commanded.

He walked over to her side and leaned his head down quizzically. A piece of auburn cowlick grazed her cheek, giving her a sensory thrill that tingled into her toes.

Marlena reached up her arms and grabbed him by the neck, kissing him full on the lips. The buzz between them surprised her. She drew back and murmured, "Thanks for being my knight in shining armor."

"Any other tasks I could do around here? How about chopping wood? I can come back when I'm done with my rounds."

She laughed.

"You're doing quite enough already. Besides, we have Apollo here to cut wood, and I'm afraid he'd be quite put out by having any competition."

"Yes, but I'd do anything you say for another of those kisses." He beamed at her in such an eager way that her eyes dropped.

"Get along with you, Eagle Scout. Besides, I'm practically an old married woman twice over. You're wasting your breath."

"Is that a fact?"

Was he posing a serious question?

She thought a moment, then offered a gentle, but serious answer.

"Yes, it is. You see, I'm devoted to Harry Drake, until death do us part, and I'm expecting he'll do the right thing by me."

"You mean, stand by you while you have his baby? Divorce his wife and marry you?"

"I don't know what it means. Only one thing has become clear to me. I shouldn't have an abortion just to let Harry off the hook. There should be a better reason than that."

Ron was smiling approvingly at her. Seeing the look of admiration on his kind face, she blushed and changed the subject.

"Ron, will we see each other tomorrow night?"

"Jiminee. I almost plumb forgot. The main reason I came by was not to lecture you about the dangers of alcohol but for a purely selfish reason."

"And that is?" She flashed a smile. He felt it inside, as a heat that was threatening to melt him into a puddle before her eyes. He cleared his throat. *Get on with it, cowboy.*

"May I have permission to escort you and your mother to the big shindig? I'm a plain country doctor, but even clods have fantasies. Mine is making a grand entrance to the Christmas Fire Night Ball with the prettiest girl in town on my arm."

Marlena pursed her rosy lips, considering.

It wouldn't hurt for Harry to see her being escorted by the town's most handsome, very eligible bachelor. It might just inspire Harry to do the right and loving thing by her (even if it was for the wrong reason).

"Why, that would be very nice, Ron," she said, flashing her amazing eyes at him. "Mother will be thrilled."

He felt crestfallen by the reply, but what he said was: "Fantastic. I'll arrive a bit early, then."

"I'll look forward to it. Ciao."

Close on the heels of Ron's departure was the arrival of Apollo Nelson, dusting off snow as he came inside with Pierre.

He walked into the kitchen where Marlena was having a light breakfast and asked if there was anything he could do for her.

She smiled sweetly and said she'd be most obliged if he would get the tallest ladder from the barn and meet her at the mill wheel.

With Apollo up on the ladder and her supervising, the two spent the next hour affixing a long, fresh garland strung with lights to the mill wheel. It had been successfully repaired and was now fully operational.

When they finished decorating it, they turned it on with an electric switch. The giant wooden wheel began slowly to rotate, making a whirring noise that was very pleasing to her ear alongside the splash of falling water. *What a soothing, natural effect.*

Through the glass wall in the kitchen, Annie was watching Apollo and Marlena work. The rotation and the lights on the garland, flashing like twinkling stars, cast a resplendent vision of light and shadow across the room.

"Isn't that thing going too fast?" Annie muttered as Chloe was heading out the door. "Apollo should adjust the speed. Someone could get hurt."

To celebrate the mill wheel's return to functionality, Marlena went back inside the house and made Bloody Marys for herself, Annie, and Apollo. This time, however, she made hers a virgin.

"What's that on your sleeve?" she asked Apollo. "Looks like a goose feather."

He swallowed a bite of egg salad sandwich, then said, "It is. I was at a feather-ticking yesterday. Jack, my oldest cousin, is getting married the day after Christmas in Bulette."

"So I've heard," said Marlena demurely. "Jack was my horse-back riding teacher. I was his worst student ever."

"Do you mean to tell me they still do feather-tickings hereabouts for weddings?" asked Annie.

"In the Nelson family they do, leastways. If someone's a-gettin' hitched, the family's obliged to put together a goose-down quilt. Now there's fewer ranches than there used to be, and sometimes it's harder to find geese to get the feathers. But me and pop went to see Mr. Scattergood last night, and he said we could pluck some of his."

Marlena said: "So you know Mr. Scattergood, do you?"

"Everyone knows him."

"What do you think of him? Is he trustworthy?"

"No man here is more so. Some say he's the only man in town to go to, if you're hard up and can't make your mortgage. He'll loan you the money at no interest and on a hand-shake, so you don't lose your house or your ranch to the bank."

"He could get burned doing that, not to mention pissing off the bank officers," opined Annie.

"Yeah, but so far, he hasn't lost a dime. And he don't care that"—Apollo snapped his fingers—"for them guys at the bank."

"Do you know why he does it?" asked Marlena.

"I think he don't like to see them old houses get bulldozed to make way for some new crap pushed through by Drake Enterprises."

"I work for Mr. Drake." She arched her eyebrows at him.

"Didn't know. I apologize if I've offended you, ma'am. Wouldn't do that for the world."

She decided to play devil's advocate. "People need affordable housing, don't they, Apollo? How is the town to grow and thrive if there's nowhere for newcomers to live?"

He scratched his chin. "Well, ma'am, what's the matter with fixing up the older houses and keepin' the trees? Why do they have to pull 'em all down, just to put up new, when the stuff they build is so cheap, with walls thin as paper and no space between houses? That's what I don't understand about this so-called development thing."

She laughed.

"Bravo. I believe exactly the way you and Mr. Scattergood do about local development, and I'd hate to see any more shoddy housing going up in this wild territory. There might be a way I can save some of the old buildings in our home town. With the help, in fact, of your Mr. Bryce Scattergood."

Apollo's face lit up, this time with more than ardent admiration of the lady's beauty. He had the eager look of a knight errant on a mission. Where had she seen look before? Why, on Ron's face, just now.

What was up with that? Did Ron seriously have a thing for her?

"Ma'am, I'd love to work with Mr. Scattergood. You let him know that, will you? Now that we have only the one horse, and the high school kid comes in twice a week, Miss Chloe's just keeping me on to be nice. I'd do anything in this world that you wanted me to. Say the word. I'm your man."

She put her right hand on his wide shoulder, which quivered at her light touch, then laid her hand on the round oak table. "I dub you a knight of the round table, Apollo Nelson."

After walking around aimlessly for awhile, Marlena went into Chloe's downstairs study. Chloe had told her she was welcome to anything in this room that wasn't under lock and key. She picked up the manuscript from the Cleveland doctors that Chloe had been asked to review in her article, on maternal attachment disorders.

These were the materials she chose to take into her bedroom with her to read while awaiting Harry's call at one o'clock. At noon, she picked up the phone in her room to make sure it was working. Chloe's expected return wasn't until three o'clock.

Everything was in order for Harry's call, provided Ron had succeeded in his mission.

Chapter Thirty Two

One by one, Ron was checking off completed missions for the love of his life.

First, he stopped at Bower of Bliss Flower Shoppe and ordered flowers for his hostess, an elegant basket of Birds of Paradise flown in from Florida. He also selected corsages for Marlena and Faith Bellum--white camellias from North Carolina--to be ready for pickup on the afternoon of Christmas Day.

Then he went into his office and sat at his desk. He was preparing himself mentally to place the call to Harry Drake, whom he'd never heard anyone say anything good about.

He now personally regarded the man in a most unfavorable light. Yet he must take the right tone with him, not judgmental but firm, a man-to-man approach.

Ron allowed himself a few moments of righteous indignation before placing the call. This powerful man was almost certainly unworthy of Marlena's love. Drake enjoyed unparalleled prestige in the community and already had a beautiful wife of his own. Yet he'd stooped to making a mockery of the titles of boss and husband.

If Ron hadn't promised he would get Harry to call Marlena, he wouldn't have been able to restrain himself from calling the cad out. But a promise was a promise, even where his opinions were in the way, and so he placed the call, meanwhile loathing himself for carrying out this particular mission.

"Merry Chrithmath. May I know who ith calling, pleathe?"

He'd reached the butler first, which was a relief. Ron guessed he could easily get past such a personage.

"This is Dr. Ron Huddleston speaking. Is Mr. Drake at home? If so, I must speak to him personally, on a matter of some urgency."

"Yeth, Dr. Huddlethon, he ith here, thomewhere." The butler sounded bemused. "I'll get him on the phone, if you don't mind holding."

"Thank you. I'll hold."

In her study near the hall phone, Lila had heard Alexander say the doctor's name to Harry. She softly picked up the phone and heard the sound of a whistled Christmas carol, "Oh Come All Ye Faithful."

Marlena would have recognized it as Typhoid Ronnie's tried and true, Tom-Sawyer-like method of dealing with stress. Indeed, Ron had the endearing habit of whistling Christmas tunes year round.

"Harry Drake."

"Hi. Ron Huddleston."

"What's this all about, Dr. Huddleston? Plague hit the town?"

"Mr. Drake, we aren't acquainted, and I apologize for disturbing your holiday weekend. But it has fallen to me to transmit an urgent message from a lady we both know."

"Yes?"

"I have a message from Marlena Bellum that it's urgent you reach her today at one o'clock by phone. She's tried to contact you but has been unsuccessful. I'm directed to instruct you as to how to reach her. That way, you can be assured only Marlena will be at the other end of the line."

And then Ron explained the signaling process.

Harry cleared his throat. "Is that all?"

"It is, but there's one additional message from me. If you fail to call her, you'll have me to answer to."

Click.

Harry looked at the phone in his hand as though it were an adder poised to strike. The next moment, he was so hot under the collar, he could barely contain himself from calling that pipsqueak Huddleston back and giving him a piece of his mind. *Outrageous! No one tells me what to do!*

This added pressure only confirmed Harry in his resolution not to make a single move to contact Marlena. They were over and done with. This third party call was only another one of her tricks to railroad him into doing what she wanted.

Signal her. What a crock of donkey shit.

He'd be forced to see her tomorrow night, but it would be in a public setting where she wouldn't be able to bare her soul. She'd get one dance, and that would be it. He slammed down the phone, making his wife jump from her seat in the adjoining room.

With the open line buzzing in her ear, Lila quietly put the white phone into its cradle. After the scoop she'd obtained from her inside source at the doctor's office, Huddleston's call proved her original hunch was right: Marlena was pregnant with Harry's child.

Slumped in her chair, Lila held her stomach, grieving her barrenness. She'd gotten pregnant when she was only fifteen. She couldn't recall the pimply boy who'd taken her to the cotillion and barely remembered losing her virginity. Then she had miscarried.

It was all hushed up, as was done in the best families. The doctors had told her parents it was unlikely she'd ever bear a child to term, as she had a heart-shaped uterus. *But she hadn't believed them then, and she still didn't.*

What was her next move? Perhaps she should get on the phone and line up a lawyer. She wouldn't put it past Harry to divorce her and marry Marlena so he could fulfill his destiny and leave his empire to his progeny, like Henry the Eighth.

Though she needed to protect her own interests, Lila found herself disinclined to do anything that would hurt the kid. She felt a keen sympathy for Marlena, who was more vulnerable than ever before, with the cat out of the bag and no commitment from Harry.

What must she be going through, in the situation that she was in? Yes, the truth was she liked the kid a lot, much more than she liked Harry. He was up to his old tricks again. This week, there'd been repeated calls from that new woman he'd taken up with--the dishwater-hair with acne and a boob job who worked in the sheriff's office.

Harry claimed the woman was calling him to get her brother a job. But she figured otherwise. Alexander said she was the town's pot connection. Just like Harry, to let the kid down just when she needed him the most.

Chapter Thirty Three

Marlena waited all afternoon for a call that never came.

By Christmas Eve, she felt depressed and restless. When Chloe and Faith retired to their rooms to wrap presents for the morning gift exchange, she pretended to go to bed, then sneaked out.

Zooming down the dark, clear road, with the snow-bank on each side up to ten feet at some points, she felt as though she were spinning through a tunnel. However, the great outdoors made her felt better-- more clear-headed and focused. She took a deep breath, then another.

With an uplift of her customary optimism, she felt sure she would run into Harry at B.L. Zebub's. He hated the holidays and would seek respite in his bar. This was a spite battle, and she had a hunch he was waiting and hoping for her to find him. She willed him to be there. *He doesn't know how important it is we meet before Christmas. Why should I hold his little power play against him?*

Half an hour later at the bar, with Sally and Coddie perched on either side, she realized her hunch couldn't have been more wrong. She felt bereft. *What had happened to her special powers?*

Sally couldn't seem to keep her hands to herself, and Coddie was stinking drunk. She needed desperately to get back to Mill's Creek and sleep, but Sally was pressing for a commitment to join her in Key West immediately after Christmas.

"We're leaving the day after Christmas. Wouldn't miss the big ball tomorrow at Miss Vye's house. Stretch has promised the Bloods we'll both be there, with bells on our toes and cocaine up our nose." Sally laughed huskily. "Just say the word and I'll buy the ticket for you, sweetie. First class, of course. We can all leave together."

"Thank you, Sally. You know I want the job, but there are a number of reasons why that timing probably won't work for me," said Marlena. "I'll let you know for sure at the party. I hope you have a wonderful Christmas Eve tonight, and Santa brings you what you want."

Sally rolled her eyes with a suggestive expression, which Marlena pretended to ignore.

Coddie had been exuberantly glad to see Marlena come in. Hoping to catch her, he'd been hanging around all day in the bar. As soon as she turned away from Sally, he hunkered down close to her and mumbled in her ear.

Did she recall flirting in the lunchroom at PAD and passing notes to him from her cubicle?

"I need to go to the bathroom, Coddie. Please let me out."

She was washing her hands when Coddie came crashing through the door. He pretended he'd mistaken the ladies' room for the men's, but she didn't buy it. He wasn't that drunk.

"All I want is to be ish your white knight in flaming--sorry, make that shining ardor."

"Don't you mean armor?"

"I mean every word I shay to you. Shay something nice to me. Shay, I love you, Coddie."

His eyeballs were the color of blood. Perhaps he was that drunk.

"I love you, Coddie. But your behavior is not helping us."

She pushed him off as he tried to kiss her, meanwhile repeating over and over again he was in love with her. Then his tactic changed.

"Does little Marlena want Coddie to challenge big bad Harry to a duel? He'll do it, by God." He slammed his fist on the marble counter.

Shirley, the bartender, came through the door at that moment.

"Is there a problem, Marlena? What's he doing in here?"

"It's all right. He'll quiet down in a minute. Leave him to me. Thanks anyway."

"Let me make love to you as a Christmas gift." He whispered the suggestion into her ear, his lips slobbering.

Coddie's next proposal was that he would tear up the divorce papers and they could wing off to Vegas to renew their marriage vows.

"I'll raise Harry's bastard as my own child."

"That's a wonderful offer, Coddie. I promise I'll think about it if you go upstairs and get a good night's sleep. I have to go to Chloe's, but I can't go until you're safely upstairs."

"Can we dansch the last dansch at the ball?" he asked owlishly. He had slumped onto the floor, which he was gazing vacantly at.

"You've got it," she said, dragging him to a standing posture.

"I always loved you, even when you looked like a flag. Lemme put it into you, jus' for one l'il second."

"I love you too, but that's out of the question."

She was maneuvering him with great difficulty through the door. She looked up and saw Ron Huddleston coming toward them.

She'd never been so glad to see anyone in her entire life. With Ron's help, she got Coddie up to his room, where he continued to rave, so finally Ron injected him with a sedative from a kit he providentially had with him.

After Coddie was settled, Ron conveyed the information that he'd reached Harry earlier in the day and had delivered the message. Had Harry called as planned?

She lowered her eyes. "No."

"Perhaps he was called away on business."

Marlena shook her head.

She was hoping Ron would invite her somewhere for a drink. Instead, he ordered her home, making it clear that there would be no bar stroll for them tonight.

"You don't look well enough to be out," he said sternly.

"What a party pooper," she taunted him, But while driving back to Mill's Creek, she thought how loving Ron was, how balanced, kind, competent, and smart. Ron would be a vastly superior father to either Coddie or Harry. They were too old and egotistical; their sexual powers were waning, and their relationship skills were woefully lacking.

Who was she kidding? Ron didn't care for her, not that way. He'd ordered her to go home as if she were a child.

Defiantly, she gunned the engine. Then she had to slow down to make the icy turn into the entranceway to Mill's Creek.

That night, around midnight, she was awakened by a sharp pain in her belly. She got up and went into the bathroom.

On the crotch of her panties was a streak of blood. She panicked.

Oh God. Please don't let me lose this baby on Christmas Eve.

She was afraid to venture very far, so she went to the window, opened it, and called out, as loud as she could.

"Hello! Is anyone out there? I need help!"

Because of his cousin's wedding, Apollo Nelson was late doing his evening chores. He happened to be walking under her window on his way to the barn.

"Halloo! Is that you, Miss Marlena?"

"Thank God! Apollo, will you come up here, please? I'm having a-a medical problem. I need for you to find my mother for me, but I can't walk. It's an emergency."

"Yes, ma'am! Have her there in two shakes."

As he took off at a gallop, she thanked her lucky stars. Her mother slept like the dead, but Apollo would prevail. A scant three minutes later, Faith was standing at her bedside in an old flannel robe.

"Lena, don't worry, I'm here."

Faith frowned at Apollo, whereupon he made himself scarce, congratulating himself for saving the day for the gorgeous doll he was madly in love with.

"I'm in some trouble, Mama. I know you know I'm pregnant. I'm afraid I'm losing the baby. Isn't that a kicker? I was gearing myself up to throw myself down the stairs, and now I'm freaking out."

"Let's see what we've got here, Lena. Don't worry. This happens to women during the first months. I'll put in a call to your doctor, if you like."

"No, let's not do that just yet. I've already troubled my doctor enough for one day."

Once she'd determined her daughter was in no real danger, Faith knocked on Chloe's door and alerted her to the situation. Chloe swiftly was there, in her flannel nightgown, with extra blankets and a comforting array of stories about friends of hers and patients who'd survived similar problems with good outcomes.

The three women had a heart-to-heart huddle in the middle of the night about the pregnancy. Then, haltingly, Marlena told them of her attempts to contact Harry. But he hadn't responded to her, remaining silent day after day, and she'd been struggling with what to do.

How did she send the message? Faith asked.

Marlena told them the message was left on his fireplace mantle days ago at the hotel, where he would be sure to see it.

"Oh my God." Marlena stared at them.

The curse! He didn't get it, did he? It must have fallen off the mantle, and he never saw it. Just like the note from Nicholas to Cassandra that lay unseen on the mantle here in Mill's Creek the night she left town. Oh my God. Letty's right. I'm accursed!

When she began moaning, the two older women feared her emotions would generate more spotting. But nothing more appeared, and two hours later, when the bleeding hadn't reoccurred, they breathed a mutual sigh of relief. With all the good nursing and comforting woman talk she'd got, Marlena had fallen asleep with a mustache of warm milk on her upper lip.

Faith whispered to Chloe, after they'd tiptoed out of Marlena's room, "She called for me, invited me here on her own accord."

"I know." Chloe hugged Faith. "Welcome home, Granny Bellum."

"Well, just don't expect home-made bread in the morning," whispered Faith. "I'm still plain old Faith who's no good in the kitchen."

"You were a good mom when she needed you tonight, Faith. That's what counts."

It was very late, but Faith found she couldn't fall asleep. Instead, she lay awake and wrestled with some demons of her own. She reviewed her life and the mistakes she had made.

In the end, she decided it was wrong of her to have duped Marlena all these years about her paternity. She saw no alternative now but to come clean about the whole rotten, filthy mess. She must confess to her daughter that Austin, though he wasn't Marlena's father, was the father of Chloe's aborted child; and that, when Austin told Faith confessed this during a drunken quarrel, Faith decided to leave Austin and go to New York to see if she could find Gordon again, using the care of her father as a pretext. Of course, she hadn't found Gordon.

When all this was acknowledged--and if Marlena was still speaking to her after these terrible admissions--she would beg her daughter's forgiveness for leaving her behind in Austin's clutches for two long years.

You knew he was a sex addict, didn't you, Faith?

Perhaps, if Marlena knew Austin wasn't her real father, she would have fewer painful flashbacks, as Chloe called them.

Having sped through her rosary, Faith fell asleep, clearer in her conscience than she'd been in many years. At four in the morning, she was awakened by Marlena. She was having more spasms, and she was anxious about them.

Faith tended to her daughter until she was soundly, peacefully asleep. After that, she slept on a cot next to Marlena's bed. She prayed to the Blessed Virgin her child would come through this crisis whole and happy.

Chapter Thirty Four
December 25, 1977

At the crack of dawn, Marlena, Chloe, Faith, Annie and Apollo quietly assembled before the tree and opened their Christmas gifts. The occasion was subdued, but joyous.

Chloe said she must go back to bed and get her beauty sleep before the big ball--this made Marlena feel like Cinderella.

"But there's so much to do!" she objected.

"Not by you, Miss Marlena. Anyway, it's all done," said Annie. "Thanks for washing the windows yesterday."

Faith took Marlena's placid retreat to her bedroom as a sign that it was time to fulfill her resolution. Without a knock, because she was too nervous even to stand at the door, she barged into Marlena's room. She found her daughter sitting up in bed, reading. Without preamble, Faith blurted out her confession.

As Marlena listened to the incredible airing of her mother's dirty laundry, her eyes grew big as saucers. As it happened, their color fit into Faith's confession.

"That's why I never commented on your beautiful eyes, Lena. They're exactly like your father's--Gordon's, that is. Luckily for me, you got the remainder of your looks from the Zanellis. Okay, from cousin Cassandra, with her red-gold hair and beautiful face and figure."

Faith said that ever since she'd arrived back here at the scene of the early days of her marriage, she'd been forced to review her own part in creating a shambles of what a solid home life should look like.

She now realized Chloe had never loved Austin, and that she, Faith, had made a terrible mistake in giving up the man she loved to marry him.

Marlena was stunned. "Chloe and Daddy?"

Hurrying along, Faith said she'd married Austin for an even more critical reason. She couldn't convince Gordon, who had got her pregnant after a single act of post-war intercourse, to marry her in the Catholic church.

She'd sought to appease God and preserve the Zanellis' respectability by marrying Austin and pretending the child was his. She had put these considerations above her own and her daughter's welfare. For her duplicity, and for leaving Marlena alone in Alta with Austin, she now begged forgiveness.

"Mea culpa, mea culpa, mea maxima culpa. I couldn't go through this holy day with the terrible sin on my conscience, not with your being so honest with me about your troubles. My plan was to convince you to pretend the baby is Coddie's. It worked for me, so it might work for you. But now I'm not so sure, and I'm ashamed of myself for thinking that way."

When she'd finished what she'd come to say, Faith stared fearfully at Marlena. She was prepared to endure a torrent of abuse or years of stony silence.

"Oh, Mama!"

To Faith's astonishment, Marlena fell on her mother's neck, weeping, and kissed her. It was the first exchange of emotion between mother and daughter in a dozen years.

"You don't know what it means to me that you've confided in me," said Marlena when she was able to speak. "I know how I've hurt you by my silence, and I'm sorry. I promise you'll be proud of me again one day."

"I've always been proud of you, Lena."

"Mama, those words are the best Christmas present I've ever had."

Mother and daughter were still sobbing and hugging when Chloe knocked.

Wiping her tears away, Faith got up and opened the door.

"Ready, you two? Annie has prepared a huge brunch for us. Then it's nap time for Marlena, seriously. You've got to get some rest, dear, before the party tonight. Doctor's orders."

Chapter Thirty Five

The last person Annie Witherspoon expected to see Christmas morning was Harry Drake outside her window. She was cleaning up the brunch remains when, unlikely as it was, there he was on cross country skis, grinning owlishly at her through the leaded glass window in his snow goggles. His nose was painted white with sun block. She screamed.

Annie had a fear of clowns, a phobia which Chloe had successfully treated her for, but Drake's sudden appearance was both clownish and unexpected.

"Must see Marlena!" he shouted as she retreated from the window. The wrapping papers from the gift exchange were still piled in a corner of the parlor, and there were a million things to do before the ball tonight. Now this blackguard appears, Annie thought resentfully as her panic subsided.

She trudged to the back kitchen door, opened it a crack, and said Miz Marlena was not to be disturbed. Would he like to come back later? Then Harry pitched a fit. She'd witnessed it several times before, when he was young man sniffing around Miss Chloe. Annie shook her head and compressed her lips into a thin upside-down U while Harry hurled aloft his ski poles, so his valet had to chase after them.

Then her mistress arrived on the scene. While Annie grumpily retreated, Chloe courteously invited her old friend in. Harry sat in Annie's nook, looking silly with his painted nose, while his hostess poured strong coffee and listened to his side of the story.

"I guess by now you know all about Marlena and me," he began in a resentful tone. "If you don't, you're the only one in town who hasn't heard the gossip."

"Yes, but not because Marlena spilled the beans."

Chloe told Harry how she'd first learned of their relationship from a colleague who'd spotted them in Santa Monica.

"Marlena was horrified when I asked her about it. All she did was confirm what I already knew."

Harry admitted he'd deliberately ignored an urgent message from Marlena, via Dr. Ron, to contact her, but that he felt justified in doing so.

"Why, Harry?"

Chloe's trained eyes flashed when he told her he believed Marlena was lying about a trumped-up pregnancy.

"I heard about her supposed condition yesterday, from Codwell Dimmer in my own hotel bar, no less. He's claiming I'm the father."

"From *Coddie* you heard that she's pregnant?"

"From fucking Dimmer, of all people."

"How very odd."

"You haven't heard the worst. I'm being framed. They're after my money."

He described how divorce papers had been strategically placed in Marlena's hotel room, clearly left out for him to see, and how this ploy had been quickly followed by others, culminating in Dimmer's sudden appearance and his claim Harry had knocked up his wife.

Then Harry laid out his darkest suspicion: Marlena was in cahoots with her husband. The plan was to pressure him into leaving Lila and marrying Marlena, so she could get his hands on his real estate holdings.

She had even masterminded over-the-top vandalism in the bar, Harry recounted indignantly, to call attention to her plight and guilt him into marrying her. "If they think I'll be railroaded and swindled, they have another think coming, by bloody Mungo."

"Who's Mungo, dear?"

"A Scottish saint. My good luck charm is a Saint Mungo medallion I wear around my neck. It was handed down to me from my father, who got it his father. I only take it off for formal occasions, like your ball tonight."

"The cursing, no doubt, was also passed down from Curly Drake. He was known for colorful language, though your father was not."

But Harry wasn't to be derailed by any side excursions into family history. He began pacing about the kitchen, shouting about Marlena's perfidious nature.

"Keep your voice down, Harry. Marlena is sleeping. She had a rough night."

There was no sign that Harry had heard her last comment or, if he heard it, cared.

"The little tramp will NOT lay a hand on my properties OR me. It'll be over my dead body. I swear by any saint you can name, Christopher, Mungo, Judas Priest, the whole bloody lot. She won't force my hand with a pregnancy that might belong to ANY SWINGING DICK IN TOWN."

Chloe threw up her hands, startling Harry.

"I'm aware of how deeply engrained is the fear of being cuckolded, my friend. Indeed, a study in New York City has recently uncovered the fact that in almost a quarter of all pregnancies, the sperm didn't belong to the named father.

"However, anyone who knows Marlena and the crazy depths of her obsession for you will never doubt you indeed are the father. Just when I think you couldn't do any worse, Harry Drake, you outdo yourself. It's amazing, what an unfeeling cad you are."

Harry stopped his pacing and stared at her in disbelief.

"Cad? What nonsense are you talking, woman? Marlena's not like us, so why are you defending her? She's a low-born nobody. I never thought of her as the mother of my child, as I did when I was with you."

Chloe found his comment to be very annoying, but all she said was "Let's not revisit the past, shall we? The present is difficult enough."

He came back to his chair, took a gulp of coffee, and sighed loudly.

"So, let's accept, for the sake of argument," said Chloe patiently, "that Marlena is indeed pregnant with your child. Now, Harry, what do you wish her to do about it?"

"I'd have to think about that one."

"Look me in the eye, my friend. Our very special Marlena *is* pregnant, and through no fault of her own. Her I.U.D. slipped. I assure you she's embarrassed, terrified, and unsure of what to do. She's most eager to speak with you about it, though I won't allow you near her now. But it's not your decision to make, whether or not she has the child. It's her body, her decision, her child, *if* she wants it."

"Oh, really. We'll just have to see about who's in the driver's seat. I could make her life miserable, refuse to acknowledge the bastard, ruin her reputation, and throw them both over the wall without a penny."

His face was dark and malevolent, the upper lip curled in scorn, the scar on his face throbbing. If Chloe hadn't been a psychiatrist, she would have visibly cringed. But as she said nothing and looked at him impassively, Harry continued on in an unbridled, belligerent tone.

"Who's to say I'm the bloody father? I'll demand proof. She's still married to Dimmer, isn't she, though she dropped his name like a hot potato. Let the lawful husband take the fall. Now I think of it, he gave me the distinct impression he wanted her back on any terms, though why he does, I'm sure I don't know."

He stroked and relaxed his jaw, which had been clenched tight.

Chloe said in measured tones, "I'm not sure about Coddie's motives in coming here or telling you the news, Harry. What I'm sure of is that it's not your money Marlena wants but rather your love and commitment."

"Come on. Knowing Marlena as we do, we both know exactly what's going on. She's a social climber in love with a fantasy, not with me."

"That may be true. But she's worried about how you'll react to the pregnancy and how it might affect your reputation. Those are the real issues for her, not her own well being. The question is, do you care enough about Marlena to consider what's best for her?"

"Oh, come on. If you think Marlena cares a fart about me or my future, you must be talking about a different cunt than the one I know."

Along with the sneer, a new thought crossed Harry's mind. His expression now contained a flash of the cunning wolf. An alarm went off in Chloe's head, and she wasn't reassured by what he said next.

"If ever there was a woman unfit to be a mother, it's Marlena. You asked me what I'd do. Why, I'd get the child away from her and raise it myself. It shouldn't be too difficult."

She knew he was already thinking of the lawyers he would hire and the judges he would bribe.

"We've been friends for a long time, Harry, but I've nothing more to say to you on this subject. Good day."

As it appeared he wouldn't be getting the sympathetic ear he'd come for, Harry got up, slammed the door, and stomped off.

But as he skied back toward Drake's Roost, fuming at being misunderstood by yet another perverse female, he was also mulling over the fact of his paternity as it began to sink in. An heir apparent to his throne wasn't something he'd thought would ever happen to him.

For, despite what he'd said just now to Chloe, he had no doubt he was the father. The rival he saw yesterday was a wretched cuckold; Dimmer reeked of the lunacy of the sterile cuckoo. Now that it was too late in their high-stakes game for a clear-cut win, Dimmer wanted the damaged goods back, at any cost. Why?

God knows, but on Dimmer's watch, what would happen to the child, *his* child?

Well, perhaps he needed to think this matter through more carefully before making any rash moves. He would be seeing Marlena later tonight, at the Fire Night Ball. Perhaps it was time they talked things over.

As Harry turned over the ski poles and boot fastenings to his valet, he told the man to have his tuxedo aired and pressed and his dance shoes shined, so all would be ready for the evening activities.

Alexander opened the door for him with the ironic smirk which he hated so much. Harry vowed once more to lay down the law with Lila; that fag had to go.

He marched through his cavernous house and entered his office, a room that was called the Board Room but which looked more like the Vatican, with a 200-foot domed ceiling. There was a lot of correspondence to go through, but he found what he was thinking about was the unexpected Christmas gift he'd received from his young mistress.

There were strange rumblings in the location of his heart. He pressed on his scapula.

Could it be love for his unborn child he was feeling?

What is love? he thought, rubbing the spot in his chest where he felt pain.

He wished there was someone to talk to about the strange sensations. He'd be damned if he'd go see that young doctor. Chloe had all but run him off; clearly she was piqued with him. *How could she think he was in the wrong?*

Harry decided to ignore both Chloe's opinion and the intermittent experiences of pain in the chest. An endless cycle of wheeling and dealing on the derailed Laramie project awaited him in the mail pile.

But, if truth be told, the wild card that occupied his mind was the one just dealt to him by his sweetheart.

Chapter Thirty Six

Everyone in the household seemed intent on mothering her.

Marlena had agreed to a nap, and she even managed to doze off for a short time. Then she propped herself back up in bed and began to wade into her reading pile again.

Yesterday, she'd bought all the childbirth books on the Alta Bookstore shelf. Dr. Ron had advised her not to read just one book on the subject, and she planned to follow his advice from here on out.

Putting her purchases together with the books Dr. Ron had given her and the books in Chloe's office, her sampling was turning into a library. *The pilot was becoming a mini-series!*

Indeed, the stack looked daunting. At the top of it was a baby name book. Atalanta wasn't on the list of A's. Anyway, would she really want her daughter to be thought of as a roamer, like Cassandra? There had to be something better, and so now she flipped into the B's. Bathsheba, Belinda, Bess...nothing there.

She began to look through the C's. When she got to Cassandra, her eyes stopped. Her mind zoomed back into the story of long ago that she was still absorbing.

Outside her window, an assortment of local characters was assembling in the same way as the bonfire builders of 1900. Children and men of all ages were all over Hatter's Field picking up sticks and long faggots. There were windy mutterings in the mountain, and a lightning storm was in the forecast for the evening.

She flipped to the back of the book, to the Z's. And there she came upon the perfect name for a daughter: Zoe, the Greek word for "life."

Yes, that was the one : Zoe Augusta Drake. They'd call her Zaddie. But she'd keep the name to herself for the moment. *No sense getting her mother's hopes up.*

First, she had to talk to Harry. If an abortion was his preference, she would agree to it with as much grace as possible.

Throwing on a fluffy red robe Faith had given her for Christmas, she went downstairs to see if she could help with lunch preparations, but one look at Annie's flushed face as she bustled about the kitchen was warning enough to both Chloe and Marlena to stay out of her way.

As the sun approached its zenith, she did more speed-reading. The terminology was both intriguing and terrifying: Lamasse, spinal block, birthing room, tubal ligation, natural childbirth, pre-term eclampsia, and so forth.

As the sun descended from its zenith, she was reading a well-thumbed copy of <u>Our Bodies Ourselves</u>, first published in 1971, which she'd picked up from Chloe's shelves. There was much more to the things happening inside her body than she would've guessed, changes in everything from hormones to hair follicles.

Of course, she told herself, it was a matter of curiosity only; despite last night, she still planned to have an abortion.

How the mighty had fallen in only a few short days. Ironic, wasn't it, how it turned out that both Chloe and Faith, those paragons of virtue, had got themselves knocked up while out of wedlock!

Now here you are, Marlena, married but pregnant by another woman's husband. *The apple didn't fall very far from the tree, did it?*

After Annie appeared with a teapot, she indulged herself in a spot of curiosity about her father, whose eyes were like hers. Faith hadn't said if Gordon was alive or dead. She recalled feeling detached from her parents. Her feeling of singularity was partly based on the fact she didn't look like either of them.

Was she glad or sorry Austin had never suspected he wasn't her father? She decided she was glad. *Despite his flaws, he loved me more than Harry does. What does that say?*

He'd sung songs and whistled them by the hundreds for her. "Baby face, you've got the cutest little baby face." At one, she could say the name of each song. She was a genius, he said, a claim which Faith vigorously disputed: "She has a gift from God."

At five o'clock, Marlena went out for a walk around the pond. The bonfire was laid and ready to be set off after the signal fire was lit on Hatter's Field. One of the distinct pleasures of the gathering tonight would be the smell of burning junipers down by the pond and a convivial circle around the best bonfire in town, with the mill wheel slowly turning in the background.

It was quiet, until she heard the sound of "ker-plunk."

She looked around and could barely make the outline of Apollo, who was finishing up with the bonfire preparations and had skipped a stone across the pond to get her attention.

"Save a dance for me tonight?" she called out to him.

"You got it, milady," he cheerily called back.

The villagers were in their homes, having a quiet Christmas supper or getting ready to go out for the evening festivities. In an hour, Chloe's guests would begin arriving. The Cajun band would start up at eight o'clock. The bonfire lighting was at nine.

Marlena thought of Harry and Lila, getting ready for the party in their cold stone mansion. Harry's silence was speaking volumes. It would serve Harry right if she had the baby, causing the maximum amount of trouble for him!

But Chloe had wisely advised her the very worst reason to have a child was to hold paternity over a man as a weapon, using pregnancy to force a man into marriage. She'd said she would prefer to see Marlena have an abortion rather than to play such a destructive game. Faith had blanched white at that comment, but she'd kept her trap shut. That must have been difficult for her, Marlena thought, with a lurch of sympathy.

Should she consider keeping the baby and going back to Coddie, as her mother so desperately wanted? She now so wanted to please her mother, but it seemed the least reasonable course of action.

First, she'd have to be utterly convinced Harry didn't want her or the baby. Second, she'd have to muster the strength to give Harry up for good, even if she still loved him. *How? Harry was the one great love and obsession of her life!*

Sighing, she looked back toward the house. It was beginning to get dark, and it was time to get dressed for the party. This day had gone quickly, but nine months seemed like a lifetime. If she had the child, what would her life look like at the other end of the term? For once, her imagination was failing her. She couldn't see a clear picture in the crystal ball. The clouds had gathered inside her head.

As if to underline her emotions, menacing storm clouds were gathering overhead. The wind had whipped up, and it promised to be a tempestuous night. The perfect environment for a Fire Night, she thought, a maelstrom above and a crisis within.

She thought of Cassandra, who'd married a man to escape her dull surroundings, only to find she was trapped here with him.

She thought of Chloe, pregnant by a man she didn't love and bravely enduring butchery to have her life back again.

She thought of her own mother in the same predicament that she now found herself in--except with fewer options.

How terrible it must have been as Faith bore her to term, all the while pretending to a virtual stranger that he was the father!

How dreadfully their decisions had turned out for these women! Though Faith had saved face with the Church, everyone had been harmed. Marlena was born into a flawed marriage and never got the parenting she deserved, nor did she know her real father. Austin got a wife who didn't love him, so he obsessed over his daughter to make up for it.

Chloe's tragedy was the saddest of all. Marlena felt sorrier for Chloe than she did for anyone. Once Faith and Austin became engaged, Chloe's hands were tied. Or so she must have thought at the time.

Come to think of it, why didn't Chloe have the baby out of wedlock and never reveal its father? That's what Cassandra had done, and with good results. Perhaps Chloe was not as brave as Cassandra had been, when it came down to it.

Perhaps Chloe isn't as brave as I am!

Suddenly Marlena realized Chloe was rooting harder than anyone else for her to have this child on her own terms, just as her own mother had done.

Marlena smiled. Chloe kept her cards close to the vest. Certainly she wouldn't admit to a hidden agenda. But she'd been found out.

One thing was clear. Marlena owed a lot to the two women who had got her through these seven days of reunion and her ordeal last night.

After the worst was over, Faith and Chloe had stood arm in arm in her bedroom doorway.

In itself the sight was heartening to behold, the two kinswomen, so different in their views but reunited after all these years in a common cause, Marlena Mae's welfare. Imagine that.

The last thing Chloe had said to her was: "Don't make a decision based on what people will say. If you want the child, have it. If you don't want it, end the pregnancy quickly and safely. We stand behind you, all for one and one for all. Be yourself."

Tonight, the outfit she would wear would proclaim she was bold and sexy. It would surely incite disapproving stares. The velvet sleeveless designer top was cut down to the navel. The skirt was white leather Paris couture and slit to the thigh. Around her neck she'd sling an extraordinarily long aquamarine boa, Chloe's Christmas gift.

Soon this peaceful home, which now felt to her like an oasis, would be over-run by noisy guests with prying, suspicious eyes. *One more grueling ordeal to get through. Help!*

She wished she could play the Clare Brighton card, stay out of sight. But she was nothing like that character, save for her dogged allegiance to a domineering wolf named Drake.

At the end of the evening, would she and Harry be reconciled? Would she still want to have his child, as she did at this moment? Or would she be thinking of Ron and how good she felt about herself in his warm presence, happy and child-like? Confusing! How nerve-wracking not to know how she wanted her own story to turn out!

"Just get through this night. Tomorrow's another day," Marlena muttered. She took one last look at the glowering sky and then went inside.

Chapter Thirty Seven

Up the long driveway trailed an ant-like army of guests, both invited and uninvited. They walked, skied, rode horses, drove, or were taxied to Chloe Vye's annual Christmas Fire Night Ball.

Early this morning they'd opened their gifts, gone to church services, gorged themselves at dinner, and fought with their relatives. Now it was time to enjoy the best bonfire and dance music in town, with refreshments catered by the peerless banquet services of the Alta Hotel.

Each guest was greeted warmly at the door by the hostess and given a nod by one or both of her two cousins, who were flanked on the outside by Dr. Ron Huddleston. He stood a few paces behind them, so as not to appear to be presuming a role beyond that of escort.

Faith had pinned her corsage on her simple and elegant black dress, a Christmas gift from Chloe.

After some consideration, Marlena had taken off the pearl-and-aquamarine bracelet and worn her camellias on her wrist.

A female guest was looking her up and down until Marlena's cheeks reddened, and she stuck out her hand. Then the woman rudely walked off without saying a word. Ron sensed Marlena stiffen under the rebuff. "You look gorgeous," he murmured to her. "Now hold up your chin and knock 'em dead."

She smiled back gratefully, relaxing. She thought, the enemy is at hand, but bring 'em on, so long as Dr. Ron was at her side.

So far, no sign of Harry. *Was it possible she'd once thought of this evening with great anticipation?*

A similar scene had appeared in her dreams, one in which she needed rescuing. Harry always appeared to save her, a knight on a white horse galloping through the flames to scoop her up and carry her off. But in reality, the dream was quickly turning into a nightmare.

From their shunning behavior and the sour expressions on people's faces when they saw her, it was clear everyone had heard enough to hate her, even if the accusations were sheer speculation magnified by hocus-pocus.

Indeed the word was out. All eyes were converging on the scarlet woman at the front door of Mill's Creek.

Rosa Brown, Lila's source, had relayed the confidential information onward to her third cousin, Letty Brown-Hawker. Word had spread like wildfire that the uppity intruder from San Francisco was pregnant, and yet no father's name was listed in the doctor's office records. *What did that tell you?*

As the line continued to grow and the people passed by, only the two lesbians, who arrived on the early side of eight, seemed genuinely glad to see Marlena. And was she glad to see them!

With a murmured word of apology to Chloe, she grabbed an arm from each of them and beat a retreat from the receiving line.

"You did this? Fabulous home. Where's the bar?" Sally said.

"In the ballroom, also known as the parlor. I couldn't wait for you two to arrive. Brrrr...the natives are giving me the cold shoulder treatment. Did you notice it?"

"Maybe the word's out about you blowing this place to go to Key West," said Stretch.

Sally whispered in Marlena's ear, pressing her arm tightly with her bony fingertips, "Never you mind her. She's just green-eyed with jealousy about the way you look. She knows I'd like to eat you alive."

Marlena grimaced. *Things would get better.*

And then, it seemed to her, things got much worse. As the three walked into the parlor where a parquet dance floor had been set up, the buzzing in the room came to an abrupt halt. It was as though everyone stopped and stared at her; then, in the next moment, they started talking again, like the cabaret scene in <u>Gigi</u>.

Her ears were ringing from stress as the three women walked to the bar, seemingly in a glass tunnel that separated them from the other guests. They ordered their drinks and stayed huddled together, which suited Sally, at least, just fine.

Chapter Thirty Eight

When the sky was pitch dark, the first bonfire of Christmas Fire Night was lit at Hatter's Field. With a roar of the crowd, the sulphurous flames leapt into the frigid air.

Next up was Mill's Creek, the juniper bonfire that was fairest of them all. It had been prepared singlehandedly by Apollo Nelson. He proudly set it off, then dutifully stayed in the shadows near the pond to take up a surveillance posture. The flames were reflected in the icicles glistening from the lower branches of the juniper, creating around the humble young man an aura of eternal brightness.

It seemed in keeping with his buoyant spirit. After a bit, Apollo took a lap around the pond to keep himself warm.

On the side of the pond nearest the house, the decorated millwheel was the crowd favorite. They stood transfixed as it rotated clockwise and the water softly splashed, a soothing sound which softened the grinding note of the mechanism.

Apollo checked its operation and then began a sharp lookout for small children wandering astray from the purview of their parents. He'd been charged by Annie to make sure no one fell into the fire, the water, or the mill wheel, so he had his hands full.

Foremost on his mind, however, was watching out for Marlena. She'd been looking dejected today, and he'd heard rumblings about her in the community, even as far afield as Bulette. He was troubled in his mind about her safety and dedicated to making sure nothing bad happened to her tonight.

Other young people were preoccupied with evading the watchful eyes of mothers and grandmothers. They slunk away into dark crevices of the mountain, near enough to the bonfires to enjoy the flames, far enough away so as not to be seen or heard as they made love.

At eight o'clock, the hostess entered the makeshift ballroom. At her signal, the Dewey Balfa Band started to play, opening with an homage to Clifton Chenier. Couples eagerly came forward from clustered chairs along the walls to sway to the music and dance.

Once the music was well underway, Chloe stopped at the bar to check in with her cousins. "Where's your mother?" she asked Marlena.

"Faith is out by the pond, presumably enjoying the bonfire. I'm having a rip-roaring time on the dance floor with my friends."

"Are you sure you're all right?"

Awful. "Never better."

"I need to greet a few more guests--I don't know where they're all coming from! But then I'll be right back, Lena, I promise."

"Don't worry about me, darling. I'm in good hands."

As Chloe walked away, her mind remained on Marlena's expression, which looked tragic and forlorn despite her brave words.

Harry and Lila Drake hadn't yet shown their faces, so perhaps Marlena was disappointed by Harry's absence.

Suddenly Ron appeared at Marlena's side, and she felt a thrill of pleasure when he said, "May I have this dance? They're uncorking a slow one."

"Certainly."

He added, "I would've been here sooner, but I needed to talk to two patients who are in labor at the hospital. There's a full moon tonight."

"Anything else going on?"

"Oh, the usual assortment of gunshot wounds, but so far no fatalities. I'll go in after midnight." *I'd prefer to go into you.*

"Gunshot wounds?"

"Oh, you don't know." He then explained a tradition, dating back to pioneer days, allowing a public display of personal firearms on two days-- Christmas Day and the Fourth of July. "Didn't you hear gunshots ricocheting off the mountain?"

"I thought it was firecrackers."

"Some here are packing."

"No!"

"Courtesy demands they check their firearms at the door. I saw a few in line."

"You're kidding! Don't they know what goes up must come down?"

I'm up every time I see you, my dearest love. Ron agreed it was a dangerous tradition, that every year the local hospital entertained an assortment of merry-makers who didn't understand Newton's Law and were its hapless victims.

They were moving to a nice ballad, and she would have thoroughly enjoyed their dancing, if it weren't for all the malicious eyes following them as they waltzed around the dance floor, pressed together.

Despite this distraction, she felt herself physically attracted to the hardness of Ron's cock against her leg as they danced. Instinctively she pressed back, and then she rested her head on his shoulder. *God, this feels good; I wish the dance would last forever.*

But the band was taking a break. The local D.J. came on and spun "Proud Mary," and then an eager circle of fruggers quickly formed. Marlena dispatched Ron to drag the lesbians into the circle. As the four commenced dirty dancing, heads flopping and hips grinding, out of the corner of her eye, she saw Harry and Lila Drake enter the room.

They were strolling toward the far end. On Harry's arm, Lila looked like a vision, more like the lady in the painting than ever before. Her dress had a gossamer sheen, and her taut breasts showed through the filminess; all she needed was a pair of leopards at her feet and a bowl of white roses in her arms to complete the picture.

Marlena felt an unusual lurch--was it jealousy, remorse, or something else?

"Are you all right?" Ron asked.

"Just another ghost sighting. Nothing to worry about."

Surely Harry would seek her out later. *But what if he continued to ignore her? She would die. Yes, she would surely die, if he delivered one more blow to her pride.*

Around ten o'clock, as she glanced in their direction, she saw Harry was standing up. He bowed to another couple nearby, then strolled out of sight, probably to the bar.

She was wondering if she dare attempt to follow him and entice him upstairs, where they could talk privately.

"Ron, do you mind if I go and see if Chloe needs any help?"

"Sure thing. Right after this next number. Let's two-step. "

Ron whirled her around and then took a stab at the move. She couldn't help but laugh. Ron was terrible at two-stepping, but his heart was in the right place.

After the number was over, they retreated to a side wall, and Ron nudged her. Harry was now sitting nearby, with his back to them. Lila was gulping down her drink. They seemed to be quarreling. Lila stood up on wobbly legs, mouthed something at Harry, her lips curling, and then wandered off, drink in hand.

She and Ron returned to the dance floor. Harry promptly strolled over and tapped Ron on the shoulder.

"I hope you don't mind, Huddleston."

"Not unless the lady does," said Ron.

Then, looking at Marlena's face, he said quickly, "Now you mention it, I was just about to see if I could make myself useful to our hostess."

"Oh, you're a darling, Ron," said Marlena.

Her face grew quite pale as Harry gathered her in his arms.

Ron reluctantly left the floor. "Hang tough, Lena," he muttered, fighting his way to the crowd to get to Chloe. He was all too painfully aware of feeling territorial toward the beautiful damsel in distress, whose love Harry so richly didn't deserve.

Fifteen minutes later, the star-crossed lovers sat facing each other on Cassandra's bed.

"Your hair seems longer," Marlena observed sadly, tracing with fingers where Harry's black hair curled around behind his ears.

It made her depressed to think of all the failed opportunities during this week when they might have had this meeting, might have kissed and made up.

And now that the all-important moment was here, she was unclear on what she wanted to say to him, even what she wanted from Harry.

Chapter Thirty Nine

The line of incoming revelers showed no sign of coming to an end. Chloe was still greeting guests at the door when Ron came up alongside her and asked her if there was anything he could do to help.

"Well, some of these folks have brought their kids, and we don't want any of them straying off and falling into the pond. Would you be a darling and check how Apollo is doing with that situation?"

"Be glad to. I'll come back with a full report."

The borders of the pond were secure, Apollo told him, as was the bonfire at the far end of it on a knell that overlooked the town. But when he returned to Chloe's side, Ron did have a trouble report, though of a different and unexpected sort.

He'd happened upon a small group of people who were clustered near the mill wheel. In the flickering shadow of the turning wheel, he had spotted the Hawkers, man and wife. Hawker was outfitted in a loose pilgrim's coat, which overwhelmed his small frame. Letty was in pioneer garb, a heavy dress that covered her all the way to her beefy ankles.

When Ron had come up to the outer edges of the inner circle, he could hear they were taking turns loudly declaiming "the presence of the devil's whore in their midst" and "the drunkenness and debauchery that has been going on in this town, threatening the very fabric of our native society."

"I didn't invite the Hawkers," said Chloe wonderingly.

"Then they're loudest, most ballsy gate-crashers I've ever seen. Shall I go back out there, take him aside, and firmly suggest they leave?"

"Well, I don't know that would do any good. Attempting to throw them out would just make them holler all the louder. But, if you could alert Apollo to their presence, that would be a good precaution. He might have to round up more security on quick notice, in case they don't simmer down."

After dispatching Ron on his mission, she turned back to her oncoming guests, a continuous stream.

Where were all these people coming from? She'd invited over seventy, but it appeared the entire town was showing up at her doorstep. She was flattered, but soon there wouldn't be room for anyone to move.

She recalled what Marlena had told her, about how all great parties are very crowded ones, with nowhere to sit. Well, if that was the criterion, this one was turning out to be a huge success.

Still, she couldn't very well relax into her role of gracious hostess, worried as she was about her cousin's state of mind. She wished she had quizzed Ron on this subject.

At that moment, Ron again appeared at Chloe's elbow.

"Oh, you must be a mind-reader," said Chloe. "There's one other favor I need to ask of you."

"Anything, but I'm afraid there's one thing I have to tell you first."

"What is it?"

He spoke softly into her ear. "Faith is out there in the crowd listening to Letty, nodding her head in agreement to every word. I think she's unaware Marlena is Letty's actual target."

"Ye gods. That's not good. Let's both go see what Letty's up to."

Chloe shook one last hand, pulled on her snow boots, and took Ron's arm. They set off at a fast clip along a dirt path close to the house that was a shortcut to the millwheel by the pond.

Meanwhile, in the flickering light-and-shadow stage cast by the turning wheel, Letty Brown-Hawker was hitting her stride, galvanizing the growing crowd against the evils of liquor and loose women, warning them darkly that Satan and his legion had reappeared among them in the guise of prominence and beauty.

Her husband had begun his circumnavigation of the pond. It was his assigned mission to find Marlena Bellum and bring the slut before Letty to face her accuser--by force, if necessary. In his voluminous coat pocket Hawker carried a loaded firearm, which he had not checked at the door. Hawker was sure that at some point, Marlena would be drawn to the bonfire, witch that she was, so he hovered in its vicinity.

Hawker had no way of knowing that his intended prey, at this very moment, was safely sequestered in her bedroom with Harry.

Now that Letty had the audience mesmerized, she was making full use of their attention. Her voice grew louder as the crowd increased. And she'd just spotted Faith Bellum standing foremost among the gaping onlookers.

Letty knew who Faith was. She was first cousin to a known witch who had caused the deaths of several natives in the early part of the century. Faith was also the New Yorker who'd brought disgrace to a native family by leaving her child and imposing on an old woman to take care of the precocious brat. Finally, she was the mother of a modern witch, the precocious brat who had lived up to Letty's expectations of evil reincarnating itself and had shown herself to be Cassandra Vye reborn and Satan's red-haired whore. Marlena had even emblazoned Satan's name on the hotel masthead. If that wasn't enough, Faith's grand-child was Satan's spawn!

"MOTHER OF SATAN'S WHORE!" roared Letty, pointing a fat finger at Faith.

Faith looked around, her face alight with curiosity about the poor, quivering culprit, unaware it was she who was being addressed. When the other people had stepped away, she hadn't noticed. Her eyes were fixed on Letty, who was moaning and drooling as if in a trance. Now Faith was left alone in the shadowy circle, face-to-face with Mrs. Brown-Hawker.

Letty madly believed she was channeling a spiteful Native American by the name of Red Cloud, an Indian rightfully incensed about Harry Drake and his nefarious real estate deals with a scam artist known as "The Prince of Darkness."

From the sideline arose a loud cackle from Thomas Hawker. He had not yet succeeded in rounding up Marlena, so he had quickly returned in time to witness the crescendo of his wife's Act One.

"Speak out, Letty! Tell Faith what her daughter is! Speak of the CURSE!"

"YOU, THERE, WOMAN. THE SPIRIT OF RED CLOUD SPEAKS THROUGH ME. HE SAYS THE WHORE WHO IS CARRYING SATAN'S CHILD IS A MENACE TO THE COMMUNITY. GET THY DAUGHTER GONE FROM HERE! FLY, BEFORE IT'S TOO LATE! THE CURSE OF GOODY BROWN LIES

ON YOUR DAUGHTER AND HER EVIL SPAWN. GOD WILL PUNISH HER WITH TWO DEATHS TONIGHT UNLESS SHE LEAVES!"

The crowd murmured as Letty held her beefy hands over her turban and her head began to gyrate.

Faith was non-plussed. The medium seemed to be staring right at her. What was this all about? She now realized the crowd had stepped away, leaving her exposed. Instinctively, she put her brown plastic purse on the ground and readied herself for whatever might come next.

The wrath of Letty and her spirit continued to pour forth, thick as pitch, into Faith's reddening ears.

"MOTHER OF SATAN'S WHORE, DO YOU REFUSE THE WARNING OF RED CLOUD? REMEMBER WHAT HAPPENS TO THOSE WHO AID THE WITCH! RED CLOUD HAS SPOKEN TO GOODY BROWN IN THE AFTERLIFE. SHE SAYS THE CURSE RESIDES RIGHT HERE. TWO MORE DEATHS WILL BE LAID AT THE DOOR OF THE WITCH YOU SUCKLED AT YOUR BREAST. MARLENA BELLUM IS THE EVIL REINCARNATION OF CASSANDRA VYE! NATIVES OF ALTA, BEWARE!"

As if on cue, the ground rumbled beneath the hag's feet. Faith blinked her eyes and shifted her stance, but stood her ground.

"I SAY UNTO ALL, THE FRUIT OF FAITH'S WOMB IS THE DEVIL'S OWN SPAWN. FROM THIS DAY FORWARD, NO MAN, WOMAN OR CHILD IN THIS TOWN IS SAFE FROM THE EVIL THAT LURKS WITHIN HER DAUGHTER. TWO DEATHS ARE FORETOLD UNLESS SATAN'S WHORE LEAVES THIS TOWN TONIGHT!"

Seemingly overcome by the exertions of the spirit within, Letty abruptly sat down at the pond's edge, her legs splayed out under her voluminous, antique petticoats. She was oblivious to the proximity of the revolving mill wheel, though her head was only a foot away from the line along which it rotated.

A shadow crossed her line of vision, and she looked up, her sweaty forehead creased and her mouth drooping. The Bellum woman was standing over her, with face ablaze, fists clenched, arms akimbo, in a military striking pose.

"How dare you slander me and my daughter?" Faith demanded. "Who do you think you are? You don't speak for God, lady. You're a bully, a fraud, and a blasphemer. God loves and protects my daughter. He'll judge the likes of you!"

"Step aside, woman," said Letty sternly, but in a weaker voice than before. "You don't know who you're dealing with."

"Oh yes I do. I'm dealing with a slanderer!"

Letty struggled to stand upright, but the weight of her old-fashioned dress was so encumbering she couldn't do it. As Faith remained in her threatening posture, Letty slowly wiped her beet-red face, which was soaked with sweat, and then spat at her.

The crowd groaned, but Faith simply wiped her eyes and jutted out her chin.

Just then, the Wyoming wind, strong as a mule and random as a roulette wheel, came up and caught the frayed end of the long cloth that was wound as a turban around Letty's large head. As the wind picked up, the turban began to unwind on both ends; yards of fringed cloth were unraveling. When the wind suddenly veered, it whipped one end of the cloth around Letty's neck and the other straight into the mill wheel housing, where it rapidly spooled.

As if a hand had reached out and grabbed her, Letty was yanked backwards into the water. In a few seconds, she appeared in the air again, but now she was bald and floundering wildly, her angry face purplish, with a long scarf tightly wound around her neck.

Huskily she shouted: "Get this off me! Shoot her, Thom!"

But Thomas was out of earshot, having resumed his pursuit of Marlena at the bonfire. Thom wasn't there with his firearm when Letty needed his assistance, and she cursed her bad luck.

Then Faith leaped into the water and began to flail at the slanderer. The older, heavier woman took a few blows before recovering and rallying. She pushed back at Faith violently. But meantime she was sinking ever lower, and her turban continued to wind ever more tightly around her neck.

Ron and Chloe arrived just in time to see both Letty and Faith in the water under the revolving mill wheel, a few feet from the pond's edge. Faith with her military posture and her agility at first had the upper hand, but Letty butted her massive head into her opponent's stomach, taking the breath out of her, and then pounded her with her fists.

Behind them, the mill wheel, glittering with its string of lights, continued to pull the turban tighter. Letty didn't seem to notice the ribbon of cloth rewinding itself around her thick neck ever more tightly and rapidly as she continued to utter increasingly soundless curses.

"Marlena Bellum carries Satan's child! Red Cloud demands she leave, or he predicts two deaths on her head this very night!" Letty pulled Faith under.

Chloe screamed and Ron went rushing forward. Faith resurfaced, gasping, managed to clamber out of the pond, and then she fainted. The ground ominously rumbled once again.

Letty was lifted up bodily from the water and spun around twice, as though she were having a fit. She fell heavily backward into the water, with the entire length of the turban tightly wound around her neck. Then she dropped from sight.

A sudden hush came over the scene.

Onlookers later said it looked as though the pond itself had heaved Letty up into the air, which offered support for the contention that the cause of death was a supernatural force.

However, there was a perfectly natural explanation for the phenomenon: Alta Mountain was experiencing an earthquake along the fault line that underlay the defunct silver mines, the first such upheaval since 1947. And this was only the opening round of tremors.

Ron jumped into the pond after Letty went down for the last time. He continued diving into it, but to no avail. Her large, limp body was too heavy a weight for him to carry aloft. Then Apollo came running up and jumped in alongside Ron.

Between the two of them, they were able to lift Letty to the surface and then out of the pond, where Ron immediately began to perform CPR. Chloe had already called for an ambulance on a guest's mobile phone, but Ron told Chloe in a quick aside that the madwoman was dead, strangulated and drowned.

While Apollo spelled Ron in the futile attempt to revive Letty, Ron turned to Faith, who was dazedly struggling to get herself up.

"Stay right there, Faith, " Ron said in a commanding voice. "Don't get up. I'll be right back." He put Chloe in charge of Faith and ran to meet the ambulance stretcher-bearers.

There was a brief lull in the action and the sound of weeping. The bulk of the crowd had fled, fearful for their own lives.

Then, Chloe was startled to hear a woman's voice in her ear.

"One down and one to go."

"Lila?"

"She's better off dead, that old publicity hound," murmured Lila drunkenly to Chloe. "She's the victim of her own ridiculous curses. By the way, have the cute doctor check her underwear. SHE is a HE; you can bet on it. Amazing party."

Then Lila trailed off in her gossamer gown, cocktail in hand, looking like a ghost from the roaring twenties. Overhead, the gathering clouds were ever darker and lightning flickered.

What next? Chloe wondered. And where were Marlena and Harry? She had not seen either of them all night. Had they chosen this accursed moment to go off by themselves? Thank God!

Among the small group of onlookers who remained, there was a general sigh of relief when, a few minutes later, Faith was pronounced by Dr. Ron to be in good condition, other than scared out of her wits and with several bumps and bruises.

Letty's mottled face already wore the rigid mask of death. After Ron pulled a sheet over her head, signaling her official demise, Chloe whispered to him what Lila had said about SHE being a HE.

"One more surprise on an unprecedented night. Please take Faith into her room," Ron said to Chloe. "I'll be up in a minute to give her a sedative."

"Shouldn't we look for Marlena?"

"First I have to find the deceased woman's husband. Or rather, the deceased man's husband, if Mrs. Drake is right. Hey, did you feel that?"

"My God, what now?"

What they felt was a violent shaking in the ground. It continued on while overhead, multiple lightning bolts rippled across the sky.

Chloe clutched Ron's arm. Faith abruptly sat down on the granite walkway that encircled the pool, grabbing onto a slab with her fingers.

They all looked at each other as the rumbling and the shifting of the earth went on for several more seconds.

When it finally quieted, the rumbling was followed by another ominous sound. There arose from the far side of the pond, where the bonfire was still brightly visible, a crescendo of raised voices.

"What next?" said Chloe, dazedly.

Chapter Forty

When the rumbling of the ground and the lightning overhead first began, Apollo was standing by the stretcher, staring at the corpse and scratching his head.

In pulling the heavy skirts back down from where they were wound around the bald head, he'd made the discovery that the madwoman had a set of hairy balls.

Was this crazy world coming to an end? Was it because of the curse his cousins had told him about? Was Marlena safe?

Smelling ozone and seeing lightning in the air, feeling the ground shift again, Apollo made haste and sprinted off in the direction of the raised voices. That was when he heard that deep booming sound, he knew what it was; it meant a tree had cracked and then crashed, uprooted by the violence of wind or earth.

Whatever was going on over there, Apollo planned to be on hand in case anyone, and Marlena in particular, needed rescuing. He took off at a run.

"Wow, an earthquake in the midst of a lightning storm," Ron said to Chloe. "God is giving us quite a show, not that we needed one. I'd better check out what those folks over there are screaming about. Stay here."

About fifty yards away from an overturned tree, in the darkness punctuated by the flickering light of the bonfire, Harry Drake was answering an invidious allegation by Thomas Hawker with a punch in the face.

But Hawker, who had his own ideas about Letty's death, was not dissuaded. From his pocket he drew a loaded pistol and began to wave it around.

"Drake, I demand you produce Satan's whore! If I find her myself, I'll kill her! Kill her and gore her and burn the heart of the devil's spawn!"

Arriving at a run, Apollo got to the two men first. He began shouting for help and began to drag Drake out of harm's way, but Drake kept plunging toward Hawker, who continued to brandish the firearm.

It was at that point the ground began to rumble in earnest, and the lightning strikes peppered the sky with blue and gold zigzags, rattling all the china and silver on the buffet tables and throwing people to the ground. Another giant oak fell. The bonfire licking the air with fiery tongues seemed to be mating with the lightning strikes.

But the two antagonists were oblivious to nature and its danger.

"Marlena Bellum is Satan's whore and carrying His child! Her freaking mother killed my wife!" screamed Hawker.

Harry roared back: "Don't you insult the mother of my child! Take that back, you sack of shit! You don't know what you're talking about!"

The ongoing rumbling of the ground and the lightning show in the sky around the circling protagonists created a stage of light, shadow, and motion that was right out of hell. Remaining onlookers fled.

Hawker wiped the blood off his face and came roaring at the bigger man, pushing Drake toward the pond with his momentum.

He would've gone into the water if Apollo hadn't caught him in time. Drake righted himself. Meanwhile, Ron had arrived and was attempting to wrestle the gun away from Hawker.

Drake was armed only with a dancing shoe that he'd removed from one foot to have something with which to battle the enemy.

The gun went off. Then Drake flung off Apollo's restraining arms and came charging back toward Hawker.

As a second shot rang out, a lightning bolt came slashing down through the sky and smashed into the pond.

A look of surprise on his features, Drake fell face down into the water.

Hawker shouted that he'd killed Drake in justifiable revenge for Letty's life, fulfilling the curse. Then he turned and ran into the shadows.

Apollo moved quickly to Drake's rescue, jumping in and fishing him out. He laid him on the ground, and Ron immediately began CPR. He instructed Apollo to run and alert the ambulance drivers to wait, that there would be more cargo on their trip to the hospital.

Ron fully expected Drake to revive. He'd been under the water only briefly, for less than a minute, and there was no sign of a wound or other trauma. Hawker's bullets had lodged far of their mark, in a juniper tree.

But when, after eighty compressions, Drake didn't begin to show any signs of returning to life, Ron listened to his heart. It was then he realized Harold Drake was stone dead, the victim of a massive heart attack. The look of surprise was imprinted on his death mask, so quickly had he expired.

In the morning newscasts, it was reported that Harold Augustus Drake, President of Drake Enterprises and the foremost real estate developer in the state of Wyoming, had died suddenly while attending an annual Christmas Fire Night Ball at Mill's Creek in Alta.

According to the coroner's report, Drake was the victim of a heart attack. It coincided with a bizarre combination of dramatic natural events. A lightning bolt had felled the oldest oak tree in the district. Simultaneously, there was an earthquake of 6.9 magnitude, the first of its kind in Wyoming.

It hadn't been established whether there was a connection beyond coincidence between these natural phenomena and Harold Drake's death, but there was a faction of natives who were quoted as saying they would never believe otherwise.

Funeral arrangements were pending and would take place in Bulette at Scottish Presbyterian Church.

An hour after these cataclysmic events occurred, Thomas Hawker III turned himself over to the authorities and spent the night in jail. He was released the next day, still claiming that his dead wife had been the victim of witchcraft and that he had unmasked Harold Drake as Satan and executed him, a fitting retribution for his conspiring with Marlena Bellum to unleash the forces of evil on an unsuspecting community of believers. He left Alta soon afterward and never spoke Marlena Bellum's name again--he feared to.

But in fact, as Ron pointed out to Drake's widow, neither the lightning nor the earthquake nor even the fight with Hawker had been contributing factors in Harry's death. Rather, it was his ignorance about the importance of cardiac symptoms.

However, there was one casualty other than the old oak tree that was directly attributable to a lightning strike. Hit by a bolt, the gold rooster at the top of the clock-tower at Drake's Roost bit the dust, having taken on the function of a lightning rod.

In the summer of 1978, when Lila was touring Europe with her sister Marty, she would explain her reaction to friends in this way: "When the two big cocks croaked at the same time, it was a sign for Lila Coffin to get out of Dodge."

A week later, Lila thought of someone who might be able to do something useful with Harry's rock pile. She turned it over to what she called "the local hysterical society." Her waggish reference was to the Northeast Territory Historical Society, headed up by Bryce Scattergood.

She'd been favorable impressed by Mr. Scattergood's mission, his demeanor, and his physique. As Marty later observed to Marlena, "Lila hardly talked of anyone else on our European jaunt."

Chapter Forty One
Rewinding to midnight, Christmas night

In the words of the Rocky Horror Picture that was touring the country in 1977, "Let's do the time warp again."

Several missing pieces from that tragic night need to be told to complete the picture, including Codwell Dimmer's role in the proceedings and also the role of Cassandra Vye, the ancestral ghost hovering over them.

For four long days, poor Coddie had been forced to cool his heels in a hotel suite, his isolation and emotional meltdown punctuated only by morning, noon, and night ventures into B. L. Zebub's, where he'd become well acquainted with the lesbians who were hoping to lure his wife to Key West. Just what he needed, more competition!

To his mind, his efforts to impress upon Marlena his desire for a reconciliation had been met with indignation, indifference, and angry outbursts. He would try once more, on Christmas evening.

Upon arriving by taxicab at Mill's Creek at midnight, Coddie was in an uproariously drunken state. He appeared at the front door as the unfashionably late guest. Then he barreled inside, unannounced.

Spotting Chloe, but not noticing her dropped jaw, he elaborately bowed to her. She was in the parlor drinking brandied coffee, exhausted from the evening's calamitous events.

Lila, who'd just accepted Chloe's gracious invitation to spend the night, was poised on the first step of the grand staircase, a large glass of brandy in her hand.

"You all sheem shurprised to shee me," mumbled Coddie. "Am I the uninvited guest to the feasht? But, no. I have an invitation." He waved it, so unsteady on his feet that he almost fell over.

From an adjoining hallway connecting the parlor to the kitchen area, Coddie's late entrance was spotted by Ron, who was tending to the bandaging of minor wounds suffered by three members of the hired staff.

While guests fled for their lives, the young people had collided with each other in rushing out to see the spectacular lightning show on Hatter's Field that had spelled an abrupt end to the party.

Ron called out, "Steady there, Mr. Dimmer. I'll be with you in a second."

Coddie ignored the call-out.

"Guess what I got. Five hundred smackaroos for good old Harry Drake, my good old buddy. I got 'em right here in my pocket--five one hundred dollar bills. Where is that snake? I've got his winnings. Two days ago he bested me on the pool table at his hotel. I didn't have it all on me at the time."

He stopped and burped loudly before going on. "You shee, ladies and genulmen. You shhhhhee, me and Harry had ourselves a sporting afternoon, during which, I'm s-s-sorry to s-s-ay, I failed to perform adequately. Conshider these silver coins for Judas. Conshider whatever. The dough belongs to Harry. Not that he needs it. Winner takes all. He gets everything--hook, line, and stinker. I mean....ha ha ha....I mean wife, I mean slinker."

No one said anything, but Lila began to giggle uncontrollably, with tears running down her ashen cheeks.

"You think ish funny, lady? I had an agreement with your husband, no joking matter, long time ago. We agreed on two rules. Do NOT fall in love with her and do NOT knock her up. Naughty, naughty. Your hubbie failed to abide by the rules, Mrs. Drake. The rules are the rules, between genulmen. Hey, did I miss anything?"

Lila hiccoughed and then said grimly. "Are you speaking to me, whoever you are? You didn't miss a thing except divine retribution. Everyone's gone home. I'm going up to bed."

Ron came in then and said, "Mr. Dimmer, the ladies are tired. Let me get you something to drink. Then perhaps you and I can take a little walk upstairs. We'll find you a place to lie down."

"No lie down, no way Jose. Came to see world's prettiest bonfire, best in class they tell me at the hotel. Came to play a game of pool with good ol' Harry Drake. Came to dance with my wife. Wassa madda? Where ish everyone? Time to party!"

"Come on, Mr. Dimmer," said Ron, taking him firmly by the shoulder. "Let's go find you some coffee."

Sitting in a corner by the fire, Marlena was barely aware that her husband had entered the room and then left it.

Marlena was reviewing in her mind the conversation she'd had with Harry in her bedroom two hours earlier.

It had been the crucial moment of decision for her. The scene was committed to memory. She was reliving it in exact detail, for the fortieth time. She assumed she would be doing so for the rest of her natural life.

Chapter Forty Two

Marlena would be willing to swear on her mother's Bible she'd heard tinkling female laughter coming from the window when she led Harry upstairs to her bedroom.

As they talked, Cassandra's mocking spirit had been everywhere.

She'd perched on a chair while Harry remained standing.

He had seemed violently angry with her.

He voiced his strong suspicion, in the roughest of terms, about her being in league with her husband to railroad him, citing the divorce papers he'd seen, the vandalism in the bar, and Coddie's claim she was pregnant by him.

Marlena was startled by his brutal and unfounded accusations. She burst into a spontaneous outpouring of tears. The young woman who had never cried in front of her lover before cried and cried and cried.

After a time, Harry seemed willing to placate her. He sat down on the chair and pulled her into his lap, stroking her hair. Nonetheless, he kept looking, surreptitiously, toward the door, as if he were expecting someone.

Look out, breathed Cassandra.

"Let's blow this scene, my love. Hightail it to Key West for New Years," Harry said, "where no one knows us. We can knit potholders on the beach and drink margaritas. This town sucks."

Marlena smiled weakly through her tears.

He held her by her heaving shoulders. At first she allowed herself to be comforted and lulled into believing his old love for her had returned.

But while she'd been listening to Harry's rant, she'd become slowly aware of a third party hovering.

Look out there, through the door.

Entranced by the echoing voice of a woman in her head, she peered carefully at the crack in the door. Then she caught sight of the ashen-haired woman crouched there, making a questioning face. Her miming was clearly intended for Harry. The woman's face was familiar, which at first puzzled Marlena, until she remembered she herself had extended the party invitation to Lorna.

When she'd entered the sheriff's office, she recalled, her old classmate had seemed grateful for the invitation, yet had acted oddly.

"Someone out there seems impatient to see you," said Marlena.

"Oh, that's nobody, just my pot connection. I told her I'd be up here with you."

He's lying.

There was a pause. Harry gaped at Marlena and then winked lewdly. It was a move which threw her, as he'd never appeared so mawkish before.

"Let's invite her in," said Harry eagerly.

"I know who she is, my love. Her name's Lorna Anderson. I went to school with her. I was supposed to ask you about finding a bloody job for her brother. I'm afraid I failed to do so, but I'm not at all disposed to talk to her now."

"She's my new pot connection."

"Yeah, you already said that."

"Works at the Sheriff's Office, no less. Well, what's the matter? Aren't you going to invite your friend in? Suddenly you don't like pot? I'm sure she's got some on her. Sure as I'm sittin' here waiting on you to be hospitable, by Mungo."

Suddenly Marlena recalled Lila saying that Harry "had someone new on the string."

Could her new rival be Lorna?

As she dully registered the new pain, Marlena could barely hear Harry for the scornful laughter ringing inside her head. Meanwhile, he was rambling on about how Lorna had sold him some pot and one thing had led to another...if you know what I mean, honey. "Let's have some fun with her tonight. It's a golden opportunity. She's up for it. Whaddya say?"

Clearly, Lorna had taken matters into her own hands. The picture in her crystal ball seemed murky and dark.

What was it I wanted from Harry? Where is Ron? I need him.

Her next conscious thought was whether sex with Harry without pot was likely to be any fun. She and Harry had come to rely on weed for spicing up their lovemaking. Otherwise, she had no use for it. Harry had just admitted smoking pot with Lorna, which was code for admitting he was screwing her.

Was that such a big deal? Suddenly she felt very tired. Harry was fumbling with his words, saying he was going to dump Lorna because she was calling the house and pestering his wife about some job.

"Dump her as a pot connection, or dump her as a mattress polo partner, Harry?"

"Come on, Marlena, invite the chick in and let's have some fun, the three of us. She's up for it; I'm up for it. Aren't you? Don't be a drag, my love."

So, she thought dully, at this crossroads in their lives, the top priority of the father of her child was to indulge himself in a sexual fantasy. His deepest interest lay in having a three-way, right here on Cassandra's bed, while his wife Lila was wandering around drunk.

What kind of a man is Harry, kid?

Her mind cleared. Suddenly she had no desire to discuss with Harry the pros and cons of bringing a child into the world. In fact, she couldn't wait to get out of his sight.

Outside the window, Cassandra was laughing at her, the dulcet tones echoing, "Lila told you so, told you so, told you so. He's a snake, he's a snake, he's a snake."

Marlena shook her flaming hair back and lifted her chin. Hands on hips, she stood up at her full height and stared her selfish lover down with her blazing eyes.

"Harry, you're a shit, not fit to wipe my ass or your wife's. Even Lorna's, for that matter. You aren't the man I thought you were. It's over. Make up with your wife, if she'll go home with you."

He wiped his face as though she'd spit at him.

"Make up with Lila? Whaddya mean?"

"Well, when I talked to Lila at Drake's Roost, she said she was planning to file for divorce. Why, you may wonder? Because you're a snake who cares for nothing but his own skin. Just a heads up, Harry; consider it a final courtesy. If you want some head tonight, you can try getting it from the lady outside the door. Giving you head has become a tiresome bore to me."

"What in the name of thunder were you doing at my home?"

"I went to see my lover about our child," she said.

His eyes veered aslant, and he looked momentarily guilt-stricken.

"Look at me, Harry. I have a new plan. It's one that doesn't involve waiting around for the privilege of sucking your dick. I intend to make a difference with my life."

"But what about Key West?"

"What about it?"

"Didn't you hear me say just now we could escape to the Keys? I'll divorce Lila. I'll dump Lorna. It'll be like the old days again, just me and you, my love. And our baby."

He flashed a lopsided vintage smile.

Is that all you've got?

He looks like a spoiled boy, she thought, one who has been thwarted for the first time.

"Well, that's a nice offer, Harry, but it's a day late and a dollar short. I'm going to tell you now a bit of the unvarnished truth about us. One day, I'll tell you the whole story about us and our ancestors."

He groaned, but she ignored him.

"You and I have hurt innocent people, and I'm ashamed of us. The way I see it, we've got serious penance to do. As you've often pointed out, there are no strings attached between us. So here's what *I'm* gonna do.

"First, I will stop treating my family like shit. Next, I'm going to Key West. Only I'm not going there with you as an escape. I'll be helping a good friend with her house and getting my own career back on track. It got stalled when I took up waiting on you. And then, Harry, I'll come back here and kick your ass!"

Chapter Forty Three

Rousing herself from the memory of those riveting last minutes with Harry, Marlena looked around, then spotted Chloe coming toward her.

"Was I dreaming, or did Coddie come in here a minute ago?" she asked Chloe.

"He did, dear. Ron just took him up to a guest room. He wasn't making much sense."

"You look exhausted. Why don't you turn in? I'll get the lights."

Chloe looked like a pale ghost of herself. She'd been endlessly walking around, helping anyone who'd needed comfort, and many had.

Marlena took a few quick steps forward, staggered, then lightly sprang onto the first step of the stairway.

"Dear, where are you going?"

"I'll be right back down. Really, I'm fine. Trust me."

"I do trust you," said Chloe, looking up at Marlena as she ascended the stairs.

But she sent Ron up after Marlena anyway.

Ron waited outside the door. He could hear Marlena speaking within to her comatose ex-husband in a steady voice.

She was there, she said, to confess to the terrible mess she'd made of things. She would be doing a lot of apologizing and making promises, so she hoped he wouldn't mind if she practiced on him.

"I've been trying to see into the future, but I've only been looking out for myself. That's not nearly good enough for the long haul.

"Everyone says I'm Cassandra. Well, so be it. Once she got her head on straight, she spent a long life doing good works for others and raising her child the best she knew how. That's precisely what I'm going to do, and I'm going to need everyone's help, including yours.

"I'm not going to run. My flag flies here, and I'll stake my claim. I'm a native and proud of it. I love the solitary mountains and the strong, physical people who know how to fend for themselves.

"I've learned three important lessons during this reunion, Coddie.

"Life isn't a speakeasy, though it's no sin to have fun. Fun is good, sex is great, but hurting others or spiting people to get your way is bad karma.

"Next, you can run, but you can't hide from who you are. The imprint is in the genes. Our instincts are handed down from a time when there were no birth control pills and no ATM's. We just have to live with what we've been handed, whether it's a kickass sex drive or a deep desire to be a nun.

"Clearly the nunnery is not for moi. I'll be exercising my God-given sex drive for quite some time, and truthfully, my instincts are somewhat polymorphous. Viva la difference!

"Finally, we're all in this together. I have family and friends who love me. I'm connected to them, as I am to this baby within me.

"Coddie, I'm sorry I was a bad wife. I'm not that person any longer, but we can't go back. You've lost a bad wife, but you've gained a best friend for life. I hope you'll forgive me.

"I used to wonder, what is destiny? Is it ancestral ghosts haunting us in the night? DNA? The minute adjustments and decisions one makes under the pressure of a particular culture? The work one does, the progeny one has? We can't begin to imagine it all. I hoist my standard and embrace my future in the here and now.

"In my crystal ball I can see some things pretty damn clearly now. I'll have my baby for everyone--for you and Lila, for Sally and Stretch, for Ron, Mama, and Cassandra. Even for Apollo and especially for Annie and Chloe. She will be a Drake, of course, for better or for worse.

"So help me God, I'll see to it she does the right thing with her legacy. No more gobbling up land for easy profits or self-aggrandizement.

"Coddie, here's another promise. I want to save as many good homes as I can, what's left of them here, starting with the only home I've ever known, the old pink house. Home building needs to be combined with nature, history, and the aesthetic needs of human beings. Home schooling is all about connectedness."

With tears welling in his eyes, Ron tiptoed away from the door.

Exhausted, he crept into bed in an empty guest room at the far end of the long hallway, having first checked on Faith and Lila. Both were asleep but restless, gnashing their teeth. It wasn't a night for untroubled dreams.

He was awakened from his own fitful sleep by a loud thump.

It sounded as though it had come from the floor, on the other side of the bed. Rubbing his eyes, he sat up and peered into the darkness.

"Where am I?"

It was Marlena's voice, calling out in a whisper.

He jumped up and was quickly at her side, helping her up. It all happened so fast he'd barely had time to catch his breath, and his heart was pounding.

"Where am I?" she repeated, in a voice drowsy with sleep. "I got lost. Am I home?"

"Yes, Lena," he said. "You're home. Everyone in this house tonight loves you and cares what happens to you. You don't have to feel scared and lonely any longer."

"I must have gone sleepwalking. I haven't done that since I was a kid." *Home. All over the world I've been looking, and here it was.*

He adjusted her filmy nightgown around her and then tucked her into the bed.

"May I stay with you?"

"Of course."

"Don't leave me, please, Ronnie."

"Go to sleep. I'll be right here beside you. I'm not going anywhere."

I want him so bad I can taste it. How can that be, after what has happened? Sex and death. Do they go together? The Elizabethans called sex a little death.

The full moon was shining through the window. It lit up the room so that their faces were both aglow.

Instinctively, they turned toward each other. She focused her eyes up at Ron in the semi-darkness, and he stood there, transfixed, as the current buzzed between them.

The loud buzz of sexual attraction was like an alarm, waking her up.

Marlena sat up in bed. "Oh, Ronnie. Are we going to have an affair?"

They kissed hungrily, their lips and tongues on fire, and she drew him onto her. They fit together instantly, and they sighed in mutual pleasure and relief.

After awhile, he said, "I can't promise you trips to the Italian Alps. I'm only a small town doctor. But I'm yours, Lena, body and soul, on this night and forever."

"I am the Italian Alps. Climb me, you beast."

Chapter Forty Four
December 26, 1977

The next day, Marlena went straightaway to Chloe in her study.

"I need to know what happened. When I last saw Harry, he was alive in my room. The next thing I knew, I was standing over his corpse."

Beside Chloe, staring down at the corpse, she had remained convinced it was some magic trick, nightmare, or optical illusion.

Chloe caught her up on what had happened to Harry.

Frantic to find Marlena after Hawker had run off into the darkness on a rampage to kill her, Chloe had immediately gone to her room. There she'd found Harry with Lorna Anderson. She omitted the following detail in her account to Marlena. Lorna had her skirt hiked up to her thighs, with no panties on, and she was hand-rolling a joint.

"What's up, Chloe?" Harry had asked nonchalantly.

There was no time to chastise him, so she rolled out the scenario.

"Letty has drowned in the pond, a freak accident. Thom Hawker's gone berserk. He's looking for Marlena, threatening revenge. He's convinced she's a witch with evil powers, that she lured them here and is personally responsible for Letty's death."

"That's shit!"

"Indeed. Do you know where she is?"

"Marlena walked out of here just now," Harry said.

His posture shifted.

"You don't suppose she's in real danger, do you?" He added, in an aside, "Well, I suppose this clears up the mystery of who vandalized my bar. I thought Marlena did it, to get my attention. I was wrong."

Chloe opened her mouth to give Harry a piece of her mind about the long list of things he was wrong about, then closed it. There was no time.

"Thom thinks the hexing backfired, that Letty was sacrificed instead of Marlena. He's out to kill Marlena, Harry, and he's armed!"

Harry's face suddenly registered horror. He jumped up and ran from the room without once looking back.

"I never saw Harry move that fast before," Chloe told Marlena. "Not in his entire life."

Three days later, at Harry's funeral in the Scottish Presbyterian Church, Chloe was still pondering Harry's uncharacteristic behavior.

So he had loved Marlena after all, she thought. Poor Harry, always one day late and a dollar short when it came to emotional commitments.

In Marlena's dream, Harry lay in a wet tuxedo by the pond.

With his monogrammed white linen handkerchief, she dabbed the bleeding welts where long nails had strafed his prominent jaw-line. His eyes were closed, but his mouth was open, fixed in an expression of surprise. There was a white streak through his black hair, or perhaps it was only a reflection of the eerie lighting. Above the pond and the shivering circle of shocked guests, the sky was filled with blue lightning. And then, just as she was about to turn away from his corpse, sobbing, he sat up and swung at her with a sword, slicing her head off.

She would awake screaming. Chloe, Faith, or Annie, and usually all three would come at a run.

Marlena insisted on sleeping in Cassandra's old room, where she'd last seen Harry. Even though the dream terrified her, she found it comforting to remain there as she grieved her lost love.

Ron came by every day, and they took long walks together on Hatter's Field, hand in hand.

Chloe marveled at how close they had become, and how happily Marlena had settled into the second stage of her pregnancy.

The Brown faction would continue loudly to maintain Goody Brown had reached out from the grave through Letty to defeat Cassandra once again, that Marlena was Cassandra reincarnated, and she had masterminded Letty's death.

That was okay, Marlena decided. Let them think what they wanted.

Marlena's focus was on saving her home with the help of her family. She'd be damned if she'd run away from those bonds of connection. At the funeral, she stood shoulder-to-shoulder with Lila Drake.

Let ignorant gossip-mongers make of us what they will.

Poor Harry, Marlena thought at his funeral.

Like his grandfather, Harry had run after strong women but didn't know how to love them. Maybe there was something to that curse after all.

Sure is, kid. Lesson one learned. Pride goeth before a fall.

Chapter Forty Five
Aftermath...one year later

There were some surprising developments that followed the dramatic events of December 25, 1977.

Lila Drake proved to be an exceptional ally in Marlena's quest to save her small town from architectural corruption. Lila lent her the money to buy the pink house from the bank, rebuild it to historic specifications, and add a new wing for Faith to live in.

At the end of probate, when she received the bulk of Drake's holdings, Lila then executed a trust devolving control of her estate to Drake's heirs when she passed.

Lila also became the first investor in the Scattergood-Bellum REIT. The enterprise wasn't yet launched. The opening was slated for the summer of 1979. Its announced mission statement was "acquiring and preserving buildings of historic and aesthetic value in the Dakotas and Wyoming."

The operation was to be housed in a portion of Drake's Roost, which Lila had already turned over to the Northeast Territory Historical Society. NTHS planned to use as seed money the revenue from the increasingly popular public tours of the mansion.

It wouldn't be at all surprising to Marlena, still looking into that crystal ball which Chloe helped her scrub from time to time, if there turned out to be a hidden agenda in Lila's investment.

She believed Lila had her eye fixed on Bryce Scattergood.

"That's my prediction. She'll marry Bry," Marlena said to Ron.

Ron repressed a smile.

It was obvious to anyone who knew both of them, that as soon as Marlena completed the finishing touches to Sally's award-winning Shell Mansion in Key West, and as soon as Lila returned from Europe, the two women would become business partners.

His own wish for the future was certainly no secret. Ron was totally consumed with Marlena, a connection so deep that their lovemaking seemed to be a dance of hearts and bones, where one couldn't be felt apart from the other.

HOME SCHOOLING: The Fire Night Ball

As she was learning to trust again, he knew the feeling she had for him was more than physical. He hoped one day they would marry.

In the past year, Marlena's life had become a joyous, inclusive juggling act. She was fully engaged in doing all the things she loved passionately and held so precious, child-rearing being uppermost among them.

The glorious natural childbirth had taken place in the best possible setting, the new Cassandra Vye birthing room, the first in Wyoming. Ron had presided over it, but the entire extended family was in attendance: Faith, Chloe, Annie, Lila, Coddie, Bryce, Apollo, Sally, and Stretch.

Ron and the others had become the choir before whom Marlena sang her causes. As listening to Marlena talk and watching her nurse were the twin joys of his life outside their bedroom, he now egged her on. She promptly set about explaining why Lila's investment was a sound one.

"It'll be a struggle, but we'll prevail," asserted Marlena in what Ron called her "mother-preacher" voice. "Affordable housing doesn't have to mean clear-cutting trees and pre-fabbed homes, my love. Solar panels, rehabs, and rooftop gardens are the future."

Ron pretended to play devil's advocate. "But, darling, will you still have time for your writing? You owe it to your readers to continue."

Marlena's self-published book, <u>Home Schooling: "How to Build a Happy Home/life,</u>" which she'd co-authored with Dr. Chloe Vye, had been a phenomenal success. Written in seven months, its first printing sold out in three. It was a compendium of advice on feng shui and post-modern architecture fused with relationship and child rearing techniques--also tips on improving one's memory.

The final chapter, "The Glass Treasure Chest," had been on Marlena's lap immediately before she went into labor.

"Publish or perish!" Marlena sang out to Chloe on her way into the hospital. Part storytelling, part architectural drawings, part how-to-do it, the essay schooled modern readers on how glass brick, vaulted ceilings, and Navaho artifacts might co-exist happily in a sunny, whimsical, cheerful home environment.

Afterward, Chloe reflected that "the mere thought of our manuscript being so close to the finish line was enough to induce Marlena's labor."

"What did you say, Ron?"

"You owe it to our extended family to keep on writing."

However, Apollo had begun bellowing "Chattanooga Choo Choo" for Zoe Augusta Drake at the top of his lungs. Marlena shook her head at Ron, indicating she couldn't hear him. So Ron tried raising his voice.

"ALL OF US CHICKENS WANT YOU TO KEEP WRITING."

Marlena was seldom alone at the pink house. Ron was a constant presence. Chloe stopped by daily, as did Lila, when they were in town. Today, Apollo, the fledging firm's first employee, was balancing and bouncing Zaddie on his knee.

Apollo paused in his singing.

"The red-head wants you," he declared.

Zaddie was sucking on Apollo's knuckle with such greedy ferocity that it was turning purple.

"Hand her over, champ."

Frowning as she smelled breast milk, Zaddie clamped on, working the nipple furiously.

Just then, Faith appeared, coming down the central staircase in her chenille robe and slippers, having been awakened from her afternoon nap by Apollo. She frowned, and he ducked into the kitchen.

Faith sat down next to her daughter on the buttery-yellow leather couch.

She detested the color, but Marlena believed yellow makes people cheerful, so she dare not say a word. Faith first looked at and then diverted her brown eyes from Marlena's overflowing breasts and engorged nipples. Then she gazed proudly at her red-headed granddaughter.

"Do you think you'll ever wear a bra, Lena? With your figure and your rise in the publishing world, I would think--"

Faith was interrupted by her daughter. "Think what you want, Mama. First hear me out."

"Uh, oh," said Ron. "Better take cover, Faith."

"Britain's next prime minister will be a woman named Margaret Thatcher. I foresee a young woman, perhaps even my red-headed daughter, on the cover of <u>Time</u> magazine in 2012 with her arms folded and the headline: 'What--Me Marry?' The old restrictions that held us back are falling like the Berlin Wall.

"Women are already well on their way to running the world, Mama, and we don't have to take our cues from outdated stereotypes. But here's what I'll do for you. If Zaddie asks me to do so when she turns thirty, then I'll start wearing a bra. But not before then. Deal?"

"Oh, have it your own way, Lena. You always do."

THE END

Free extras for Anne Carlisle's Readers

Readers may contact and follow Anne Carlisle on her website, www.annehcarlislephd.com. While there, please enjoy the free extras, such as discussion with other readers and the author, the main character's diaries, and excerpts from published or upcoming books.

Below is an excerpt from HOME SCHOOLING: Cassandra's Story by Anne Carlisle, coming soon.

Prologue: December 21, 1977

Flickering candelaria were everywhere, along the window sill and the hard pegged floor.

In her long white night gown, with her amber eyes glittering and her beautiful face serene, her cousin Chloe Vye resembled a white witch, or so thought Marlena Bellum.

Settling into the sofa, Marlena prepared herself to take in every syllable of the long-awaited secret story.

Cassandra's Story Begins: October 27, 1900

Cassandra crept up to her cold bedroom (Chloe began) and gazed out from her casement window, using her grandfather's spyglass. She scanned the cold, vast immensities of Hatter's Field.

To her impatient view, it appeared barren and immovable, as if nothing had ever changed here since the days of the glaciers, when woolly mammoths roamed the arid plain

She saw that at last twilight was approaching, and the gas-lamps of Alta's three hundred or so settlers were coming on. The stars sprinkled across the sky and the home fires in the little mountain town appeared to converge in the emptiness where mountains end and the vast high plain begins.

Cassandra could remember her arrival last year when she was not yet twenty, just rounding the bend in the road from the south in a small brown surrey. She had strained forward eagerly to catch her first glimpse of the town where she'd soon be hanging her best lacy bonnet, unaware it would be hanging on a nail by a raw wooden door.

Progress had been slow behind the tired, single horse plodding along the lonely, narrow road past Hatter's Field. On each side of the muddy thoroughfare were frozen sheets of snow, layer upon layer, as far as the eye could see. A dark, brooding mountain towered over the town like a pitiless ancient god.

The terrain she'd stared at with mounting anxiety was constituted in a way so wild and resistant that even back in the greedy old homesteading days, no one had ever made a move to tame or claim it. The land had irregularities not caused by plows and pickaxes but rather by the geology of the last climate change.

Having flourished into young womanhood in the much more densely populated East, where she fancied herself a Progressivist, she could think only of how horribly isolated the town appeared under that endless, vast, unforgiving sky.

The native biddies had been very quick in picking up on Cassandra's disdain, and it wasn't long before she became a target for malicious gossip. People are apt to be suspicious of a proud, beautiful, exotic creature who sets herself apart from them, and there was no hiding one's opinions from public scrutiny in such a tiny settlement.

In 1900, even the largest Western towns consisted in no more than a thousand men, women, and children living in pine cabins or frame clapboards. A handful of shops provided the necessities: saddle and leather goods, hardware, dry goods, barber-dentist, cobbler, blacksmith, and butcher—plus thirteen bars and one busy local jail, as a rule.

The three hamlets of the northeastern district were unusually tiny, with a population of no more than two or three hundred in each remote location. They also claimed the distinction of being an exception to the rule in regard to drinking establishments.

Among the three, there was only one bar, the Plush Horse Inn & Saloon in Alta. It had a ten-foot tall music box in one drafty corner, which also made it the sole entertainment center. The Plush Horse was owned by Augustus "Curly" Drake, who was a relative newcomer and therefore viewed with some suspicion despite his boyhood having been spent at a prestigious school in Scotland. The fact that he had a law degree, was a handsome bachelor, and owned property made him immensely popular with the native daughters.

His deceased father had been president of the Colorado Silver Mines, but none of Drake's history cut much mustard with the local religious faction, given his choice of business. It didn't help matters that the Plush Horse was located not fifty yards from the graveyard of the Methodist church, where every proper citizen of Alta was expected to attend on Sundays.

Noted (and frowned upon) exceptions to the rule were the new inhabitants of Mill's Creek and, excused on a monthly basis, the native sons who were having their hair cut. This service was performed free of charge and regardless of the weather by Mr. Fairwell, by trade a cobbler, on the broad, pillared porch of his pretty Victorian house on West Street, as it had recently been named.

As any Western historian could confirm, a town where women and the church dominated the social order rather than the saloon-keepers was an anomaly. In Alta, the natives' piety was an tradition passed down from a severely strict, "low" sect among the original homesteaders. Only a few of those families remained, including the Brightons, Fairwells, Bottomlys, Harrisons, Simmonses, Hawkers, and Browns.

One native daughter, Widow Zelda Parker Brighton--she was also the biggest landowner and thus the most respected person in Alta--had descended from families of missionaries led by the Reverend Samuel Parker and Dr. Marcus Whitman.

As the church denomination was Methodist, so the church structure was plain, with no steeple. The itinerant pastor was Bill Dodge, a well-liked man with a wife and three small, solemn children. Attending church on Sunday was not only a requirement for being in good standing in the community but it was also a prime source of gossip.

For the natives of what had been a remote, sparsely settled U.S. Territory, gossip was no inconsequential matter.

News traveled slowly. The assassination of President McKinley that would occur in Buffalo the following September was not heard of in the district until Christmas, as the telegraph lines were down.

Sometimes not knowing the social trends back East was disastrous. For example, the collapse of the fur-trapping business back in the 1840's, which decimated entire communities and the fortunes of most mountain men in the West, was directly attributable to the decline in fashion in the East of the beaver hat. But who knew?

For the all-important dissemination of gossip, besides church services there were the Plush Horse, the community grapevine, and a series of bonfire celebrations held at the end of October, Thanksgiving, and Christmas night.

Fire Nights, as they were called, were the time-honored, surefire way to find out who was traveling south to Casper or east to Rapid City and whose husband had been spotted making cow eyes at Diane, the buxom barmaid at the Plush Horse.

The tradition went back a century or more to rituals of the local tribes—first the Shoshone and later the Lakota Sioux—who had used the base of the Hat as a place to congregate and worship their nature gods. They set ablaze pine logs and sagebrush and danced solemnly. The dancing was of a pattern that held dire meaning for those white settlers who knew of the Ghost Dancers.

By the dawn of the twentieth century, the lighting of bonfires during autumn and winter had been assimilated by all homesteaders as a venerable practice and, by some at least, constituted an excuse for a night of unbridled debauchery.

The one at hand was very special indeed, being the first Fire Night of the brand new century. The highpoint of the evening would be dancing once the bonfires were lit, beginning with the largest at the Hat.

The exact locations and times for the firings were announced in church and posted at gathering places. The order was strictly followed, a throwback to earlier notions about appeasing an Indian god. The district's native sons would use a firing technique that resembled a modern telephone chain. Brush would already have been collected and the faggots bundled in all the outlying hamlets and neighborhoods of the district; the male citizens of Alta, Aladdin, and Bulette were to a man expected to participate.

The bonfire at the Hat would be answered as quickly as possible by a second, a third, and so forth, until all the fires were raging, sometimes as many as thirty, sometimes as few as eight, depending on the bitterness of the weather.

The quickness of the teams in answering would be a matter for bragging rights, as was the size of a particular fire, its color, and its visibility from miles away. Once lit, beginning precisely at nine o'clock, the bonfires would be manned for several hours by boys and men, designated by virtue of a foolish willingness to risk their lives, as lightning strikes were very common during fall and winter up along the Hat.

As to the color of the fire, it was generally agreed that the best appearance to be had was at Mill's Creek, which was graced by the largest grove of junipers. It was a disappointment, then, when its new owner had let it be known he was declining to participate.

"There will be no bonfire at Mill's Creek pond tonight," Captain Marcus Vye had sworn as recently at four o'clock. He was at Bottomly's Butcher Shoppe, where the native men congregated each morning and also in the afternoons before community activities.

In truth, Vye's wood was very dear to him, as he was saving it for the last Fire Night, on the evening of Christmas day. It was his secret plan to throw a Christmas Fire Night Ball in honor of his beautiful grand-daughter Cassandra, who had graced his bachelor residence since the preceding winter.

CPSIA information can be obtained at www.ICGtesting.com
Printed in the USA
BVOW082307060812

297209BV00005B/91/P